Praise for Katie Khan and
HOLD BACK THE STARS

"Taking 'star-crossed' to a new level . . . [and] cinematically styled . . . *Hold Back the Stars* is a tale of first love that will appeal to fans of David Nicholls's *One Day* (2009) and of Jojo Moyes's romances."

—*Booklist Online*

"*Hold Back the Stars* is a high-stakes, high-concept, high-flying (or floating) love story that marks Katie Khan as a bold new talent. I raced through it. All the obvious 'out of this world' comments apply."

—*New York Times* bestselling author Matt Haig

"Gripping from the very first page, *Hold Back the Stars* is a rare combination of thrilling action, deep emotional depth, and intelligent ideas. The most unique love story I've read in years, it's sure to take the world by storm."

—*New York Times* bestselling author Rowan Coleman

"Prepare to shed tears."

—*Heat*

"This is a stirring, unique, and beautifully crafted story on the complexities of first love that will stay with you long after reading. This is going to be huge."

—*Image*

"Dazzling . . . a truly stellar debut, full of wonder and heart. I'm sure it's going to be a megahit."

—Emma Jane Unsworth, author of *Animals*

"A beautiful, moving, truly original tale. I loved this book for taking me by surprise."

—Renée Knight, author of *Disclaimer*

"Terrific . . . A beautiful story."

—Samantha Shannon, author of *The Bone Season*

hold back the stars

KATIE KHAN

GALLERY BOOKS
New York   London   Toronto   Sydney   New Delhi

G

Gallery Books
An Imprint of Simon & Schuster, Inc.
1230 Avenue of the Americas
New York, NY 10020

First Gallery Books trade paperback edition February 2018

GALLERY BOOKS and colophon are registered trademarks of Simon & Schuster, Inc.

For information about special discounts for bulk purchases, please contact Simon & Schuster Special Sales at 1-866-506-1949 or business@simonandschuster.com.

The Simon & Schuster Speakers Bureau can bring authors to your live event. For more information or to book an event, contact the Simon & Schuster Speakers Bureau at 1-866-248-3049 or visit our website at www.simonspeakers.com.

Interior design by Davina Mock-Maniscalco

Manufactured in the United States of America

10   9   8   7   6   5   4   3   2   1

The Library of Congress has cataloged the hardcover edition as follows:

Names: Khan, Katie, author.
Title: Hold back the stars : a novel / Katie Khan.
Description: New York : Gallery Books, 2017.
Identifiers: LCCN 2016040736| ISBN 9781501142932 (hardback) | ISBN 9781501142949 (trade paper) | ISBN 9781501142956 (ebook)
Subjects: LCSH: Outer space—Fiction. | Love stories. | Utopias. | BISAC: FICTION / Literary. | FICTION / Romance / General. | FICTION / Action & Adventure.
Classification: LCC PR6111.H355 H65 2017 | DDC 823/.92—dc23
LC record available at https://lccn.loc.gov/2016040736

ISBN 978-1-5011-4293-2
ISBN 978-1-5011-4294-9 (pbk)
ISBN 978-1-5011-4295-6 (ebook)

part one

part one

one

THIS IS THE END." They lurch into focus: Carys is breathing hard, a gasping panic filling her fishbowl helmet. "Fuck," she says. "I'm going to die." She reaches toward Max, but the motion rolls him away, out of her grasp.

"We're not."

"We're going to die." Her voice is choppy with shallow breaths, the sound loud in the glass of Max's helmet. "Oh, god—"

"Don't say that," he says.

"We are. Oh, god—"

They are falling in space, spinning away from their ship, two pointillist specks on an infinitely dark canvas.

"We're going to be fine." He looks around, but there's nothing out here for them: nothing but the bottomless black universe on their left, the Earth suspended in glorious Technicolor to their right. He stretches to grab Carys's foot. His fingertips brush her boot before he's spinning away and can't stop.

"How are you so calm?" she says. "Oh, hell—"

"Stop, Carys. Come on, get it together."

Her foot tumbles up in front of his face, and his face swings down by her knees. "What should we do?"

Max pulls his legs up to his body as far as he can, trying, through the panic, to calculate if he can change the axis on which he's rotating. The fulcrum? Axis? He doesn't know. "I don't know," he says, "but you need to calm down so we can figure this out."

"Oh, god." She flails her arms and legs, anything to stop their trajectory away from the ship, but it's fruitless. "What the fuck are we going to do?"

Hit harder by the impact, she is spinning away at a faster pace than he is. "We're being pulled apart as we fall, Cari, and soon we'll be too far to get back to each other."

"We're falling on different trajectories—"

"Yes." He takes a moment to think. "We need to get back to each other," he says. "Now."

"Okay."

"On three, swing your arms toward me as if you're diving into a swimming pool." He demonstrates the move. "Bend your upper body as much as you can. I'm going to try to kick my legs toward you, so grab me. All right?"

"On three."

Their audio crackles.

"One."

"Two—"

"Wait!" Carys puts up her hand. "Can't we use the impact to change our course back to the *Laertes*?"

With matte black sides and no lights visible in the hull, the *Laertes* lies abandoned above them, a ship passing in the night. "How?"

"If one of us hits the other hard enough," she says, "would it push them back?"

Max thinks. Maybe. *Maybe?* "No. Let's get us tethered first, then worry about that. Before it's too late—I don't want to lose you out here. Ready?"

"Ready."

"*Now.*"

Carys throws her body forward as Max throws his back. Her arms fly out as he kicks his legs up toward her; for a second they're suspended, like inverted commas, before the swing pulls them parallel. They come up level and she grabs his legs, hugging his feet. "Got you."

Now falling head to toe, they use their arms to rotate clockwise, cartwheeling slowly along with each other until, finally, they're face-to-face.

"Hi." She puts her arms around his neck. He takes a tether from the pocket on his thigh and gently wraps the floating rope around them, securing her to him.

MAX CATCHES HIS BREATH. "We need a plan." He looks back at the *Laertes*, lurking in the shadow of space as they fall farther from it with every moment. "We need to get help."

Carys has pulled herself around to Max's rear, where she's rummaging in the back of his silver suit. "Who's going to help us? We haven't seen a single soul for—"

"I know."

"We have lights," she says, "rope, water—why didn't we take propellant? We're so stupid."

"We had to try—"

"We should've taken the time. You should've let me go back and get the nitrogen—"

"It was an *emergency*. What did you want me to do? Watch your head shrink as you suffocate and die?"

She swings back around so they're helmet to helmet and looks at him in reproach. "That's not how it happens, and you know it. The EVSA said head shrinking was a twenty-first-century myth, propagated by bad movies."

"The EVSA said a lot of things. The EVSA said we'd be totally safe, and nothing would go wrong." Max taps the blue European Voivode Space Agency badge on the arm of his suit. "They also got us to sign a risk-assessment waiver, if you remember."

"I can't believe this is happening." She looks around. "Shall we try Osric?"

"Yes. Of course. Yes!" He hugs her sharply.

Carys pulls her flex down across her knuckles and moves her fingers to type, the strip of mesh webbing measuring her muscle reflexes and finger movements across an invisible keyboard.

Osric, do you read me?

She waits.

Are you there, Osric?

I'm here, Carys. There is a *ping* in her audio and the words appear in blue on the left side of her helmet glass.

"Thank god. Max, I've got comms with Osric." *Can you call for help?*

Certainly, Carys. Who would you like to call?

Base? The EVSA? Anyone?

"Ask if there are any ships nearby," says Max, "just in case."

Is anyone within distance to rescue us, Osric?

No, Carys. Sorry.

Are you sure?

Yes, Carys. Sorry.

Can you talk to Earth?

No, Carys. Sorry.

She screams in frustration, the sound distorting inside her helmet and through their audio. *Why not?*

My receptor was damaged in the accident. I believe Max was trying to fix it when we lost oxygen, Carys.

Fuck.

Pardon, Carys?

Sorry, Osric. Typo.

No problem, Carys.

We've got a big problem, Osric. Can you help?

How would you like me to help, Carys?

She sighs. "Max—I'm going around in circles talking to this thing."

He rubs the sleeve of her suit. "I didn't have time to connect my flex, Cari, so you'll have to, for now. Find out anything you can. Any vehicles in the neighborhood?"

She shakes her head.

Osric, she flexes, *can you send the* Laertes *to us?*

Negative, Carys. Navigation systems are unresponsive.

Can you move her?

Negative. Navigation systems are unresponsive.

Turn her?

Negative. Navigation systems are unresponsive, including the guidance system that would allow me to rotate the *Laertes*.

If she could bury her hands in her hair, she would, but they're held captive in gloves, her tawny plait encased in the glass fishbowl helmet. The small daisy tucked behind the helix of her ear has fallen slightly out of place. *Can you help us calculate how to get back to the ship?*

Carys? If I might suggest, something more urgent is pressing—

Calculate how to get back to the ship, Osric.

Situational Analysis is telling me the trajectory you're on allows no path back to the *Laertes* without nitrogen thrusters, Carys. Have you got nitrogen thrusters, Carys?

Can you stop putting my name at the end of every sentence, Osric? Certainly.

Thank you. No, we don't have propellant. Any other way?

Please wait while Situational Analysis calculates.

Hurry. "Osric says we can't get back to the ship without thrusters."

Max grimaces. "Definitely not?"

Carys? Something more urgent is pressing—

Hang on. "What else can we try? Osric says the navigation systems are offline. Shall I ask if—"

Carys?

What, Osric?

Situational Analysis is showing that your air canisters are not full.

We were outside on the Laertes *for quite a long time.*

The sum of the remaining air and the used oxygen does not equal the cumulative total.

What do you mean? Speak European, Osric. Please.

Your air canisters were underfilled.

What?

Additionally, Situational Analysis detects they are leaking.

"What?" Surprise makes her forget that Osric can't hear, so she quickly types again. *What?*

You both have damage to your oxygen canisters.

How much air do we have left?

"Cari?" Max says.

Calculating . . .

Hurry, Osric.

I'm afraid you have only ninety minutes of air remaining, Carys.

two

CARI. WHAT HAPPENED?" Max grips her shoulders, but she cannot be calmed. "What did Osric say?"

Sorry for saying "Carys," Carys.

"Ninety minutes," she says, taking big, racking breaths. "We've only got enough air to last us ninety minutes."

He reels back, stunned. "Can't be. It can't be. We should have at least four or five hours. We—"

"We're going to die, Max. Really soon." She holds back tears as he searches for the right words.

"We'll have to get back to the ship right away," he says finally. "We need to find a way back, then we'll fix the breach in the *Laertes* from where we hit the asteroid belt."

She gulps, and he looks at her.

"First things first, you need to stop panicking. You're using up your air more quickly."

"Our air is leaking," she says.

He jolts. "Is it? Now?"

"Now. Osric says there's a leak in the tanks."

"Both?" he asks.

"Both."

"Fuck." This time it's Max who swears. "We'd better patch them immediately." He looks at her, gauging the extent of her panic. "Shall I find the hole in yours while you catch your breath?"

"No, it's okay," she says, her heart clattering, "I'll do yours first." Carys loosens their tether and they roll away from each other almost balletically. "Make a shape like a snow angel," she says, taking him by the wrist and ankle. The single layer of fabric that sits against his skin and forms a pressurized, resistant surface against the vacuum of space, like a wet suit crossed with chain mail but completely malleable for human movement, feels soft beneath her touch. "Don't let go of my hand."

Max stretches out his hands and feet, hovering at her waist height. Carys bends so the surface of his suit is at eye level, still holding his hand. It's not the easiest thing to do, as they're not still—they're falling in perpetual motion, in darkness, in what feels like a godless place outside Earth.

Moving quickly, she runs her hand and her eyes across his metallic silver pack. Each section is divided into smooth, molded grooves, the blue readouts on the side the only dash of color. Carys searches all the way around, until she catches sight of it, right at the bottom: a small puff of escaping air molecules, almost imperceptible to the naked eye were she not searching desperately for it, and were the molecules not floating in their newfound freedom from gravity. "Got it." She pulls tape from the pocket on her knee, a patch kit always within reach, and smooths it over the canister, making sure the molecules can't escape around the sides.

"Done?" Max asks.

Osric, she flexes, *did that fix the leak?*

The blue text appears on her glass, accompanied by the somehow soothing *ping*. Affirmative, Carys.

"Done." She nods to Max, exhaling hard.

"We'd better do yours."

She hesitates. "It wasn't meant to be like this—we're not even supposed to be here."

"Come on, Cari."

"We've only got ninety minutes of air remaining." Finally a sob escapes, a short burst drowning out his reassuring talk, his air of calm—because this is what he does under duress. Detaching himself from confrontation, from stress, from her overwhelming emotion: this is what he does. He'll make a joke in a minute.

"Well, I don't know about you," he says, "but I'll be putting a very bad review of space travel on the MindShare."

"Shut up, Max," she says, though his predictability soothes her somewhat. "This is no time for your shitty sense of humor."

"I know."

His jokes always appeared at the worst times: during astronaut training; at funerals; the first time they'd met.

"What are we going to do?"

"We're going to calm down, regroup, and then I'm going to save you." He smiles. "Like I always do."

* * *

THEY'D MET THREE MONTHS into Rotation when, as a new resident in a new European city, Carys was picking up more languages in the region's language lab. Styled like a retro coffee chain, the Voivode's language lab had generic down-lighting, faux-leather sofas, and the smell of a thousand low-quality Arabica beans over-roasting in the skillet. "My colleague has moved here from Voivode 11," Carys had said to the instructor as she scanned down the list of dialects spoken across Europia, "so I need to learn modern Greek, please." A jaunty poster behind the counter declared: "Learning five languages lets you talk to 78 percent of Earth's population."

The instructor emitted a beep and green light, then guides and courses promptly started projecting at Carys's workstation.

"Thank you." She pulled the flex across her hands and began the thankless task of copying out the Greek alphabet over and over. Halfway through her third go, she remembered dinner. A waterfall of real-time information moved across three walls—"Wall Rivers" displaying a constant, scrolling feed of news, weather, and updates. Carys quickly flexed a short query on the MindShare, the local channel. *Does anyone know where you can buy goose fat in Voivode 6?* The words appeared in perfect Spanish, where they pulsed for a few seconds on the wall before being lost in the river of comments, questions, and anecdotes in multiple languages taking place all over the Voivodeship. She reached omega and reversed back up the Greek alphabet.

Ping. Carys looked up; someone had answered.

What do you need goose fat for, in this day and age? It was written in French.

Feeling rebellious, she flexed back in Catalan: *Cooking.*

Ping. Romanian. *Why are you cooking, in this day and age?*

Roast potatoes. Portuguese.

I said why *are you cooking?* German.

Her Germanics less strong, Carys switched to Italian, the start of a smile twitching the corners of her mouth. *New neighbors. I'd like to serve them crispy roast potatoes. Any ideas?*

Italian, again. *About your new neighbors? None. Sorry.*

In a game of linguistic one-upmanship, this language repetition was a small victory, and she smiled openly this time. *Perhaps you're one of my neighbors. Maybe later I'll serve you a roast potato so rubbery it will be like chewing a bouncy ball. Then would you wish you'd helped me track down some goose fat?*

Ping. *I don't trust strangers to cook for me.*

Surely strangers cook for you at the Rotation restaurants? she flexed.

Not really. I'm a chef, so it's easy.

Carys paused. *You work at the RR?*

Yep.

Great. Perhaps you can help me with some cooking advice. Do you happen to know where I might find some goose fat around here?

No answer.

Please? She added a smiley face to soften the tone.

Ping. *Try the classic supermarket just off the Passeig.*

Thank you.

They even sell food in cans, if you can believe that, in this day and age.

You're obsessed with "this day and age," Carys flexed back. *That's three times.*

Who isn't? So much has changed.

True. Thanks for your help, I'll head to the supermarket later. She finished six iterations of the Greek alphabet and removed the mesh from her wrists, roast potatoes in seven languages on the brain.

CARYS STEPPED OUT INTO a beautiful September evening, the tickle of a breeze drifting through the ruins. Smooth glass and steel structures erupted out of bricks and foundations from buildings long gone, their ghostlike shells preserved and structurally supported with all-new interiors. Here and there, the remains of narrow alleyways and tall, plastered walls jutted up and out, strengthened by steel girders. Inside, the ruins contained rooms formed from vast sheets of glass: a gleaming modernity Russian-dolled within fractured, ancient structures.

The light was fading to an orange hue as she walked across the café-filled squares, hugging bare forearms to her chest as her chip lagged, pausing her on a corner. "Cheer up, love, it might never happen," came a call, and she turned her wrist over with irritation.

"If the meteors start wiping out humanity, I know who I want to be first," she muttered, as her chip finally updated her on which way to go.

Reaching a wide, cobbled street lined with trees, Carys turned off into a row of shops, the fronts sagging with age and propped up by steel girders. A multicolored curtain of beads marked a small entrance, with "Fox Supermarkets" illuminated above the window. A newspaper placard stood outside, flashing: "US fallout finally at safe levels."

She eyed the headline for a moment, before pushing aside the beads with a rhythmic crackle and heading into the supermarket.

Old-fashioned wire baskets and carts lined either side of the doorway. In aisle eight, a man was kneeling on the floor stacking canned goods. "Sorry to bother you," she said, "but can you point me in the direction of goose fat, if you have it?"

He turned. Dark, slightly curly hair, falling down in front of blue eyes already entertained, like she'd missed the joke. "You must be Carys." He finished stacking a small shelf with cans and, standing, handed one to her. "We spoke earlier. Hi."

She stretched out her hand, baffled, and took the can. "You—wait. What?"

"On the MindShare."

"But didn't you say . . . Aren't you a chef? At the RR?"

"No. Yes. Nearly." He had the grace to blush. "At least, I will be. I did all the training on my last Rotation, so I'm hoping the restaurants here will take me on. As soon as someone helps me with the family business"—he gestured at the shop around him—"I'll be off, I hope."

"Right," she said, turning the can of goose fat in her hand. "I hope you find someone."

"Thanks," he said. "What do you do?"

She hesitated. "I fly."

"Kites?"

"Shuttles."

He made an impressed face. "Cool."

Carys took a small step backward. "I hate to run, but I'm late getting this dinner started. Thanks for your help, and . . . it's nice to meet you."

"No problem. I'm Max, by the way."

"Carys." She stuck her hand out awkwardly, and he shook it. "How did you find my query?" she said.

"Queries with food keywords are routed here, on the MindShare. They're flagged for the shops and restaurants to answer."

"That makes sense." She nodded, turned, and started to walk away. "Thank you."

"And," he called, at her back, "your profile picture is cute, so that helped."

Carys looked over her shoulder. "Shop manager, chef, *and* online stalker? You must be busy," she said, though her tone was light.

"Three full-time jobs," he said. "Plus you responded when I wrote in French—the language of my last Rotation."

She raised an eyebrow and turned back to face him. "Really? I presumed you were using the translation chip for our conversation." She gestured at his wrist.

"Nope."

"Me neither," she said, and they both smiled. "I was based in V8, too. Two Rotations ago. Down in the south, by the sea."

"I spent three years in Paris. It's where I learned to cook—I make a mean soufflé."

After a beat, she said, "Listen, I'm having a few of my new neighbors over for dinner tonight. Just a bunch of people, to help us make friends. Nothing fancy, I don't know any of them from Adam. Would you like to come?"

"I'd love to. Who's Adam?"

"It's an expression. But I can see from your grin that you know that, and you're teasing me. I'm adding teasing to the list next to light stalking. So tonight—eight p.m.? I'll flex you the address. Bring something. Anything." She repeated the nodding-turning-walking routine. "Good. See you later."

* * *

CANDLELIGHT ECHOED OFF SIX crystal wineglasses and water tumblers, as the dinner party was in full swing. Two of Carys's living-room walls were given over to Wall Rivers: huge, in-built screens, one showing a stream of news, the other the chatter of the MindShare; she had turned the text on both walls a warm orange. The building's former barrio front cast shadows of balcony bars into the room, the noise of the sea snatching through the ancient shutters. Serving dishes offered a buffet of roast chicken, vegetables, Yorkshire puddings, and Carys's much-heralded roast potatoes.

"Yorkshire puddings with chicken?" said Liljana, one of Carys's new colleagues. "Isn't that a little . . . ?"

"Unconventional," said John, a structural engineer and her new opposite neighbor, as he reached for the serving spoon. "Where I'm from you eat what you like, and forget the conventions."

"Where are you from, John?" said Carys, shooting him a look of gratitude.

John shifted uncomfortably. "Well, like all of us, I don't really know. But my first memory is from Voivode 3. I was five. My nana took me to get fish and chips, but I only wanted pudding. I was fussy, I hadn't eaten a full meal for *ages*. The chef at the RR put the two together and gave me a deep-fried chocolate bar, with chips." Everyone around the table started laughing. "I know. But I was young, and it did the trick—it got me to clear my plate. Nana rewarded me for finishing a meal, so I cleared my plate for the rest of the month."

"I'll drink to that." Liljana raised her glass, and the table followed. "To clearing your plate."

John beamed as the group clinked glasses. "What about you, Liljana, where have you moved here from?"

"It's pronounced 'Lil-*i*-ana,' " she corrected. "I know it looks different written on the MindShare."

"Apologies, Liljana." He got it right this time. "It's a pretty name."

"My parents were on Rotation by the Adriatic when I was conceived, hence the name, though my heritage is pure African. I last lived in Voivode 1."

"Heritage," mused Olivier, whom Carys had met at the language lab and invited along on a polite whim. "Us third-generation Europeans don't really get to talk about heritage all that much."

"Voivode 1?" said Carys to Liljana, ignoring Olivier's interjection. "How did you find life in the central Voivode?"

"Utopian," said Liljana, and the table laughed. "Very proud, still."

"And so we should be," said John. "Living freely, independently, in ever-changing, mixed communities—lots to be proud of."

"Hear, hear," said Liljana, before gently posing the utopian pledge: "In whose name do you act?"

"Not God, not king, or country," the group responded.

"In whose name?"

"My own."

Olivier took the opportunity to pour himself more wine. "But it is interesting, is it not," he said, swirling Pinot Grigio in his glass, "that we no longer talk about where we're *from* but where we have been?"

"That's the joy of Rotation," said Max. "Seeing the world, living in different places, no three years the same . . ."

Liljana shrugged. "Europia's now so big, we don't need to live in the same place twice. Mainland Europe, Russia, the treaty with Africa, soon Australia . . ."

"I've lived in the same place twice." Astrid sat forward. "I was named in the northern Voivodes, and on my sixth Rotation I was sent back there. It was beautiful, living once again in Scandinavia for a little while. But very cold."

The group laughed. "Where's the coldest place you've lived?" asked John.

"Russia," said Liljana, "V13. The Space Agency offices there frequently hit minus ten."

Olivier shivered. "Ireland."

Carys raised an eyebrow. "Ireland? The coldest?"

"Lightweight," tittered Astrid. "I've been there and it was positively balmy."

"I lived in Voivode 5 three Rotations ago, and it was freezing," insisted Olivier. "Did you go to a bar on the River Liffey, where they sing folk music?"

Astrid shook her head.

He was undeterred. "Truly a fantastic place." He glugged some wine and slid from his chair. "Carys, I think you would like it. I sang a song there once—a classic love song. I will sing it to you now."

Oh, god. "Really, there's no need. Max brought pudding—"

Olivier picked up a guitar and, as Carys cursed her mother for making her look after the damn thing, he began strumming and walking toward her.

Oh, god, oh, god. She prayed fervently that he wouldn't sing directly at her. As he opened his mouth and began to sing—

"Let me help," said Max, moving to clear the plates in front of Carys, subtly shifting between her and her admirer. Looking around the table, he asked, "Anyone for dessert?"

"What a great idea," she said.

"Perhaps you could give me a hand," he replied, as Olivier strummed violently on the guitar behind them.

"Certainly." She tried to edge out from where Olivier was still performing but he leaned in, wine fumes swirling on his breath.

As Carys recoiled, Max reached across and put his fingers over the frets, and the sound fell away with a muted metallic *waaaah*. Carys's suitor stopped in confusion. "Dessert?" Max asked sweetly.

Defeated, Olivier slumped back into his chair, and Astrid patted his wrist. "Some people don't understand great art." She refilled his wineglass, turning her body toward his. "They just don't."

Max and Carys carried the plates into the kitchen, and she pulled the door shut behind them. She leaned back against it and exhaled. Max joined her. "Damn," she said, looking up at the ceiling. "That was intense. Thank you."

"I can't believe people do that at civilized dinner parties. Do you think," he went on, "he wanted us to join in and . . . jam? I could've jumped in on some bongos, Liljana could've clacked together some spoons as a makeshift maraca . . ."

"Olivier's head could be rammed between some huge cymbals . . ."

"That could certainly be arranged."

"I could leap on the keys . . ."

"You play the piano?"

Carys nodded.

"That's cool. Where is it?"

She stretched her fingers, still holding the plates, and smiled.

"Oh, of course. You can play the keys anywhere. It's just—you had a traditional guitar. In the other room."

"That's my mom's. We swap, depending on who's in the cooler climate. She says humidity wrecks the instrument, or something. She's obsessed by it, actually. I'm the guardian of Gwen's guitar, for a limited period only."

"So she'd be sad if she knew the abuse it's seen tonight?" They laughed again, quietly, and Carys put the plates by the sink. Max flicked out a cotton tea towel and placed it over his shoulder as he laid out six dessert bowls, humming Olivier's tune, and they both giggled. "Where's your family now?"

She propped herself against the counter, watching him fill and dress the bowls. "My mom and dad live in V14, this time. My brother is working on the aid teams in the former United States—"

"Shit. Really?"

"Yes. We haven't heard from him in a while—as expected, I guess, but it's hard. I suppose comms isn't as important as getting food and water to survivors."

"At least it's a little safer now," he said. "Did you see the news?"

She nodded.

"If the nuclear fallout is decaying, maybe they can start to rebuild."

"Hopefully. There are so many displaced—and desperate—people over there." They were both quiet for a moment. "And finally, my sister is in the Portuguese Voivode."

"Ah," said Max, as he ran the tea towel around the rim of the bowls with his finger. "Hence your mad Portuguese skills earlier, on the MindShare."

She smiled. "You caught that, huh?"

"How many languages can you speak, anyway?"

"Five, maybe? Six? Soon to be six. I've started learning Greek. Can you really speak all those languages?"

"Do I look like someone who relies on his chip to translate?" He raised his eyebrows.

"No," she said, appraising him. "You look like someone who

works hard." She reached out and turned over his hand. "A grafter." She realized how cheesy this was and blushed. "Someone who earns his keep. Who keeps a shop running because you promised you would." She paused. "Am I close?"

"Closer than most people."

"Really?"

"Yes. Mainly because you're standing about a foot away from me." She rolled her eyes, and a clank of laughter from the next room brought them back. "So," he said, in a different voice, "you fly shuttles, dislike being serenaded, and ask people who've lived on Rotation their whole lives where they're from?" He tilted his head, looking at her speculatively.

"Ah," she said, starting to wipe the counter. "I always forget that when I'm around people like Liljana, I have a huge tendency to put my foot in my mouth."

"What do you mean, 'people like Liljana'?"

"Proud. Utopian. Believers."

Max tilted his head. "People like me, then."

"Yeah?"

"Yeah," he said. "My family . . . We're passionate about Rotation, and why it matters."

"Moving around, living alone in different cities matters?"

"Yes."

Carys shrugged, her face neutral. "Then my upbringing was probably a little different from yours."

"How so?"

She moved the roasting dish, stirring the fats and oils, and the smell of roast chicken rose up again in the kitchen. "That's a whole other story for a whole other time. Shall we get this dessert out?"

Something played across his face as he deftly picked up four bowls and balanced them across his wrist and forearm. "Sure. And perhaps later you can tell me about your heritage."

"Perhaps," Carys said lightly, heading toward the kitchen door with the other two, "but please don't say 'heritage' around Olivier. You'll send us third-generation Europeans over the edge."

* * *

"THAT'S RIGHT," SAYS CARYS. "You've always saved me, Max. A real white knight." The dusk of stars surrounds them as they fall, suspended like puppets on the string of space. A small rock whips past, and she shudders. "But this is more serious than my roast potatoes."

"At least you're a little calmer," he says, "and using the air more wisely."

"All right," she says, "you can stop patronizing me. I'm back. I'm here. I'm breathing." She looks around at the darkness, then back to the blue readout on their air supply. "What the hell are we going to do?"

"Don't worry," says Max. "I have a plan."

three

HE UNTIES THE TETHER and they come apart, still tumbling away from their ship. "It's your turn to be a snow angel," he says, taking her by the wrist and ankle, "because the first part of the plan is to find the leak in your canister."

"Oh, god," she says, watching the white rope float between them, trying to quell the rising terror as it threatens to surge again. She hands him the tape and he searches for escaping molecules, like she'd done with his. "It's tiny," Carys says. "You might not be able to see it. Put the darkness behind—it's the only way it'll show up."

Without saying a word he maneuvers Carys until he's looking out into the solar system, away from Earth, the purple of the Milky Way laid out behind her.

"You know," she says as a distraction while Max hunts for the outflow, "there are more stars in space than there are grains of sand on every beach on Earth."

"That's terrifying."

"Some say there are ten thousand stars for every grain of sand. Imagine how much bigger some are than our sun."

After a few moments he puts his gloved finger over a tiny wisp of air. "It's on the bottom."

"So was yours. Can you patch it?" she asks.

"Yes." He sticks down the tape, rubbing hard to make sure it's secure, and sighs with relief. "That's done. Now stay still—I want to see if this will work."

"If what will work?"

Max feels his way around Carys's air supply until he finds the manual override on the different compartments, then the tube running from her pack to her helmet. It's embedded deep within a groove, and he despairs—it's not going to come away easily.

"Max?"

"Give me a second. I have an idea but I need to think it through for a minute."

"Are you crazy?" she says. "We don't have all that many minutes left."

"Half of one, then. Trust me." He gets his fingers around the tube and twists hard, feeling it give slightly. Rolling it between his forefinger and thumb, he twists again, unscrewing the air supply from the long thread holding it in place. At the base of her pack, the rubber compound bends in overrotated spirals, bunching as Max turns it at the top. He carries on, regardless, though it's awkward.

"How are you getting on?"

"I need a nozzle," he says. "What could we use?"

"How big?"

"Small." He holds up his two fingers pressed together. "This narrow."

"We have the tube for the water pack," she says quietly. "But if we take it then we can't—"

"We have the other pack. That will last us . . ."

"Last us, what—eighty-six minutes? Is that all we're trying to survive?"

"No, of course not. But if we don't try and save ourselves now it won't matter if we have two days' worth of water. Nothing will matter after we run out of . . ."

They look at each other, saying nothing.

He puts his hand on hers. "Please."

"You're right," she says, putting her other hand over his. "You're right. We have to try."

"Thank you."

She fumbles for the lights and water pack and detaches the white transparent straw, holding it out for him, a tiny token of hope against the vast backdrop of nothingness. He reaches for it—"Make it count," she says—and takes it gingerly between finger and thumb.

He pinches the straw into a funnel, bending the plastic to make the shape hold. "I'm going to leave you enough oxygen to last a minute, and seal off your supply. Conserve it the best you can, okay?"

She blinks, then nods.

"This will be over soon." He finishes unthreading Carys's tube from her air supply. "Get ready."

"What for?" she whispers.

"Try not to talk. Breathe slowly, if at all. And don't panic." He disconnects her tube and mashes the improvised nozzle into the end. At the same time he presses the manual override on her pack, forcing a jet of oxygen to hiss out through the straw, pushing her body forward in reaction. She advances an inch or so, and he laughs with relief.

"It's working!" He lets go of her hand as she moves forward a fraction more, watching the oxygen hiss.

"Wait—" Carys shakes her arms, reaching and grabbing at him. She can't speak freely until he reconnects her air.

"You're moving, Cari—"

Frantically, she signals at him, her green eyes pooled. The oxygen is going too fast, she's not traveling far enough—

She's not traveling far enough and he is wasting her air supply. He grabs at the back of her pack and, panicking now, all thumbs, re-attaches her air, screwing it in the wrong way. The bunched base of the tube recoils, and he grasps it as it spins out, dispelling yet more oxygen into the ether.

Every second counts.

He pulls her tube back and turns her air supply into the groove, winding it in place.

"Max," she gasps.

"Are you all right?"

"Were you making a propellant?"

"Yes."

"I could never travel far enough like that. You need to heat the gas to make a thrust," she says, beads of sweat floating at the side of her face inside the fishbowl helmet.

"But," says Max, "I thought it would work if the pressure—"

"No." Carys makes to wipe her eyes but can't, so she shakes her head from side to side to clear the fluid. The beads of liquid pool into her hair, halo-braided around her head, away from her face. Her adrenaline is flowing and her heart monitor beeps. She swipes the alarm away, but her heart rate continues to rise.

"I'm sorry," he says.

Her alarm beeps again. "A thrust would need to be pressurized."

"I didn't know. I'm sorry." He reaches for her.

"I can't believe you were going to send me back on my own without even talking to me about it."

Max's hand stops midway to her. "That's what you're really annoyed about, isn't it?"

"How much air did I lose?"

"Not too much." His eyes flick to the gauge on the side of her pack. "I'll make up for it—we'll use my pack next time."

"Next time?" she shouts, her voice distorting. "Now I have less air than you, so you're probably going to have to watch me die. Good one."

"Don't freak out. I was trying to help."

"Yeah, but you didn't. And now I have less time with you to figure this out."

"If it had worked, you would've been safe. You might've been rescued—"

"Jesus." Carys shakes her head. "I don't need a white knight, Max."

His voice is plaintive. "I'm just trying to do the right thing."

"It's not your job to save me."

* * *

HE'D LEFT THE DINNER PARTY around midnight and she'd seen him to the door, leaning against the frame, her arms huddled inside her cardigan against the chill.

"Thanks for tonight," he'd said. "Thanks for inviting another total stranger around for dinner."

"Thanks for making my roast potatoes look good." They laughed. "What are you doing tomorrow?"

"Working at the shop. You?"

"Same, working."

And still he'd lingered. "Learning more Greek anytime soon?"

"Oh, undoubtedly."

"At the language lab?"

She nodded.

"Good. Then I'll know where to find you." He waited. "Catch you soon, Carys."

He looked back a couple of times, her silhouette illuminated in the orange glow of the streetlights as she moved from the doorway.

It didn't take him long to get home. The chip on Max's wrist recognized his place as he approached and the door clicked open, the metal bolt springing free across the wood. The lamp in the hallway switched on automatically as he entered, but unlike the built-in frames covering the walls in Carys's home, filled with photos streamed from her chip, Max's hall frames were bare. Pictures from the last Rotation's inhabitants still hung on the kitchen walls, where Max would cook beneath them, oblivious to their smiling faces and superior sunsets.

He thought of something Carys had said earlier that evening at the party, about how she'd decorated the moment she moved in, reaching out on the MindShare to new neighbors as well as streaming conversations with her friends and family in other Voivodes. Her life was full of people, full of noise and mess. "You really want this lot in your house round the clock?" he'd said, waving at Astrid and Olivier hooking up on the sofa, the latter sloshing wine out of his glass onto Carys's pale rug.

"Why not?" she'd replied. "It beats being alone all the time." He wasn't sure he agreed.

Max walked upstairs, taking care to avoid the creaking floor-boards. He stepped soundlessly into the bathroom, punching the pad to program his tooth cleansing. He leaned against the sink, looking hard at himself in the mirror, still feeling the flicker of her gaze and knowing he didn't want the night to be over, not yet.

HE TOUCHED THE SHOULDER of the guy on the door of the club, who let him straight in—Carys wasn't the only one who'd ben-efited from Max's help on the MindShare. It was nearly one in the morning but the Dormer was busy for a Thursday, as groups of new friends, on their new Rotations, cut loose ahead of the weekend in the bar downstairs and on the glass dance floor above his head. He looked up, admiring the vivid patterns created by the footfall of danc-ers: wherever they moved, the touch-sensitive glass lit up with bursts of color beneath their feet. The effect was captivating, and the only decoration the converted church really needed. After Europia had united "belief systems" into "faith" (and nonbelievers into "no faith"), many of the old religious buildings were repurposed, their striking architecture becoming iconic settings for the Voivodes' nightlife.

"Max! Over here," Liu called from the tatty chesterfield sofas by the bar-altar downstairs. A renowned Chinese dissident, Liu always drew large crowds with his wild stories. A group of girls, clearly not yet comfortable in their new clique, surrounded him, and Max walked over, smoothing down his day-old T-shirt and brushing his hair off his face.

"Hey," he said. A chorus of different-pitched "hey"s floated back at him, and he smiled genially.

"I didn't think you were coming out tonight," said Liu, standing to rest his arm on Max's shoulder in the favored Voivode greeting. "I thought you were done for the night."

Max shook his head, and a girl wearing a slashed red dress jumped up. "We've heard about you," she said, "the famous Max."

"Oh?"

"There's no need to be so coy." She licked salt from her wrist and tipped tequila into her mouth. Max noticed that her lips were the exact same shade as the dress. "We've all heard you're an astronaut who's going to save the world—"

Max looked alarmed. "Liu, come and help me carry some drinks." They walked to the bar, settling against the ancient wood while a round of tequilas were poured in front of them. "What the hell's going on, mate?" he asked.

"Oh, you know, the usual," said Liu, looking like the Cheshire cat. "Are you getting these?" He pointed at the drinks lining up on the bar.

"I can't afford them on my nonastronaut salary."

Liu smiled more broadly. "I've warmed them up for you."

"You didn't even know I was coming."

Liu began to laugh and clapped Max on the back. "Then it's damn lucky you're here, because I can't help these women, can I?"

Max jabbed him in the ribs. "You idiot."

"I just hoped you'd show, like usual, and if not, at least I'd have made some new pals, blinded by my fabulousness and desperate to know my famous astronaut friend."

"That's a dangerous game," said Max. "I'll probably serve half of them in the shop tomorrow."

"Do any of these people look like they make their own food?" Liu made a skeptical face. "Exactly."

"Nobody does."

"Precisely. Not much danger in our little mythology."

"*Your* mythology," Max said, and Liu started laughing again. "I met a girl tonight. Today. In the shop."

"Sandy from the shop? Blonde Sandy? How did it go with her?"

"Not her. Another one."

Liu nodded sagely. "Women are like buses."

"Come on, man," said Max, "the way you're talking—"

"Don't worry, I'm all about gender equality, so I objectify men in the exact same way."

Max knocked back one of the shots and winced. "I don't doubt it."

"Go on, then," Liu said. "Tell me about your new girl."

A familiar beat started, and the group on the chesterfields screamed, moving like a swarm up the stairs and onto the glass dance floor. Max took a moment, watching them overhead, then said, "She's—I could talk to her. About real things."

"Things?"

"Things. The way *we* talk. Not about hookups, obviously." He turned round, propping his elbows on the bar. "But unlike these guys . . ."

"And Sandy," said Liu.

"Unlike these guys and Sandy," amended Max. "It just felt more substantial, if you know what I mean. Everything else feels so . . . transient."

Liu spoke quietly. "Rotation *is* transient, Max."

"I know. It's never bothered me before. I've always quite liked getting to live on my own—doing what I want, when I want. Then moving on just as it begins to get a bit dull."

"That's certainly a novel way to describe the ideal of Individualism," said Liu.

"Everything in my own name, that's what the rules say. No national identity, no religious divide, no distractions or serious relationships until we're established. But—"

"I don't believe it. Maximilian, speaking out against Rotation?"

Max shrugged. "Oh, calm down, I'm not about to start a revolution. Just—maybe—*transient* might be rubbish."

"I suppose," said Liu, reasoning it out, "it's made us rush to have sex with pretty people, because we'll live somewhere else in a few years' time. And I'm very okay with that."

"Right. And there'll be plenty more fish in the next sea."

Liu was quiet. "Overused metaphors aside, Max—"

"Oh, you know what I mean, don't pretend you don't. This girl, Carys, she's different."

It was Liu's turn to look alarmed. "Different? Maximilian, you're not considering . . . ? Not at the age of twenty-seven. Not here." Max was silent. "And not with a girl called Gary."

"Cari, you idiot. Carys. It's Welsh." Max laughed. "I know. I know."

"You've lived in Europia all your life, haven't you? Because I came here from China—our rather reluctant, rather oppressive ally. I may be relatively new to Europia's customs, but the Couples Rule is one that really seems to work. In whose name?"

Max fidgeted on the spot before answering with the pledge's response. "Not God, not king, or country."

"In whose name? Your own," Liu finished before Max could answer. "Not in your girl's name, your boy's name, your family's surname, or even your children's names. It's a better society if everyone can give their all. So we all contribute toward the utopia as an individual, until such a time we can begin to think about settling down and starting a family.

"And the Couples Rule currently states an age for that, of at least thirty-five." He threw back his drink. "Individualism means freedom when you're young, family when you're old. What more could you want? It's perfect."

"I know," Max sighed.

"Don't call her," advised Liu. "It's more hassle than it's worth. It's not like anything can come of it."

The girls came back from the dance floor, visibly more bonded as a group than before they'd left. A splinter cell disappeared off to the bathroom while the girl in the red dress slid over to Max, leaning over the bar to take a long sip from his straw, her eyes never leaving his face. "Do you live nearby?" she said.

"Near enough."

Liu smiled and moved away, and the girl held out her hand, nails veneered in acetate red to match the outfit. "I'm Lisa. Do you like my dress?" She pulled her body into an unnatural pose and Max gave her a long, appraising look.

"It's certainly something."

She leaned toward him. "Let's go back to your place."

"Not tonight."

"Mine, then?"

"I can't."

She pouted. "If the meteors end the world tomorrow, wouldn't you wish you'd come back with me tonight? It's not far."

"Are you always this direct?"

"Only when I want something." Lisa snaked her arms around his neck.

"Does it usually work?"

"Every time."

Max looked down at her. "Right, then. I'd better . . ." He trailed off as she put her mouth over his, and said nothing as she led him by the hand toward the exit.

*   *   *

HER WORDS HANG IN the space between them, the heat of their fight cooling as quickly as it had erupted.

"I have to try and save you up here, Cari. I have to put you first." He looks at her, his face desperate.

"Why?"

"Because I never did down there."

"What do you mean?"

"Everything you hate, everything you thought I wasn't . . . I never deserved you, not from the very beginning." He shakes his head. "I even went home with someone else the night we met. And the night before that." She doesn't say anything, and Max looks as if he wishes the confession would fall back into his mouth. "I never should've—I suppose now's not the time."

"No," she says, "it's exactly the time. I—"

He fingers the rope tethering them together. "I'm sorry."

"I know."

"My timing's terrible."

Carys thinks about how to explain what she'd done after they'd met. "No, Max. I mean, *I know*."

four

CARYS KNOWS THAT with only eighty minutes of air remaining it would be self-indulgent to talk more, but she can't resist the opportunity to discuss something they've never touched on before. She picks up the end of the tether, loose from where Max had untied her to travel back to the *Laertes*, and begins to tie a substantial sailor knot so they won't come apart again. Their ship may be damaged, but getting back to it is their best hope for survival in the vastness of space, and Carys wants to ensure Max will not be able to send her back to the ship without him. Wherever they go, she wants them to go together.

"After we met, Max, when we'd had that connection—horrible word—I thought I'd see you again. But then I didn't hear from you." She looks up at him, speaking quickly, hurrying to get the words out as she handles the rope. "You know this, I think. I worked from the language lab where you knew I'd be, I asked a lot of cooking questions on the MindShare—nothing." She touches the hooks on the side of his pack thoughtfully, then turns a loop in the line, sliding the end of their tether through the hole she's created.

"What you don't know is that I even went to the supermarket, where a blonde with a name tag told me it was your day off." Carys doesn't mention how Sandy had rolled her eyes when she had asked after Max, quipping "Another one!" when Carys added, somewhat unnecessarily, that Max had helped her on the MindShare then come along to her party. "You and me both, honey. He's always helping the pretty ones."

"I'm sorry," he whispers.

She shrugs her shoulders inside her suit, then twists the top of the rope back through the loop in a figure eight. "A few weeks after that, I went out for Liljana's birthday at a club, a former church with a light-up dance floor. This guy was making moves on practically every woman there. I watched him for a bit. He was clearly gay, but the women were so flattered by the attention they didn't seem to notice. He was basically performing.

" 'And now,' " Carys puts on a deep voice as she secures the bowline loop to the hook on the side of Max's pack, " 'the man himself, the greatest living astronaut still alive and not yet dead,' " playing to the floor like a ringmaster. " 'It's Maximilian.' And there you were."

Max stares. "Why didn't you say anything?"

"Hey. My feelings were hurt—you never called."

"I—"

"I know. I get it. I turned back to the bar, so you wouldn't see me, and once you'd drifted off I had a chat with the ringmaster."

"Liu?"

"Yes."

"You spoke to Liu? He never said."

Carys shrugs, eyeing the blue oxygen readout nervously. "We don't really have time for this," she says.

"I know. Tell me quickly what Liu said. Then we'll get back to that." He points at the *Laertes* where it lies above them in the blackness, a breach evident in the hull. Debris floats around the hole, freed from gravity, like bathwater circling a drain.

She repeats the loop in the rope on her side, circling the other end of the tether and pulling the bowline tight so it will survive a strong tug, if necessary. "I told Liu it'd be a funny kind of astronaut stacking shelves off the Passeig. He had the grace to blush—with the grin of a man who'd sold his sister to the circus."

"Naturally. That man is wicked."

"I asked why the ruse and he suddenly became quite serious. Liu said he needed a shtick, something to entertain people. With the asteroid field in the news all the time, Europia's morbid fascination with space made it an ideal gambit. His words, clearly, not mine."

"Clearly," says Max. "You'd never call space a 'morbid fascination.'"

"The man's a born entertainer. I don't know why he doesn't have his own channel yet."

"He might by now, particularly if the world down there knows the part he played in getting us together. Not that I understand for a second why we *are* together, if you knew all this when we met."

She laces the tether around their packs before securing the rope with a safety knot at each end. "I liked you—you were interesting to talk to and made me feel wanted. I was insecure enough to be flattered, I'm fine with that. But I've never got why you needed the astronaut line."

Max rests his hand on the rope. "It made people think I was somebody."

"I thought you were somebody."

"I worked in a shop."

"So?" She's exasperated.

"Most people get to do what they love in Europia," he says, "and I didn't."

"You wanted to be a chef. Why not use the chef line?"

He smiles regretfully. "Not very out-of-this-world, is it?"

"And space travel is glamorous?" Carys looks around. They are falling in the interminable dark, strung together at the waist.

She flicks the tether with her wrist and a pulse moves between them, like a heartbeat. "There," Carys says, briefly satisfied by the stress test. "We're not going to come apart now. It would take something quite sharp to slice through this."

"Like a micrometeoroid?" Max says. "Because there are plenty of those beneath us. What are we going to do?"

"I'm thinking," she says. Their tumbling has been a little smoother since they patched the leak, the small outflow of escaping molecules from their tanks making their fall erratic. Max had made a nozzle and used oxygen. What if—

"I couldn't call you, Cari."

Dammit. She screws up her face.

"When we met . . . You know what I believe. What I believed."

"Yes."

"And you were—are—a full-fledged pilot, and I was managing a shop."

"But you ended up with a job where I worked."

"You'd only said you flew shuttles. I thought you might work for an airline. I didn't know you were there when they approached me."

"You didn't apply to the EVSA?"

"No," Max says, "they found me."

* * *

HE'D BEEN WORKING AT the shop for nine days without a break when they came. He'd wanted to call Carys, but he was dimly aware that liking someone—really liking someone—was unsettling, and a part of him didn't want to face the risk. His parents had come together in their mid-to-late thirties, following the rules; he had almost a decade before he could find a Carys to apply with, if he wanted to settle down. But still . . . he wondered. What if? There was no rule against flings—the Voivodeship seemed to thrive on them. Rotation was meant to keep you individual, free from national identity or an allied social pressure—but that didn't mean you had to be lonely. Perhaps he'd manufacture a meeting somehow. The Voivode was small, they'd met once already . . . how hard could it be?

Their vehicle had crept into the Passeig del Born like mist at midday, the oxygen-fueled engine whooshing on the cobbles, and Max had pushed aside the beads covering the supermarket door to watch. Three men had got out: an elderly gentleman with a walking stick and double-breasted pinstripe suit, flanked by two security guards in sunglasses. With surprise, Max watched as they walked toward his shop, dipping their heads to enter and pausing as they took off their shades, their eyes adjusting to the light inside.

"We're looking for Max Fox," one of the guards said.

"Right," said Max. "Can I ask what for?"

The suit stepped forward. "It's confidential. But there's nothing to worry about, so if you"—he leaned back on his stick and gazed at Max—"happen to know where Max is right now, you might just change his life."

Max swallowed. "Well, there's an offer I can't refuse. Hi, I'm

Max." He lifted his arm in the traditional Voivode greeting, and the other man laid his hand on Max's shoulder in the appropriate response, cuff links flashing under the strip lighting.

"Good to meet you. Sorry to be so formal, but if you can display your chip to my esteemed colleague . . . That's perfect. Thank you.

"The name's Aldous," he said. "I head up recruitment at the EVSA, sourcing talent from the Voivodeship to join our space program. We've heard great things about your knowledge, and we'd like to invite you to join us as a specialist technician."

"I'm sorry. Is this a windup?" Max put down the canned pineapple he had been holding.

"Absolutely not."

"Did Liu send you? I'll kill him."

"Who's Liu?" Aldous didn't bat an eyelid. "Max, we're hoping that, like you said, it's an offer you can't refuse." He adjusted his cuff. "You've singlehandedly responded to the majority of Mind-Share food queries in this Voivode since the second-draw Rotation kicked off five months ago, and you've been recommended to us directly."

"I have?"

"You have. Do you like to cook?"

"I studied under Van der Kamp in Paris," Max said, the timbre of his voice betraying a hint of pride.

Aldous nodded his approval. "Do you want to come with us?"

Max ran his hand through his hair. "The thing is, this place belongs to my family." He waved at the shop. "I have to run it through Rotation, and there's one in every Voivode. I can't leave for an audition or the application process—I'm committed indefinitely."

"We would provide a full-time manager to look after your father's supermarket in your place, providing daily and weekly updates. Would that prove satisfactory?"

Max gaped. "While I apply?"

"Permanently. Max, our recruitment works on a recommendation-for-role basis. Do you understand what that means?" Max began to nod and midway turned it into a shake of his head. "It means we only hire people we're told specifically by our own employees are suitable for the job. This, if you like, is your application. There is no other way for you to join us. There is no ad for this role. You cannot apply at a later date. So, I'm afraid we will need an answer now."

They stood in silence, momentarily interrupted by Sandy's blonde head appearing over a breakfast-cereal display that wobbled dangerously.

"It sounds," said Max, "almost too good to be true. You need culinary people on your space team?"

Aldous arched an eyebrow. "Even cosmonauts have to eat."

Max rocked back and forth on the balls of his feet, his hands deep in his pockets, weighing his options. "Okay," he said slowly. "Count me in."

"Someone will be along to collect you tomorrow. Have your things ready for 0900 hours." The curiously dapper Aldous then dipped the brim of his hat, and the three men walked out, leaving Max staring after them.

* * *

CARYS LOOKS AWAY, WATCHING the darkness falling across parts of Earth as the sun sets down there, though not up here. "It's amazing, really. You got a mixture of the job you wanted and the job you pretended to have to get laid."

He winces but ignores the jab. "They said it was on the volume of culinary MindShare queries I'd answered."

"Recommendation for role." She nods.

"I used to think us meeting again was total chance," he says.

"At lunch? Yes."

"I couldn't believe it when I saw you again. My life was turning around and I was getting to do amazing things. I could finally say I was an astronaut, give or take—"

"I bet the girls loved that—"

"And I was getting into a really good place, when there you were, the one I'd stupidly let get away." He pauses. "Cari. You told me two minutes ago you'd always known what I was like."

To avoid the circular argument to which all couples are prone, where they've gone past anger and made up, only to end up back at the start after one barbed comment, Carys simply says, "Sorry." Then she can't help herself. "But you did just call me 'the one that got away.'"

"So?"

"'One' implies 'of many.'"

"No, it doesn't." Max sighs. "It implies I knew I'd missed an opportunity with you. You lingered in my mind, but we weren't allowed to be together like that—not yet—and I wasn't in a place to do anything about it." Their eyes meet. He puts his hand over hers on the rope and looks her straight in the helmet. "Why are we focusing on this?"

"You're right," she says, looking down at the blue glow of Earth beneath them in the darkness. "We've got stuff to do. Now, hold still."

five

AS THEY FALL steadily away from the *Laertes*, Carys twists to read the air gauge on the side of her pack, then looks instead at Max's air supply right in front of her. Seventy-five minutes. Their air has dropped by five minutes while they've been talking. Christ. She runs her hands over his pack, feeling for different compartments along the smooth, grooved surface. "Our best shot is getting back to that ship, am I right?"

"You are."

"Even though it's damaged," she says, grimacing, "our odds are much better there, if we can somehow fix the breach and regain control of the *Laertes*."

Max nods.

"I'm going to ask Osric about the expelled carbon dioxide."

She flexes quickly, her hands moving in front of him. Almost instantly, the gestural technology arranges her muscle movements into combinations of letters, then the letters into predictive text, and finally the text into the most likely word within context. Incorrect sentences are replaced with a swipe. It's almost seamless but, like most software, not without the occasional autocorrected typo. She pauses to read Osric's response.

"Are you going to tell me why?" Max asks, gesturing at her flex.

"Yes." She finds the override button on Max's pack and fingers it momentarily, wondering whether to press it. "Osric says oxygen is stored in the top," Carys reads from her glass, "with the carbon dioxide trapped in a copper mesh just below it."

"Okay. What are you thinking?" he asks.

Carys's hand is still toying with the plastic button. "You tried to use oxygen as a propellant. Why not the carbon dioxide? We don't need it."

"Oh."

"It's worth a shot, anyway?"

Max makes a face. "Was it obvious? I'm an idiot."

"No," says Carys. "The thing is, it's not stored as a gas. The suit freezes the expelled carbon dioxide in the ventilation flow. The whole system is a heat sink."

"Which means . . ."

"It's a frozen block. And to use it as a propellant, we'll have to stop it freezing."

"Okay," he says. "Let me know when you've figured that out."

She stops and looks at him.

"Sorry. You know more about this than I do."

"Sort of—between me and Osric," Carys says, to appease him. "The carbon dioxide is frozen in the wire mesh at minus 140 degrees." She scans the readout from Osric. "It's then dropped into an ice chest and fed back into our helmets to defog our visors. So we're going to need"—she pauses, thinking about it—"to disrupt the flow before the CO_2 hits the copper mesh and freezes."

"And how do we do that, genius?"

"We take out the wire mesh unit."

He's surprised. "You want to remove part of the pack, out here?"

"What other choice do we have?" she asks.

"What if you drop it?"

"It'll float. Or you can hold it for me."

"But then"—Max's voice goes quiet—"surely the carbon dioxide won't be expelled from our suits. We'll be breathing it."

"It won't matter if we're heading back toward the *Laertes*."

"It *will* matter if we pass out," he says reasonably.

"It won't matter if we make it back."

He pauses, only for a fraction of a second. "Okay. Go on, give it a try." His heart is racing as he turns away from her, giving easy access to his pack. "Do your thing. Go, team," he says.

"Right, then. I'm going to take out your mesh unit and disconnect the ice pack, and without those two cold elements the gas *should be* warm enough—"

"Less *should be*, please. More *definitely*."

"The gas *should be* warm enough," she repeats, as she flips open the middle compartment of his suit. "And then I'm going to use the exhaust flow as the funnel." She hesitates for a second, then presses the molded plastic button to the side. The compartment slides forward and opens with a puff. Carys pushes out the section with her fingers, the cone-shaped mesh slipping forward, icy cold. She grips its casing, then takes out the mesh, letting it hover in the vacuum of space, suspended in free fall just like they are. "Here," she says, gently batting the piece toward Max, who catches it in his gloves.

Osric, Carys flexes, *I need instructions for freeing Max's exhaust flow.*

Hello, Carys. I must warn you that the removal of the copper mesh will result in hypercapnia for Max.

Define hypercapnia?

Unconsciousness. The exhaust flow will generate one pound in expelled carbon dioxide, but Max will breathe triple that amount of recycled CO_2 in his suit in the same time period. It will not be enough to propel him, but will affect his breathing and conscious state.

How far will it propel him?

Not far enough, Carys, before he will certainly become hypercapnic.

"Give me that cone." Carys's tone is abrupt, and Max jumps.

"What?"

"I need to put it back in."

He passes her the wire mesh. "Reinsertion: imminent."

Sorry, Carys. The molecule sieve is a complex piece of physics.

"Patronizing asshole," she mutters, and Max looks up.

As you can see, by removing the adjacent mesh you have direct access to the primary oxygen supply of Max's suit.

Carys pauses.

"Are you all right?" Max asks, concerned.

She turns to him, a smile threatening to appear. "Hold the cone for a sec, will you? We're going to try something else."

Max looks confused.

"That was plan B," she explains. "Now we try plan C."

"A better plan?"

"Yes."

"Good. We had ninety minutes, Cari. Now"—he looks at the

gauge, then bites his lip—"seventy-three. Let's try whatever we can to get more."

"Okay," she says. "Let's work out how to do this chemical reaction."

"Reaction?"

"I'm going to change the chemical formula of the oxygen in your tank." She points at his pack. "Behind you."

Max moans. "Chemistry. Never my strong point. I didn't get past the birds and the bees."

She looks at him in amazement. "Max, that was biology."

* * *

HE HAD BEEN SOME way in front of her in the line for lunch the first time she saw him again, laughing loudly at something she hadn't heard. The EVSA canteen was alive with voices and the raucous crash of kitchen pans. He'd caught the sun, and the contrast of his tanned face and the speckled, freckled bridge of his nose with his white teeth was striking. She closed her eyes and forced herself not to turn and slide away as the adrenaline kicked in—this was what she'd wanted, to see him like this. *He's not all that. He's just a human.* She looked down at her standard-issue blue top, took a deep breath, and leaned forward on the pretext of inspecting the meat.

"Is this beef?" she asked, moderately loudly, and the server beeped. Up the line, he didn't turn at her voice, and she mentally cursed. She stepped out of the line—"I think I want vegetables today"—and wandered over to the veg counter, now only inches in front of him.

"May I have some broccoli, please?" She addressed the server, and at the edge of her field of vision, she saw him turn. "And some potatoes, if you have them."

"Roasted?" he said, moving to stand next to her, but directing his question at the server. "You know, there's a secret recipe for great roast potatoes. Do you want it?" He stage whispered the answer: "It's goose fat."

"Some things never change," said Carys.

"And yet," he said, turning to look at her, "everything seems to have changed."

"Hi, Max."

"Carys." He offered a respectful bow in her direction, his wavy hair sticking up every which way.

"You remember my name," she said, lifting her plate. "Fancy seeing you here."

"How very droll you are. You say it like it's a given, but really, of all the places in all the world . . ."

". . . you walked into my canteen," she finished. "It is quite far-fetched. How are you?"

The humor dropped out of his eyes. "I wanted to call you."

"Yeah?" She was taken aback by his change of pace but grappled not to show it.

"Really." He was earnest.

"It's not a big deal."

"I held myself back from calling you every day for two months. My family—"

She bounced her hip off the veg counter. "You're getting a little ahead of yourself," she said, keeping her tone light. "I thought we might talk about the weather." He smiled but didn't go on. "Fine." She sighed. "You didn't call."

He paused. "I thought we might be too different."

They were both wearing the same blue EVSA T-shirts, holding

identical trays, standing in the same cafeteria in Voivode 6. Carys looked at him cynically.

"I wasn't sure what to say," he added.

"You had plenty to say when we met," she teased, "in all kinds of languages."

"That was good, wasn't it?" he said.

"It was very good." He beamed, and she felt her insides unravel. "Very smooth."

"It wasn't an act," he said. "It wasn't something I put on to impress you . . ." She raised an eyebrow. "Unless it impressed you?"

They laughed, and Max snatched a look at her: lean and strong from the EVSA training, with long, tawny hair cascading over her shoulders, a few strands glinting gold under the artificial lights of the canteen. "It's nice to see you again."

"And you."

"Held any impromptu jam sessions recently?"

"Not really," she said. "I've been steering clear of men brandishing guitars."

"Good call," Max said, when the walls flashed green, indicating the afternoon sessions were starting. "Damn," he said, "I haven't eaten yet, but I have to get back." He started piling his lunch between two slabs of bread. "My little brother's favorite. Kent will eat anything if it's inside a sandwich," he explained.

"Kent—like the politician?"

Max nodded. "One and the same. Named after our very own utopian founder."

Carys struggled not to grimace.

"What can I say? My parents are devout. Look, can I see you again?"

"I'm not sure," she said.

"Please?"

"I don't know." She *umm*ed and *aah*ed, moving her plate to the other hand.

"Tonight?"

"I can't—"

"Please, Carys. There's something I'd like to show you. It's a once-in-a-lifetime thing." She laughed again, and he pulled a face. "I just played that back in my head and, yes, it sounded like a pickup line. But, seriously, there's something happening tonight that I was going to do on my own, but I'd love to take you. Can you be free?"

"Maybe."

"Please?"

"I suppose," she said, giving in, "if you turned up at the door to my apartment, and it truly was a once-in-a-lifetime thing, I would *consider* coming out."

"Amazing," Max said, pushing the bread down on top of his lunch. "I'll come get you at ten. You won't regret it."

"I CAN'T GET ON that."

"Try it—she's a wonderful ride."

"No way."

"Try it." Max and Carys stood in the street outside Carys's home, facing each other across a hybrid bicycle. Max held the handlebars toward Carys invitingly, and she crossed her arms. "Come on, I brought this one for you," he said. "Mine's around the back."

"No, Max. It's not the bike I'm scared of, it's the others on the road."

"Oh. That's fair enough—people are crazy out there."

"Damn right they are. I can't get on that thing when trams are flying past at a hundred miles an hour."

"Would you prefer us to walk?" he said.

"Yes," she said. "Sorry."

He sighed and pushed the bicycle into the side alley, bolting it to the ground with a liquid lock he took from his pocket and spread across the front wheel. It solidified and he pushed the bike once, to make sure it couldn't be moved.

"Wait." Carys had the inexplicable feeling she was, somehow, already ruining the memory of tonight by not being game enough. That somewhere in the future she'd look back and remember them careering on bicycles through the city at night, her hair streaming in the wind as he turned toward her in joy. She knew this was one of those times she needed to get herself out of the way, to move her cautiousness to one side; that this might be a person who responded less to what an evening looked like on the surface and more to the energy given off in the moment. "Bring that bike back here."

Max whooped and pulled off the lock with a flourish. "You won't regret it, Gary."

She swatted his arm. "Carys. Cari, if you're feeling fond. 'Shithead,' if you're not."

He placed the bike in front of her. "You got it. Now, on yer bike." He grinned, and she threw her leg over it, pulled out, and flew down the street into the night traffic.

He raced up on the other hybrid bike to where she was waiting at the lights. "Damn, you're fast. I thought you weren't confident on these things?"

"You're going to have to listen a little harder," she called. "I said it was the others on the roads I feared. Not myself." The lights changed and she tore forward, her pilot instincts kicking in as she swerved across the steel tram tracks. A silver hybrid tram pulled alongside her, its gleaming pistons the length of the carriage releasing gasps of oxygen with every push and pump.

"Carys," Max called. She didn't hear. "Cari! Hey, Shithead!"

She turned her gaze back to him. "Yes?"

He smiled. "Take the second left onto the Passeig."

"We're going to the supermarket?" she called in surprise.

"No, dummy. How about you let me lead?"

"That would do nothing for my ego," she replied, racing off once again into the traffic, the headlights catching her in silhouette.

"In that case . . ." Max put on a burst of speed, cutting around another cyclist and veering momentarily onto the slope of the sidewalk, using the downward ramp to pick up momentum. Carys, in turn, diverted down the first road on the left, switching to manual and pedaling hard, flexing the gear changes as she leaned into the corner and swung around to beat Max to the supermarket.

"For god's sake," he said, panting, as he pulled up seconds later.

"Don't like to be beaten?" she teased.

He put his feet down and caught his breath. "I'm more into teamwork."

"Where are we going, then?"

"This way," he said, and they rode off in parallel, talking a hundred miles per hour.

They pulled up next to a fence of wrought-iron fleurs-de-lis, the ancient railings trying to contain the overgrown hedge, which threatened to tumble into the road. Max and Carys stepped off the hybrids, secured them, and made their way toward a gateway almost concealed by wild shrubbery. He unlatched the iron gate, pushing hard to open it, and they walked through, their footsteps hesitant in the darkness. A narrow path wound around to paved stairs.

"Are we allowed . . . ?" She thought better of it and began to climb through the shadows.

"Probably not." Max's voice was hushed.

A moment later: "No lights?"

"None."

"Creepy." They walked up the steps in silence. At the top of a short hill, the path widened out to reveal the cityscape lit up in the dark, a jumbled scene of glass and steel structures inside crumbling Spanish ruins. Directly in front of them stood a short, darkened dome with closed shutters on the roof. The wood was weathered, with weeds and shrubs growing up around the door.

Carys gaped at the building in front of her. "Is that an observatory?"

"Come on." Max took her hand and she jumped at his touch, recovering quickly and walking with him toward the structure. He pushed once, twice, before the door gave and they climbed in.

"How did you—"

"You ask a lot of questions."

"I panic a bit when I don't know what's happening. I like knowing how things work—and where I am. How you found this place. Why we're here. I had no idea that any of these had survived."

"I found it a couple of weeks ago. It's old, from when observation was mainly Earthbound."

"Wow." Carys took a few steps inside the tiny building and rested her hand on the large wooden beam dividing the room, like the boom on a boat. "Does it use only visible light?"

"I don't think so."

"It uses only visible light," she said, her eyes laughing a little as she corrected him. "It's a really old piece of kit."

He shrugged good-naturedly. "Want to see?"

"It still works?" She looked at him in shock.

"That's why we're here." Max began to set it up, pulling open a musty wooden shutter and pushing the telescope out through the porthole. "It's the last night for thirty years when you can see Saturn from this part of Earth with the naked eye."

"But the space missions?"

"With the naked eye," he repeated, smiling. "Above us, where we are right now. I want to show you the rings of Saturn."

"That's pretty romantic."

He smiled wickedly. "I have my moments."

"So I see."

He moved her to face the telescope. "Turn the lens to pull the focus."

Carys leaned in and gasped. Flat in the eyepiece sat Saturn: small and round, ringed perfectly by lines of gray. "It looks like a drawing. That can't be real."

"It is." Max took a step behind her. "I've heard it gets better the longer you look."

As her eyes adjusted and the cloud of asteroids above Earth shifted and moved, the black of the sky drew the sphere even further into sharpness and she saw that the tonal colors of Saturn's rings had a purple tinge. He took another step. "Amazing, isn't it?"

"Breathtaking." She turned and grinned at him, then leaned back into the eyepiece. "I want to fly up there one day."

"That would be incredible. I love the stars."

"Me, too." She gazed in silence at the rings of Saturn, watching as her eyes pulled the planet into focus once more. "None of the EVSA pilots have been able to get out farther than Earth's mesosphere since the meteors arrived."

"You will."

"I hope so," she said, as a shower of meteors lit up the image in the telescope, momentarily obscuring the planet. "I want to see the night sky without the fireworks—I haven't been above the stratosphere yet."

"So what do you do all day?"

She smiled, still looking at Saturn through the lens as it surfaced in the dark once again. "Space agencies have always recruited pilots. I fly shuttles for the EVSA inside Earth's atmosphere, and I'm learning to fly higher—mainly simulations and parabolic flights at the moment. But one day soon I might get to go up to the asteroid belt, maybe try to find an exit path through it. They're mapping the asteroid field at the moment. I'd like to see Saturn without a belt of rocks masking my view."

"You will, I know you will." Gently, he lifted her hair and dropped a kiss on the nape of her neck.

She pushed herself into his hand, and he ran his thumb down and across her bare shoulder. "And what do *you* do all day?" she asked, keeping her tone light.

Max let her hair fall, fanning across her back, as he stood motionless behind her. "I thought I was going to be on the culinary team, cooking for astronauts like you," he said, "but they're moving me toward nutrition and research."

"Interesting."

"It's certainly unexpected for somebody who already had three full-time jobs." His hand followed the curve of her shoulder to her waist.

"Remind me?"

"Shop boy, chef, and online stalker of Caryslike humans."

"I remember." She paused. "Do you do this with all the girls?"

"Cari," he said levelly, "I think it's fair to say everything I'm doing with you is a first."

"Like what?"

"I don't know . . . Breaking into abandoned observatories to watch celestial once-in-a-lifetime events. Pursuing something with you. Wondering what the skin on the nape of your neck tastes like." She flushed, and he laughed. "You're different, and it's making me wonder if I can be different, too."

She turned her head sideways to look at him, resting against him.

"But we can't break the rules. I don't want to be kicked out of Europia—if the Voivodeship's Representatives found out—or my family . . ."

"For one tiny relationship?" she said, keeping her voice light. "I can't believe they'd bother."

"You'd better believe it. I've heard all kinds of rumors, people being asked to leave when they've knowingly gone against the rules and guidelines." He dropped another kiss on the back of her neck. "Look back at the night sky," he whispered. "Focus on the rings." She leaned back in and he held her waist, feeling her breathe against him. As Carys stared at the rings of Saturn, visible for the last time for thirty years above where they stood, Max traced circles across her neck and back with his hands, holding her and keeping her warm.

six

Seventy minutes

I'M GOING TO change the chemical formula of the oxygen in the tank behind you." Carys stops herself glancing at their depleting air gauges.

"Okay," Max says, intrigued.

"I need to think it out for a sec. I need to think about oxygen."

"Can I help?" His face is doubtful, his all-too-brief astronaut training being what it is, but Carys nods, thinking aloud.

"Oxygen was originally called 'fire air'—it's actually a great energy force. Very misunderstood. There are lots of types of oxygen: dioxygen O_2, ozone O_3, O_4—they discovered one in almost every century, in that order."

"What's your point?" Max jiggles, a little impatient.

"Science both advances and undermines itself over time. If we live long enough, most theories we currently accept as fact will be proved false. There is always better, more advanced science out there—we just have to advance our own knowledge first."

"Like the world being flat." His gaze drops to the curve of Earth, a sea of meteorites clustering on the horizon below him.

"Exactly. As our physics becomes more advanced, the oxygen becomes more advanced. That's not a coincidence. We learn how to apply more complicated science to oxygen, and then the oxygen itself evolves.

"In 2001 it turned out O_4 wasn't O_4, but was instead a cluster of pressurized oxygen molecules used in early twenty-first-century rocket fuel. Very powerful red oxygen, O_8—the most powerful."

"Okay, I'm with you, as far as my lack of chemistry allows me to be," Max says. "You're going to do something fancy to the oxygen and turn it into fuel."

"Oxidizer."

"You're going to do something fancy to the oxygen and turn it into oxidizer."

"Precisely," she says.

Max holds out his gloved hand in a high five, which Carys briefly touches with her palm.

Osric, she flexes, moving her fingers as though she's typing on a QWERTY keyboard that isn't there, her flex registering the patterns. *Confirming I can set off a chemical reaction with some of the oxygen in the pack to form an oxidizer?*

Hello, Carys. If you can generate a reaction with resultant double-rhomboid symmetry, you would be able to use that as an oxidizer.

A powerful oxidizer?

Yes.

Explain double-rhomboid symmetry?

We're talking about O_{16}, Carys.

Yikes. She takes a second to think, looking toward Earth with its lucid greens and blues of land and ocean, her eyes lingering on the surprisingly brown desert and drought where the United States used to be. *What happens if we can't create enough pressure?*

You might create a different allotrope.

Would that be bad?

Not necessarily. If you can create O_8, the Situational Analysis measures a 50 percent probability of this working as an oxidizer powerful enough to be used as propellant.

So it's worth a shot, she flexes, and as an afterthought adds, *Thank you.*

You're welcome.

In the back of her mind she notes the absence of her name at the end of that sentence, but continues to plan the chemistry.

"How's it going?" While Carys has been flexing to Osric, Max has become even more aware of their predicament. His eyes dip to the meteorites below, and back up to the *Laertes* above them. "All good?"

"Not bad. Osric says we have to create O_8." She plays it down, gauging his reaction. "Red oxygen."

"You want us to create red oxygen—out here?"

"Yes."

"In space, with no controls. Red oxygen." He looks cynical. "Not in a lab."

"No."

"In space."

"Yes."

"With no tools."

She comes clean. "Actually, for a better chance of survival we need to create O_{16}."

"What?"

"Black oxygen. But Osric says if we can get close to O_8 we'll have a shot."

"Black oxygen," he echoes. "That's impossible."

"We have to try." Her voice is thin, pleading. "Come on, Max. We have to try."

He looks up, scared. "All right. What do we do?"

Carys. The word flashes in blue to the side of her fishbowl helmet glass, unbidden, and her adrenaline jumps.

Yes, Osric?

The panels of your suit are detecting a large influx of ultraviolet.

And?

Are you in direct line of sight to the sun, Carys?

Carys looks back to the ship and sees the full glare of sunrise from behind the hold. *Yes. We've fallen farther from the* Laertes, *so we're no longer in the shade.* She begins once more to work at the back of Max's pack, reaching in past the hole for the mesh cone and up toward the oxygen supply.

Carys.

What, Osric? "I'm busy," she mutters, switching off Osric's audio *ping* alerts before her heart gives out with the adrenaline.

You must not affect the oxygen under ultraviolet rays.

Carys pauses. *Why?*

A chemical reaction between oxygen molecules under ultraviolet radiation from the sun has a high probability of creating trioxygen.

"What's going on?" says Max.

"Hold on a sec."

"Tell me—"

Carys, trioxygen will not work as an oxidizer or propellant, and if you breathe it—

"Cari, what's happening?" Max grabs her arm.

"Something about the sun—"

The back of Max's pack flicks up where she's unhinged it and floats, so she shakes off his hand to hold on to it.

What if the molecules are still inside his pack? she flexes.

Negative, the trioxygen levels are too high.

"Cari, I swear—"

"For god's sake, wait. Osric is saying something about the oxygen in ultraviolet—"

Osric? Define trioxygen.

Trioxygen, O_3, alias ozone. A less stable allotrope of dioxygen O_2—

"Carys." Max sounds despairing.

"Fuck." She holds on to his arm. He is still clutching hers. "Fuck." Carefully she takes the mesh cone from him and places it back in his pack, clicking the unit shut, then letting go, so she's connected to him by only the tether rope. "It won't work."

"Why?"

"The risk is too high. If we don't succeed in creating red or black oxygen, we could create O_3. Because of the sun."

"Ozone?"

"Yes." *Osric: list medical ramifications of breathing ozone.*

Side effects of ozone: induction of respiratory symptoms. Decrements in lung function. Inflammation of airways. Respiratory symptoms can include: coughing; throat irritation; pain, burning, or discomfort in the chest when taking a deep breath;

chest tightness, wheezing, or shortness of breath; and, in some cases, death.

Righto.

"I wish I could talk to Osric," says Max. "I hate not having my flex."

"I'm not sure you'd want to read the stuff he's telling me right now." Max grimaces, and Carys proffers her wrist in his direction. "I'm sure we could reprogram mine somehow, if you want."

"There's not enough time. You carry on." His eyes flick down to her dropping air levels.

"Okay."

Osric, she flexes on a whim, *can you move the ship to block any ultraviolet rays from the sun?*

Negative, Carys. Navigation and guidance systems are off-line.

Oh. A second passes. Then: *Can you make our conversation also appear within Max's suit?*

Yes, Carys. Would you like me to transmit this dialogue to appear on Max's helmet visual, with any expletives scrubbed?

He's not a child. You can leave it verbatim.

Affirmative.

A second later Max's glass flickers to life with the blue text of Carys's entire conversation with Osric, left-aligned within his field of vision. Max blinks and looks up, scrolling back through the exchange. "He talks differently to you."

"Nonsense."

"He does. Christ, Cari, those are some substantial medical warnings about ozone you've got there."

"I know, but are any of them worse than certain death?" she says.

"If we try, but fail, we'll end up damaging our lungs. But isn't it better to try in case we succeed, and then we can live?"

"You mean," he says, "better to have a shot at a damaged life than no life at all?"

She nods.

"I don't know if I agree."

Carys stares. "Really?"

"Not when the risk is to you."

"Well," she says, "technically the risk is to you. We're trying this with your pack."

He laughs and it sounds like a hiccup. "Oh. That's fine, then."

"Really? Max? Did you mean that?" He's distracted, blinking as he reads the conversation between Carys and Osric. She tries again. "Max. Say something. Did you really mean that?"

He doesn't answer.

"Max?"

"They're not very good at being proactive, are they?"

"Who?"

"Osric. The EVSA. Almost everything Osric has calculated for you he's done because you've asked."

"I guess that's the limitation of the system," she says. "It's reactive."

"I wonder if they'll evolve that in future versions."

"Probably. Proactive intelligence can't be far off."

Max is still reading her text on his glass screen. "Cari. Osric said the *Laertes* navigation and guidance systems are offline. Ask him what systems are *online*."

Osric: list operational systems.

A reel of blue trips down the glass of their helmets. Life support;

air recycling; the greenhouse systems: photosynthesis, solar panels, irrigation; waste disposal; gaming; gravity simulation; lighting; water supply . . .

"The greenhouse," Max says.

"What about it?" she says.

"The plants need light. Activating the greenhouse routine would open the additional solar panels. Look at the position of the *Laertes*—it would have to turn the panels toward the sun. Activating the greenhouse routine *would rotate the ship*."

"You're right," says Carys, and Max bounces. "It won't bring the *Laertes* back to us," she says, though she finds his excitement contagious, her voice blooming with renewed energy. "But it might block the sun and stop your pack from creating ozone."

"And it wouldn't hurt to swing her a tiny bit closer."

"Plus the air lock would be facing us, if we did manage to create a propellant. But the important thing is the sun would be fully shielded."

"Sounds good to me."

"Let's do it. We should do it." Carys bobs up and down. "Shall we do it?"

Max smiles at her. "Hell yeah."

Osric: Initiate greenhouse routine.

The greenhouse routine was last run twelve hours ago. The ecosystem does not require more photosynthesis. Potential danger to plant life: high.

"That's it! I'm going to strangle him."

"It's a computer. He doesn't know what he's saying. Tell him to do it," Max says. "Flex so hard Osric feels the pressure of your fingers around his virtual neck."

Override. Initiate greenhouse routine.
Confirm password?
Password is FOX. Thank you.
Confirmed. Initiating greenhouse routine.

Max and Carys stare at the ship, watching intently as she lies on her haunches. Nothing happens. They flick their gaze from each other to the ship. Finally the *Laertes* begins to move: two poles extend from either side, swiveling in their sockets, like the cannons of a battleship. "Isn't it eerie," says Carys, "that when we were inside we could hear every scratch of metal, but out here it's utterly silent?" Another pause, then the *Laertes* slowly, slowly swings around ninety degrees. Her long starboard bow now faces where Carys and Max are falling.

"Very eerie."

At once the poles erupt, ballooning in silent slow motion as the solar panels open, like umbrellas against a downpour. White and silver, the panels are pockmarked with damage from the asteroids, but the remaining fabric lights the darkness as it stretches into wide squares, adjusting to face the sun. Max and Carys fall into shadow, and they cheer. "That was amazing."

"I've never been so happy to see a solar panel in my life."

"Incredible."

"Look—you can see the air lock now."

He rubs her arm, lost in the moment. "What now?"

They look at each other, and she bites her lip. "I guess we get on with this chemical reaction."

ONCE AGAIN, CARYS DRAGS herself around to his back, where she fiddles with his pack. "You're sure about this?"

He nods. "Do we know how to heat the oxygen?"

She stops and looks at him, so he turns to meet her gaze. "I told you, Max, it's a heat sink."

He snorts. "As if I know what that means."

"We remove the ice chests and we alter the temperature of the cryogenic oxygen with this very handy temperature gauge."

"Surely it's capped."

"Yep. But there's a pressure gauge, too."

"God, they really think of everything." He pauses. "Apart from all the obvious things."

"And instructions." She moves her hands across the silver compartments, fingering the flexi-tubes, the electronic gauges with numerous numbers and readings displayed in a bright electric blue. "We're going to heat it and add pressure."

"I wish Osric could tell us what to do."

"It's not in his remit," says Carys, "which sucks."

"He can run systems on request, and auto-alert when any fail. That's it?"

"And list probable outcomes through Situational Analysis."

"Right, like your ozone side effects—which scare the hell out of me."

"We should decide what we're going to do if this works," she says. "If we can create an oxidizer propellant, you'd better be ready to zoom back toward the *Laertes*. You reckon it's still in range?"

Max shrugs. "You're the one who'd know."

"Let's presume so. It can't hurt to be closer, even if we don't reach it this time. I guess we'd better face you the right way."

"Cari—"

"The oxidizer will propel you forward—"

"What's wrong?" he asks, stopping her babble.

"I'm worried the oxidizer is going to be unstable, jetting out of the back of your pack."

He raises his eyebrows. "And . . ."

"And if I'm behind you, it's going to push me away and yank the tether and we're going to be jerking all over the place. So we'd better untie the rope—"

"Carys, will you listen to me? If you succeed in generating O_{16}—*if*—it's going to be so powerful that us jerking around as we fly back through space is going to be the least of our problems."

She says, in a very small voice, "You think?"

"I do. Don't you dare untie yourself."

"All right."

"Do the reaction, then get yourself around to the front and out of the way of the thrust, okay?"

"Okay."

"I hope we don't die," he says and, on impulse, she throws her arms around his neck, hugging him.

"We won't. We've already had our share of bad luck."

Max clasps her to him, frustrated at the lack of genuine physical touch, their bodies encased in suits. They stay like that for a moment.

"How much time do we have left?" she says, and he flicks his eyes down.

"Sixty-five minutes." He thinks about all the times he's slept in for longer than an hour, staying in bed for more time than they have remaining now—what a waste.

"It's only up from here," she says. "Shall we press on with getting back to that stupid ship?" She points at the *Laertes*. Then, suddenly, "What the—"

"Watch out!"

Huge cubes of compacted waste fly toward them, smashing into Max, who spins off with the impact, yanking her tether so Carys is thrown, too. In the distance the *Laertes* has its starboard hatches open, facing them.

Osric, Carys flexes, but it comes out garbled as her fingers spasm in panic. *Osric—*

"What the—" Max twists and rolls, his hands locked into fists on the rope.

"Watch that block!"

"Is it a purge? Why is there a fucking purge?"

Osric!

Debris soars past them both, pushing them farther away from the *Laertes* and closer to the peril of the asteroids beneath.

I'm here, Carys. Are you all right?

Why is there a purge? she flexes to Osric, trying hard to control her muscle movements to type as they spin away, farther from the ship.

This is a scheduled dump. The carbon dioxide was expelled ahead of schedule because of the auxiliary greenhouse routine. The scheduled dump was brought forward.

"Carys!" calls Max. "Do not get separated right now. This rope—Concentrate—"

"Override," she shouts instinctively. *Override scheduled purge, Osric! Make it stop!*

Confirm password?

FOX. MAKE IT STOP—

"Hold on to the rope," Max shouts, as they're spinning in different directions, bodies jerking and writhing in their desperate attempt to stay together. She seizes the cable and pulls herself the short distance toward him, reaching out to lock her arms with his. Around them, molecules bounce, like snow globes, alongside huge cubes of compacted waste, ejected into space with a silent hiss.

"It's stopping . . ."

"The hatches are closing."

"We've got to try to hit a block. It might help slow us."

"We're falling toward—"

"I know. We'll be destroyed. Stretch your legs! *We've got to hit this block!*"

"If we end up down there . . ."

"Star jump. Snow angel. *Now.*"

They stretch out, their muscles and tendons splayed, making their footprint as large as possible so they catch on the biggest of the purged blocks. They bounce on and off and begin to slow, as the cube skitters off in the opposite direction from their impact. They continue to fall, slowly and more evenly, but still falling.

"We're farther away than ever." The solar panels on the *Laertes* are the size of cocktail umbrellas, the idea of creating enough black oxygen to get back to it now a distant fantasy.

seven

I'M GOING DOWN Under for a little bit," Carys had said to Max out of the blue, a few weeks after their trip to the observatory.

"What for?"

"Check it." She pointed to her headband.

"Deelyboppers?"

"Check. It." At once the two strands sprouting from her head flickered to life, the words "GO TEAM" appearing in red LED lights over her hair.

Max was surprised. "You're going to the Games?"

"Yep." Carys flexed her wrist, and the writing on her capital-letter crown dissolved and changed.

"That's awesome. My little brother would love those. Holograph?"

"Something like that."

"Make it say 'YOU SUCK.'" She changed it to "F*CK YOU," and he punched her lightly on the arm, laughing. "That's unlike you to self-censor."

She threw the deelyboppers at him, still finding their rhythm of playfulness. "I'm so excited! I've always wanted to go."

"Me, too," he mused. The Voivode Games were held every other year to welcome the newest territories to join the Voivodeship. This year was extraspecial: the Games were to be held in Australia, the country located farthest from the original European Union, and the most recent convert to Europia. Russia had caved ten years previously, unwilling to stay isolated in the aftermath of war, and treaties were in place with Africa. China, reluctantly, was allied with Europia, though that didn't stop defectors like Liu from moving across, causing much consternation in the People's Republic.

"I've got something to tell you," he said, suddenly grave, and her stomach clenched. They'd snatched a few moments like this across the past month, interspersed with light references to it not being "against the rules to hang out," but she feared at any point Max might shutter down.

"Oh?" She promised she wouldn't care when he did, and yet . . .

"I'm going to the Games, too. With the EVSA."

"Oh!" Carys put her hands over her eyes, laughing.

"I won tickets in the staff lottery."

"So did I."

He joined in her laughter. "I should've guessed. Half our company is going."

"Oh, well—it's something fun we get to experience together."

"I guess so. Just . . ."

"Be cool?" she finished.

"Exactly." He reached over and took her hand. "We're friends embracing the spirit of Europia together. There's no need to give the game away."

Carys nodded. "Got it. Individuals, to the last."

"That's the ideal."

She sighed. "Will you come and see the koalas with me, at least?" She walked toward her rucksack by the door.

"They can give you chlamydia."

"What?"

"Humans can catch chlamydia from koalas. Fact."

"That's disgusting." She mimed retching, then turned serious. "I thought that had been eradicated. We're supposed to be living in the perfect age."

"A perfect world, a modern utopia, sure," said Max, looking reasonable, "but one in which you can still catch sexually transmitted infections from koala bears."

"I'll see you at the air terminal?" she asked, heading for the door.

"Going already?"

She tilted her head. "I like to be early."

"You're not *flying* the shuttle," he teased, walking over to her, "but if this is the last time I'm going to see you in private—"

He pulled Carys toward him, bending his head to meet her lips, his hair falling across his forehead. She swiped it gently to the left.

"I'll walk you to the junction," he said as they broke apart.

She opened the door to the street and he pulled her out of the way of a tram passing inches in front of them. "Fuck," she exhaled, "it's perilous living here. Remind me why, again?" They stood pressed to the doorframe as the carriages rattled past with their signature whooshing sound.

"Great transport links."

"And the downside," said Carys, as Max stepped across the

tracks, "is the small danger of death every time you leave the house."

"We all have to die at some point," he said. "Life's nothing without the threat of death."

"Morbid," she said.

"Truth."

"Morbid truth."

His face took on a belligerent intent as they each stood on either side of the tracks outside his house. "If that tram had been about to hit me, you'd have found superhuman strength to save me."

"And what if I hadn't?"

"We show our true colors facing the end," Max said. "The woman who finds superhuman strength to lift a car off somebody trapped beneath, the man risking his own life to push a stranger's child out of the way of oncoming traffic. Heroic acts, when we're facing death. Or sometimes less than heroic acts—cowardice. You can't hide who you really are, at the end of everything.

"But the amazing thing, Cari, is these heroic stories are becoming more common than those about passersby doing nothing."

"You don't sound like you," she said. "You haven't been talking this . . . epic."

"It's because of Europia," he said simply. "We're doing what we want to do, rather than what we ought to do. We're becoming a better people."

"Better people."

"What?"

"Better people. Not *a* better people."

"Oh, shut up," said Max. "It's true."

"You really believe in it all." Her voice was quiet.

"Yes." He indicated for her to step across the tracks and walk with him to the tram station, but she did nothing. "You're upset because I mentioned the Voivodeship."

"No." She adjusted her rucksack straps and jogged past him. "You mentioned the ideal."

MAX ARRIVED AT THE air terminal and joined the group without meeting Carys's eye, smiling as he saw her look pointedly at her watch. He'd turned up only a few minutes before their commercial jump-jet was due to take off.

As the EVSA group snapped into their seats, Max slid into the chair beside Carys at the last moment. She rolled her eyes. "Back for more?" she whispered.

"I thought it might be a good idea to sit next to the person who can fly the plane in an emergency. So when they ask, 'Are there any pilots on board?' I can put you forward. Make myself look good."

"A model citizen."

He dropped his voice substantially. "It's really important that, for all intents and purposes"—he looked around to satisfy himself that everyone within earshot was engrossed in the preflight briefing—"I *am* a model citizen."

She guffawed.

"No, really." He stayed looking straight ahead. "I have to be. I'm from a founding family, Cari."

She was taken aback. "Really?"

"Yes. My grandparents worked to establish Europia after the war. My living relatives are very, very invested in it."

Thinking about her own relatives and upbringing, Carys said nothing, biting her nail as the jet began its vertical takeoff. As it rose up into the stratos, waiting for the world to turn before it came back down, Carys whispered, "In whose name do you act?"

"My own, Cari. I have to."

She nodded and turned away toward the window.

"Are we flying over the Middle East?" Max asked, straining past her to see.

"What's left of it," Carys replied. "There's no water, anywhere. It's a desert."

"How many people died out there?"

Carys didn't look away from the window. "Most of them."

"My god. I wonder who came off worse: the United States or the Middle East."

"There was no winner. You can't walk out victorious when you've maimed a continent."

"And you say Europia isn't the ideal . . . ?"

"He'll have the lamb," she told the steward, making a *baa* noise under her breath.

"You calling me a sheep?"

She slid the tray toward him. "Eat up."

"You know," he said quietly over the hum of the engines, taking a morsel of lamb between his teeth, "being one of the herd isn't really what it's about."

As they soared down from the Kármán Line, the light outside turning back from night to day, she began to laugh. "I know, Max. Individualism." She watched unperturbed while he clutched the armrest as they planed across a pocket of air, the jet bumping over turbulence. "It's what makes me so lonely."

"Surely it's worth it, though. A bit of loneliness, I mean. It's much harder to declare war or drop a bomb on a place where you've lived for part of your life, where your friends may live, or where you might live on your next Rotation."

Carys didn't look at him. "Doesn't stop me feeling lonely."

Leaning toward her as the jet dipped down on her side, shifting position subtly with the movement of the plane, he spoke directly into her ear: "You've got me." He touched his little finger against her hand. "Carys? I said, you've got me."

As they landed she released her belt with a brisk gesture and stood to retrieve the luggage, her voice low. "Do I? Would you really defy your family?" She gazed down at him, and he looked remorseful. "That's what I thought."

THE EVSA GROUP ARRIVED at the stadium in the early evening, the dry heat from the setting sun hitting their northern-hemisphere temperaments squarely in the face. "AC," squeaked Carys, as they broke into smaller groups. "The next chip OS update should have air-con." Sweat dried on their skins almost instantly, the humidity in the air next to nothing.

"We're not in Europia anymore, Toto."

"Who's Toto?"

"No idea, I just heard it somewhere." Max laughed.

"And, technically, this *is* Europia now."

"It's a totally different type of heat." They joined the lines snaking toward turnstiles with chip readers and fixed flexes, into which each attendee slipped his or her wrist to select options on a screen. "Which—"

"Carys!"

They were interrupted by a man and a woman weaving through the lines like gerbils in Perspex tunnels, heads down with purpose.

"Liljana!"

"Sorry we're late," Liljana called, squeezing past others apologetically to reach them. "I had to find a faith house."

"Great timing," replied Carys, nodding at the approaching turnstiles as they fell into line, putting their hands on each other's shoulders with affection in the expected greeting.

"So we'll be a foursome?" Liljana gestured to them, and after a second Carys nodded.

"Lili, you remember Max?"

"The king of dessert," said Liljana, eyeing him. "This is my new friend Sayed."

"Nice to meet you," said Sayed. "Are you all EVSA from V6?"

"That's right," said Max. "You?"

"I'm there, too. I work with Liljana on the Rover missions."

Max smiled. "That's awesome. I'm moving between nutrition and experimentation. And Carys is cooler than all of us lab folk—she's a pilot."

Carys gave a faux salute.

"Sayed is new to Rotation," Liljana said, "so you must be kind to him."

"Life in the big V treating you okay?" Max asked.

"Fine," Sayed said, shuffling forward in the line, "just fine. A few adjustments to make, languages to learn and the like. So many languages."

Max laughed. "That will definitely be an adjustment. My dad had me out on Rotation from the age of six."

"Six?" Carys, listening in, was aghast. "That's so young."

"Founding families set an example, I suppose. Good for the soul. Do everything in your own name for a few decades."

Sayed murmured the affirming noises of the newly indoctrinated. "Are you marking your chip for the lottery?"

Max squinted against the haze of the evening sun. "Maybe. You?"

"You should totally do it," Carys said.

"You should, too," said Sayed. "Perhaps we all should."

Liljana shuddered. "Not me. But, Carys, you should put in for the tacticals. You're a natural problem solver—you'd be amazing."

"Damn right," she said. "I've been practicing for months, just in case."

Together they stepped into adjacent turnstiles and Carys put herself into the lottery, selecting categories and punching her choices into the screen. Security was tight at big events after the terror attacks that had led to the war in the former United States, and as a new European resident Sayed was held up at the gates.

"What did you go for?" she asked, as Max freed his wrist from the chip reader and walked into the Park. "Brute-strength lottery?"

He pulled his body into an underwhelming muscle-man pose. "Oh, sure. Weight lifting. Mixed martial arts. Judo." Carys looked half stricken, half in awe, and he laughed.

"Great," she said. "We'll be flying bits of you back in doggy bags."

In the center of the Park stood a smooth colosseum made from glistening glass. This was rare in the Voivode: unlike the juxtaposition of modern with ancient found elsewhere, the Park for the Games was always a completely new construction. Ergonomic stadiums and sleek arenas were dotted about in all directions, and music played from every corner, a melting pot of different traditions—jazz guitarists with marching drummers, rappers on stages with flautists.

Lines of flags billowed in an automated breeze, their fabric changing digitally every few seconds to show the regional pattern of each Voivode. Interstitial blips displayed the tricolor design of the Games.

"Take our photo?" Carys proffered her lens to Max, as she and Liljana put their arms around each other, smiling into the camera.

"Now you two." Liljana took the lens as Carys and Max gave a clumsy thumbs-up, the flags wavering behind them.

"Another," she called. "Closer." They caught each other's eyes. "Go on," Liljana urged. "Squeeze in nice and tight." After a beat Max nodded, lifting his arm up and around her as Carys stepped into his body, smiling hard. "What a beautiful couple you would make." Liljana laughed as she showed them the photo. "It's almost a shame about the Couples Rule, no?"

Carys guffawed rather too loudly. "In his dreams."

Max made a face. "If she's lucky, I'll call her in ten years. Where to first?"

"Athletics," said Sayed, catching up with them and looking at the itinerary. "I've just grabbed us front-row seats."

Without saying a word, Max took Carys's lens and swiped the photo into his account as they walked toward the colosseum.

The pristine track was laid in a looping figure eight, the symbol of infinity. Injection-molded orange polymer seats ringed the arena, stepped all the way back to the gods. "Epic," they breathed, as screens lining the open-air roof threw lights up into the sky.

Eleven athletes paraded out to enthusiastic cheers that hushed immediately as the time came to call the lottery. Liljana looked questioningly at Max and Sayed, and they shook their heads—their chips hadn't been marked. A cry went up from the far left of the arena, and a man from the crowd jogged down to the podium, where he was given the necessary kit. All around, screens proclaimed the collaboration of Europia, through the interactive joining of participants and spectators. The man from the crowd joined the athletes to rapturous applause and took his place in lane twelve. As the achievements of elite outliers can only be truly appreciated next to average ability, one spectator went up against the professional athletes in every sport, providing context for the audience at home.

"Who are you going to play with?" Max asked Carys. This was the second interactive element of the Games: the functionality to follow one particular athlete and feel every bump, breath, and tumble.

"Average Joe over there," she said, gesturing toward the layman from the crowd. "Let's see how it feels to race the best in Europia."

"Right, then," he said, as they pulled the oculus screens from the seats toward their eyes and synced with the chips on their wrists. "I'll go with lane eleven, to see how it feels to beat your man in twelve."

"It's on." They sat forward, as did the viewers watching from home across the Voivodeship, when music with a heavy beat pounded out in the stadium. The athletes saluted the spectators, loosening up on the spot, then dropping into a crouch on their marks in each lane. The crowd hushed. With an explosion, the runners jerked forward, Carys's Joe stumbling out of the blocks and lumbering along the track.

"You picked a lame duck." Sayed laughed as Carys groaned, the oculus showing the elite athletes gliding effortlessly into the distance. Her heart raced as her chip synced with Joe, her body pitching suspiciously right as he shambled down the track, clutching at a stitch. Max and Liljana, on the other hand, had their heads thrown back in elation as they soared down the track with the professional runners, their hearts pounding an organic, healthy drumbeat. Liljana's athlete won and she leaped to her feet, arms out like an eagle's wings, whooping as she hit a euphoric high. Around the stadium, the winner's other backers leaped up, too.

They removed the screens as, around them, the crowd laughed and chattered about what they'd experienced, cheering the competitors as Carys's Average Joe beamed and took a bow, panting heavily.

"What's next?" said Liljana. "We should get a wager on. I like my chances of picking only winners today."

"A few more races here, then Aquatics?" suggested Max. "Let Carys get her breath back."

THE POOL IN THE Aquatics Center gleamed like glass as the excited murmur of the crowd bounced off the water's surface and echoed around the hall. Liljana led them up to their white seats, each with its own oculus. Carys trailed behind, exhausted from following the "ordinary" spectator participants in the Games they'd watched so far. The digital fabric flags wavered in the same breeze, even indoors, the smell of chemically clean water tickling people's nostrils.

By rote the athletes came out, and the now well-versed audience hushed in advance of the spectator lottery.

"Shit."

Max turned to Carys. "What?"

"Shit." She rummaged for her flex, pulling the mesh strip across her knuckles, looking at the chip on her wrist.

"What?" Liljana and Sayed turned to see what was happening.

"My chip was marked."

"For the swimming?" Max started laughing. "I hope you brought your suit."

"It's not funny. Shit."

"But, Carys," said Liljana, leaning over, "I thought you only put in for the tactical games?"

"I did."

"But this is an all-female strength race."

"No shit." She looked at Max. "What am I going to do?"

"There must be a mistake," Max said, shrugging.

Sayed looked serious. "You have to do it, Carys."

"What?"

"The chances of you being picked are very slim. The chances of you ever being picked again, even slimmer."

"Sayed is right. You should do it," said Liljana. "You'll never get another chance."

"I can't."

Max stopped himself from taking her hand as another announcement called for the winner of the lottery to step forward. "Do it, Cari. I know you wanted to whip some men in the tacticals, but this will be fun. Nobody will judge you for not winning a strength race."

She looked at him with despair. "I'm not a good swimmer, Max. When I—"

"Splash along," advised Liljana. "No one expects you to win."

Sayed was intense. "You'll look back and wish you'd taken part. It's only four lengths, Carys."

"It's the medley—that's four different strokes."

The last call for the lottery went up and Max, egged on by Liljana and Sayed, pulled Carys to her feet. A cheer erupted from the seats surrounding them, ricocheting around the arena as the crowd realized the winner had been found. He pushed her gently toward the steps and Carys walked with trepidation down to the pool, looking back up at her friends. Max signaled for her to smile, drawing a sweeping curve across his face with his hands, and she, in return, grimaced.

"Are you going to participate with Carys?" asked Sayed.

"Of course," said Max, pulling the oculus to his face as Carys was introduced to the crowd, then given a kit and pointed swiftly to the changing room.

"Not me," Liljana said. "I'm on a roll."

Sayed leaned forward. "Sometimes people find greatness when they don't expect it."

"Funny," said Max, "I was saying the same on the way here."

Carys came back out in a wet suit and the crowd thundered its appreciation as she took her place on the starting block next to the athletes. Max inhaled hard as she dived into the water at the pistol shot, his heart jumping in sync with hers. Sayed, also participating with Carys, felt every stroke of her scrappy butterfly as she plowed through the water in her first length, the elite swimmers gliding along in front.

"She's doing really well," he called to Max, and Max nodded.

Her return length—backstroke—went a little awry, as Carys bumped into the ropes between the lanes, and some of the audience gasped. Those participating with her, like Max and Sayed, were breathing hard.

It was at the turn into the third leg that things started to go really wrong. Taking her last breath in the middle of the pool, then stretching to touch the side on her back, Carys could easily have pulled her legs into the wall in an open turn, then taken off on her front. Caught up in the moment, though, she went into an underwater backflip turn, tucking her legs into her stomach and driving off into breast-stroke under the surface. Her air intake mistimed, Max and Sayed felt trouble from their chips as the desire to breathe overran her.

Carys went still in the water.

Max gulped for air, gasping as he felt virtual water flood his mouth and lungs, like many of the spectators around him. He wrenched himself from his oculus and ran down the Aquatics Center steps. His chip's sync lifted as he ran toward the deep end, a cry going up as the medics plunged into the pool, grabbing Carys's body where it floated in the water, her arms listless at her sides.

"No!" Max shouted in horror, as Sayed and Liljana started running down behind him.

A dysfunctional murmur went up from the crowd as the sync was manually lifted from those participating with Carys, while the other members of the audience following the elite athletes removed their screens with shock as they realized what was happening.

The flags stilled and flashed red, as the live broadcast to viewers at home signaled an accident. They all watched as the paramedics pulled Carys from the water. "Shallow-water blackout," said the medic, as the elite swimmers climbed from the pool and stood to one side, respectfully.

Max put one hand on the crowd barrier and vaulted it, then rushed toward where Carys lay motionless on the floor beside the pool. "Is she okay?"

"Please—let us do our job." The medic pushed on her chest once, twice, a steady three times, his clasped fists making the shape of a ventricle. Carys's heart did not beat a response.

Max fell to his knees behind the medic, reaching for her hand. "Carys."

"Please, sir." He repeated the rhythm.

"Cari."

"Cerebral hypoxia," said the other medic, as the first pinched her nose and began to administer mouth-to-mouth. Liljana stood watching in horror, unease flickering across her face as she realized how many pairs of eyes were on the young, beautiful couple framed by disaster: Max on his knees by the turquoise water, Carys's hair spilling out from her swimming cap like the lady of the lake. Somewhere an executive pondered what to do if she died on the live broadcast.

The medic breathed into her mouth once more. With a ripping shudder, she coughed, pool water splashing from her mouth, and cried.

"Cari." Max squeezed her hand, crying, too. She turned her head, tears mingling with pool water across her face, and he crawled toward her, resting his forehead on hers. "I'm sorry."

The flags flashed and turned back to white. The crowd shouted with relief, cheering on the girl's survival, and Carys held up her hand from where she lay for them to see she was alive.

Liljana called their names and Max blinked.

The spell lifted as he remembered where they were. While the medics gently moved her, to the arena's applause, Max, torn, felt he should step back, scared of having revealed so much, so publicly. What if the EVSA crews were watching in the Park? Or his family at home? His eyes darted across the crowd and met Liljana's disapproving gaze, but Max bit back his concern, still holding Carys's hand when she pulled at his wrist.

"I told you I wasn't a strong swimmer," she whispered.

"I know. I'm sorry I made you do it."

"You didn't."

I did, he thought.

"I couldn't hold my breath. I just couldn't."

All around the grounds, large screens replayed Carys's triumphant survival on a loop, showing Max dropping his head to hers over and over.

eight

CARYS AND MAX fall into the *Laertes*'s waste nebulae, fastened to each other at the waist, tipping farther and deeper into darkness. Shadow creeps over them, the only light emanating from their suits and fishbowls, their shiny silver arms held high above their heads as if they could feel or stop their fall. They can't.

"If we end up down there . . ."

"What do we do?"

". . . the asteroid field will kill us."

The entrails of a micrometeoroid sail past, popping soundlessly like an expiring sparkler. "Did you see that?"

Carys groans, her head between her raised arms. "We don't stand a chance out here—even the damn stars and rocks are dying."

"*Almost* no chance. What were you saying?"

"Is there anything we can do?"

Max shakes his head with sorrow. "I don't think so." They look at each other with dread as another small rock whips past, the same as the asteroid fragments that hit their ship and cracked their solar panels, the regular cacophony that accompanied the creaks and snaps of expanding metal as they went in and out of sunlight. Out here, the fissures and collisions of the rocks are more menacing in their silence. "We've fallen into the asteroid belt."

There had been widespread panic when it had first arrived: works of art locked away belowground; faith houses preaching the apocalypse in all forms, pulling out sermons from every belief system across history as they searched for learnings or meaning; the aftermath of the nuclear war between the United States and the Middle East calming in the face of the bigger, more universal, threat; the expedited joining of Russia to the Voivodeship. And yet the asteroid belt had simply hung there, suspended above Earth. Some rocks smashed into the land and sea, but the great majority stayed up above the stratosphere, ringing the planet. Earth's remaining nations came together to pool research both on meteoroids up in space and on the fallen sparkling rocks down on the ground—collecting geodes became rampant and profitable. The EVSA scrambled to write flight simulations and map routes before the best astronauts went up, though all proved unable to get out past the field.

The planet was, for the foreseeable future, hemmed in and held captive from the rest of the universe. Our solar system went unexplored; deep space was quiet. After two hundred years of the world's greatest scientists declaring our future would lie above us in the stars, that the salvation of mankind lay in exploring the wider galaxy, humanity was once again Earthbound. The clock had been turned back two centuries, philosophically and technologically, by a ring of rocks.

Carys and Max hold on to the rope tethering them together in the asteroid belt, quiet and contemplative. "We have less than an hour left."

"I don't know what to do." Max's honesty is brutal. "We're too far away now, and anything we try will probably be prevented by a meteoroid. We've done everything I can think of."

"Is it worth going over what we've tried?" she says gingerly. "It might spark something."

"I don't know."

"There has to be something."

"I don't know, Cari, all right?" His voice splits on the last words. "I don't know. Do what you want, because I'm done."

"If we had propellant—"

"We don't. You shouldn't start that bargaining crap, wishing we had stuff that we can't get."

"But if we'd only picked it up . . ."

"I know it's my fault." His voice turns shiny and hard. "I'd do anything to go back and strap it to my pack in the air lock. But I didn't. I feel terrible, but we can't change it."

"Hey," she says, reaching for him, "I don't blame you."

"Blame?"

"Max, calm down, please."

"You're the one talking about blame."

She takes a deep breath, unsure how to proceed. She wants to find a way to get through this and to survive, but Max has turned furious. She tries again. "Can we run through what we've done so far?"

"I don't want to make a list of my mistakes."

"Stop it. Just stop it." She screams in rage, exhaling a huge chunk of air.

He looks at her in surprise.

"I want to run through everything we've done."

"You shouldn't breathe like that," he says. "You're using up your air."

"Oh, yeah? And what do you care? You've given up."

He plays with the blue EVSA badge on his arm. "I haven't," he says more gently. "But I don't have any more ideas. We can't create propellant, and even if we could, we're too far away to get back."

"Fair enough," says Carys. "But at the very least, we've got around sixty minutes with each other, and I'd rather spend it being positive than giving up."

Max looks at the gauge on the side of Carys's pack, once again noticing it's lower than the amount he just heard her say.

"Come on," she says. "What did we try?" She looks hopeful, and he steadies his temper, resigning himself. One more splinter of rock flies past them.

"We tried to expel unpressurized oxygen as a propellant. Didn't work."

"Okay."

"Stupid. Sorry."

"Doesn't matter. What else?"

"Then we tried heating carbon dioxide. Changed the plan to the impossible: creating red or black oxygen."

She rolls her eyes. "Didn't work, because of the sunlight. But we're no longer in direct sun, so is there any point in trying that again now?" They look around at the surrounding darkness, their backs to Earth. It seems as if the moon and a swath of distant stars would take hundreds of lives to reach; and even they disappear into the pinkish folds of the Milky Way, making Carys and Max feel desperately small.

"We're too far, I think," says Max.

Carys scrolls back to the conversation with Osric about oxidizers and calculates for a second, then drops her head. "Confirmed. We're now too far away to get back to the *Laertes*. What else? We asked

Osric to navigate the ship, which he couldn't. He listed on- and off-line systems."

"Online—Osric only listed online." Max ducks as another meteoroid, this one the size of gravel, flies past, almost hitting his boot. "We need to be careful. If one of these microrocks hits our glass, we're done for."

"We're falling toward the largest, so it's inevitable." She checks another point off on her fingers: "We initiated the greenhouse sequence, which turned the *Laertes* and opened the panels, blocking the sun, but causing a purge."

"That bastard purge."

"Awful," she agrees. "Didn't see that coming."

"Being hit with toilet waste really is a kick in the teeth in this situation." He thinks for a moment. "Is there anything else we can do that would send something from the ship toward us?"

"Is there any point? The momentum from there"—she points—"to here, would only carry us farther away."

"And we don't have a life raft, nothing like that."

"No life raft," she confirms.

"Nothing on the *Laertes* that's intelligent, or that we could instruct." He again looks hopeful and she's lifted, momentarily.

"I could ask Osric?"

He nods and she begins to flex.

Osric, are there any drones left on board?

She waits, but Osric doesn't answer.

Osric?

Max watches her questions on his screen.

Hello, Carys. There's a lot of interference so not all of your words are being picked up.

Are there any drones left on the Laertes?

Negative. Two drones are out on recon and currently out of range. Two are acting as patrol satellites.

Damn.

She waits for the blue "Damn" to appear on their glass, but it doesn't, so she flexes again.

Damn.

It doesn't appear. "What the . . ."

Max peers at her. "What's happening?"

His audio crackles inside her helmet, so she quickly checks the speaker system, then inspects the flex around her wrist. "Can you hear me?"

He looks perturbed and shakes his head.

"What about now?"

Again he shakes his head, gesturing to his ear, his concern growing.

"Fuck." She looks again at her wrist, and again at her comms system, with its volume controls on the inside of her arm. She points at him in panic, mouthing for him to speak.

"Have we lost comms?" Max asks, but she can't hear him. She reaches out to touch him, trying to get through somehow. Max glances around wildly, mouthing words she cannot hear.

"I don't want to be alone," she says. *Osric?*

Carys. The words flicker on her screen. There's a lot of interference, and you're falling out of range.

She's stricken. *What?*

Don't waste time. What do you need to ask?

Max shakes her arm but she shakes him off, holding up her finger. *What?* she flexes.

You're falling out of range and will shortly be alone. Carys, what do you need me to tell you?

Max grabs her again, reading her conversation with Osric inside his fishbowl, but she can't hear what he's clearly shouting, and she's running out of time.

"Roads gone fly?" she interprets helplessly, shaking her head. "What?"

Roads gone fly. The lip-reading makes no sense, she has no idea what he's screaming for her to do. Carys hesitates, thinking about how she wants the next hour to play out, then makes a decision.

How do I restore comms with Max?

Max throws up his hands in dismay.

Carys, your audio is currently routed through the *Laertes*, then back into each of your chips. Switch on proxi—

"Osric?" she says, her voice desperate.

Nothing.

Osric?

There's only silence. She puts her face into her hands, as much as she can with the Plexiglas, then looks at Max again. In case Osric is still online, she flexes quickly: *Thank you, Osric.* It does not appear on their glass.

Max looks back at her and shrugs. They have no way to communicate—they're entirely alone.

* * *

CARYS'S NEAR-DEATH EXPERIENCE AT the Voivode Games drove a desire in her to feel, somehow, more alive. They went to bed, finally, nervous and too tipsy, overtly aware that it should mean something. But they'd doused their fear and expectation in alcohol, which made it hazy—she'd pushed him back on to the sofa and climbed on top of him, tearing at the neckline of the old navy fisherman's sweater he was wearing.

"*Whoa!*" Max had laughed, grabbing her wrists as she caught a thread, pulling the ancient garment out of shape.

She sat back, her face struggling to keep up with its own expression. "Whoa?"

"I didn't mean 'Whoa, stop,' " he whispered, pulling her down into another kiss, but misjudging it so she toppled toward him, her face crashing against his chest. "There's a chance," he said, "that we're a bit drunk."

She pulled herself back up, looking down at him, her hair unspooling from the plait across her shoulders, blonde at the ends where it had been lightened by the sun. "You think?"

He started laughing, and she began unbuttoning her shirt. He held her by the hips, gazing up at her, blinking away his spinning vision.

"Take me into the other room," she said.

"Sure?" he asked.

"Of course I'm sure," she said.

"I really want to."

"Me, too."

He stood up from the sofa, her legs around his waist, and carried her like that through to the bedroom as she kissed him. "Do we need to think about . . . ?"

"It's fine—I have a triple-A," Carys said. "We're safe." She lifted the hem of his sweater impatiently and he fumbled to take it off as he laid her on the bed.

"Are you okay?" he asked as he peeled down her trousers, pushing his thumb into the arch of her foot as he lifted her leg. Carys tensed and stretched out her calf muscles in response. She gasped as he trailed his hand up her inner thigh, teasing. In retaliation, she hooked her leg around him and yanked him down suddenly toward her on the bed.

"Stop asking me if I'm sure and if I'm okay. I've never wanted something this much in my life." Biting her lip, Carys unzipped his fly and he watched as she pushed him into her. He thrust once, twice, three times, though god this was happening quickly, into her, the girl who'd haunted his thoughts and had a body like—

He came sharply, gripping her in his arms. They lay like that for a moment, before he said quietly, "I'm sorry."

"Don't be silly," she said, her voice distant. "It doesn't matter at all."

"It does. I was just so—"

"No big deal." She dropped a kiss on his shoulder, drew herself up from the edge of the bed, and walked across the dark room, her pale skin lit only by the moonlight. He watched her, confused, as she picked up the fisherman's sweater from the floor.

"Can I wear this?" she asked, pulling it over her head. It fell to midthigh. He nodded, and she stepped into the kitchen. "Do you want anything?" she called.

Relieved she wasn't simply leaving, he called back: "Some water would be great."

"I'll be one minute."

He lay gazing at the light from the road running across the ceiling as each hybrid went past, his head spinning with alcohol and from what had happened. But when she hadn't come back after five minutes, he began to worry.

Max found her curled on a chair in the kitchen, silhouetted by the moonlight flooding in from the sheet-glass doors. Staring out at the ruins of brick foundations that were used to mark a garden, she was biting her fingernail and jiggling the knee she'd tucked under her chin.

"You okay?"

She didn't answer.

"Carys?"

"Hey," she said, with a smile that didn't reach her eyes, and eyes that wouldn't meet his.

"Can you look at me?" He approached gently, placing his hand on her back.

"I think I've sobered up now," she said, still not looking at him.

"That's a shame." She glanced up at him, annoyed, but he continued, "Because I haven't."

She buried her head in her arms. "I'm an idiot."

"Don't be ridiculous." He sat down next to her. "I'm the one who's an idiot—I couldn't control myself."

"Neither could I."

"But I couldn't make it—I mean, I wanted it to be amazing for you, but . . ."

She raised her head and finally looked at him properly, a tendril of hair falling across her green eyes. "I don't care about that, Max."

"It's embarrassing."

"Hardly."

He sat back. "No?"

"It's a compliment, really."

"Well, yeah, that's exactly what it was."

"I'm sorry I was weird," she said. "I was just scared."

He brushed the hair out of her face and tucked it behind her ear. "Why were you scared?"

"Because I like you. And I wanted you to want me." Self-consciously she untangled herself and stood to make tea.

"I do want you," he said. "Even though you turned a bit primal."

She hid her face in the sweater and they laughed, the tension finally broken. "Sorry." She looked straight at him.

"Me, too. I think you're amazing, and I'm sorry we were so nervous that we rushed it." He walked over and she looked down, so he lifted her chin. "But you know there's an upside."

She arched an eyebrow.

"We've done it now. Which means we can do it again."

She was laughing as he put his lips on hers and pushed his tongue between her teeth. As they kissed, Max slid his hands down her body, feeling every curve as he moved down to her thighs and lifted her onto the kitchen counter. She moaned and buried her head in his shoulder. Max trailed kisses over her as she crossed her legs around him.

"Thank you," she whispered.

"What for?"

"For wanting me even though I'm an idiot."

"That's okay," he said, kissing her next to her ear. "I'm an idiot, too." She wound her arms around his neck, and his hands went to her hair as they stopped laughing, the kick in their bellies telling them that this time it was very serious indeed.

nine

MAX AND CARYS can detect that they're angry with each other from their body language. Inside the glass fishbowl his face is screwed up as he mouths words she cannot hear, his hands gesturing faster than a chef chopping vegetables. Her posture, meanwhile, is defeated, her back curved in a slouch, though her body is moving—victim to the perpetual motion of microgravity.

"I know," she says, though he cannot hear her. "I asked Osric the wrong question. I wasted the chance, and you're angry with me. I know."

They have lost comms. They cannot speak or hear each other's voices. Osric is gone. In the silent aftermath, Max's frustration has ballooned into anger and Carys, bored of his antagonism, lifts her wrist in front of his face, waiting for his full attention before pressing her fingers against her thumb over and over in the international gesture for "blah, blah, blah." His antagonism surfaces once more, speaking words she'll never hear but he'll always regret.

They fight on in silence for a few moments, drifting on a course to darkness. When they're done, Max pulls himself tight into a ball, his arms braced around his helmet, knees against his chest, and screams. He screams for the helplessness of their situation, left stranded and undertrained by the EVSA, floating into the night. He screams that he should not be here now, with her, that he tried everything to stay away, to abide by utopian law, to leave her alone. But most of all he screams for the peril that she's now in by his hand. In an hour—less—she will die, and he will have to watch.

She does not hear his scream. She watches him curl and turn fetal, tremors rushing over his body as he expels the emotion. She can see it traveling along his skin and out from his limbs. Watching his collapse, Carys knows there's a sound she can't hear and, momentarily, she's glad.

She reaches out and puts a hand on Max's arm, which he tries at first to shrug away, but she insists. "I'm sorry," she whispers. "I'm so, so sorry."

Slowly, he puts his hand over hers, patting it affirmatively. Okay, he says, with that gesture. He's coming back.

He unfurls gradually, his legs straightening like those of a diver in flight. His arms relax, spreading out from the tight, braced coil he had become. He lifts his head and breathes slowly and deeply. The tether rope between them billows slightly at his waist from the movement, and he yanks it so she is pulled toward him, like a move from the tango.

She looks at him. Max puts his hand on his heart, his blue eyes apologetic.

"I know," she says. "I'm sorry, too."

He lifts his fingers against his chest twice, like a heartbeat.

Carys looks at the gauge on his oxygen, clocking that it's dropped to fifty-something minutes. She wonders what to do; how they will communicate now that they can't speak, if they might still manage to get back to a life together, taking for granted the ability to talk. Gently she spreads her fingers wide, like a starfish, to activate the flex mesh, then types across random QWERTY keys. Nothing appears on her glass—she had hoped it might still appear on his. She shakes her head and he looks questioningly at her, so she shakes it again. He shrugs. He doesn't know what she means.

She thinks back to what they learned at school about communication, other than European languages. The thing is, nobody actually knows Morse code. Most know "SOS" and, if advanced, maybe their own name, but not the entire system.

Carys dismisses semaphore—she's not trying to land a plane out here. She could wave fabric or rope or the water sachets up and down in front of Max, but there's no way she can remember all of the individual characters, or be sure he would even know—

She thinks.

He touches her shoulder, questioning.

Wait.

He touches her again, and she lifts a finger to pause him, still thinking.

He raises his eyebrows.

In a flurry of motion she beckons him with her hands, indicating that she wants to get behind him or turn him somehow. Max nods and Carys feels along his body, pulling herself forward until she's at his shoulder, maneuvering behind him. She reaches into his pack to where earlier she spotted water and . . . lights.

She pulls out an LED flashlight and puts both hands on it, concentrating on activating the beam. Letting go of Max to look down at the flashlight, she floats a little away from him, so the tether shudders.

The LED clicks on and Carys waves the beam full power in front of him, blinding him, so he shields his eyes with his hands.

"Sorry," she says, which he can't hear. She points to where it disappears in the dark, the beam away to one side. Bright though it is for them, it is an infinitesimal dot on the canvas of the galaxy. Max looks in the light's direction, wondering if she's using it to signal anyone, if she's spotted salvation in some form. As he turns he sees no life raft, only a largish rock cascading about a mile away, and shudders. They have fallen deep within the asteroid belt.

Carys shakes the flashlight to regain his attention and he nods, and she gestures at the beam, waiting for him to nod again.

Okay.

With steady hands she drags the flashlight in a slow line, pulling the tiny shaft of light through the darkness. At the top, she loops it around, bringing the curve back to the line's midriff. She looks at him.

"P?"

She smiles and nods, praying Max said "P" and not one of the many words "P" rhymes with or looks similar to in lip-reading. She pulls the flashlight once more in the same shape, and before she's finished Max taps her arm and says again: "P."

Carys shakes her head no. She repeats the shape, gesturing for him to keep watching, and at the line's midriff she slashes out a line on the diagonal.

"R?" Max mouths.

She gives him a thumbs-up and swiftly draws a circle with the light.

"O." Max looks at her in bafflement. "PRO. Professional? Promise? This is the world's most unfulfilling game. I've no idea. Carry on."

With serious concentration, she slashes the light beam in an X.

"P-R-O-X. Proxy?"

"No."

"Proxy. What do you mean, 'proxy'? What's a proxy? Munchausen syndrome by proxy. A substitute. Alternative. Vote by proxy. Death by proxy." He looks at her. "None of these."

Exasperated, she shakes her head, watching his monologue run on. She gestures with her hands, him to her, then her to him, pointing at the space between.

"Yes, we're both here." He repeats the gesture (him to her, then her to him) and she rolls her eyes. Picking up the flashlight, she draws a single line: "I."

"I. Or one. I? You, what?"

"Not I, Max. Not I. PROXI." He cannot hear her, and she realizes she'll have to start at the beginning again. If they can't figure this out, there will be so much they cannot say. What can you say, at the end of it all, with only body language? They've been through so much. With stretched patience and still clutching the flashlight, she holds out her arms before scrubbing the air clean with her hands, making the sign for "cut," indicating he should forget everything he's seen. She quickly runs through P-R-O-X—

"I'm an idiot. Proximity. You're talking about proximity." He mouths it to Carys, and she puts her thumbs up, gesturing at her flex, then mimes typing to Osric.

"Oh." Max scrolls back quickly through her last conversation with Osric:

Carys. There's a lot of interference, and you're falling out of range.

What?

Don't waste time. What do you need to ask?

What?

You're falling out of range and will shortly be alone. Carys, what do you need me to tell you?

Roads gone fly.

How do I restore comms with Max?

Carys, your audio is currently routed through the *Laertes*, then back into each of your chips. Switch on proxi—

Max reads "roads gone fly" and groans, then nods at her that he understands. He'd missed it before, Osric's last instruction: they must figure out how to switch on proximity to be able to talk.

"Proximity," Max mumbles, as he scrolls through the blue text in his glass fishbowl, moving the block of conversation to one side to explore changing the settings. "I've never done this before."

Carys raises her facial features into a question—does he know? She shakes her head, indicating she doesn't.

"Me neither, Cari, me neither." Max scrolls through brightness, contrast, and color settings to no avail. "Not there." He switches his attention to the aural controls on his arm, pushing aside volume, clarity control, and EQ. As if anyone is going to worry about how much treble and bass one hears in space.

He looks at her helplessly. He points to his ear, shakes his head, then points to the screen and shakes his head again.

She scrolls back to Osric, thinking hard.

Carys, your audio is currently routed through the *Laertes*, then back into each of your chips. Switch on proxi—

She whacks Max in the chest. "It's in our chips." She knows he can't hear her, so she points at her wrist: "Chip." Recognizing that the word sounds like "ship," she jabs several more times at her wrist, and he smiles as he grasps the meaning. Swiftly she rolls through the various settings in her chip to the ones rarely used. She finds the right default and holds out her wrist for him to see. He mimics the settings on his. With a crackle of sound, at a much higher volume than their previous audio routed through the *Laertes*, their comms burst to life with the most beautiful sound she can imagine: "Hi."

They hug and laugh together, in full stereo sound.

"Carys?" he says. "You know when I was offered my job?"

"That's the first thing you want to talk about?"

"I was thinking about it when we couldn't speak. I wanted to ask you. I want to know."

"Ask me what?" she says.

"They said it was on a recommendation, from the number of MindShare queries I'd answered. But you can only be referred for employment by an existing employee."

She fiddles with the tether. "We've been over this."

"When I saw you again," he says, "when I found out you worked at the EVSA, too—the coincidence of it . . ."

"Yes."

"That's one of the lessons you learn as you get older. There's no such thing as coincidence. Did you refer me, Cari?"

"Does it matter?"

"Did you get me my job?"

"Yes." She doesn't attempt to deny it, and he nods.

"I thought I got it off my own bat."

"You did."

He laughs, a staccato bark that splutters and muffles their helmet sound systems. "You intervened to make my life better after meeting me once?"

"Twice. We'd met twice."

"Are you mental?"

"No. Yes." She knows she will struggle to explain. "When we met, I could see you weren't happy. You were trapped in the shop out of familial duty—you said as much. Then I spoke to Liu that night at the bar and he told me about the 'gambit of space,' as he'd put it, so I thought I could help you use your absolute skill—because, Max, it is a skill—to achieve the story he was using about you. 'The world's greatest living astronaut still alive and not yet dead'? Why couldn't that become true? Why couldn't it be you? The EVSA needed a technician specializing in food and you'd done all the hard work—I simply pushed that work over to the right people."

"Why, Cari?"

Silence.

"Why me?"

She tries one last time to explain: "I didn't know if anything would ever happen between us, not then, but I thought it might be better to try to make *you* happy. Rather than sitting around waiting to be made to feel good, I could crack on and help make someone else's ambitions come to something, for once."

He falls away from her for a moment, letting it sink in. "So all this time," he says, "we've joked that I saved you when we met but, really, you saved me."

part two

part two

ten

IT WAS SUCH a simple question that Carys hadn't even thought to ask. They were happy, spending casual time together at work and intimate time together in secret, when half the Voivode started preparing for their next Rotation.

It began with small things, which crept into larger significance: first came the blink-and-you'll-miss-it, imperceptibly polite social withdrawal, as some Europeans inevitably realized their time together as neighbors was up. The MindShare saw a steep increase in online chatter, wild guessing, and research into potential future Voivodes, though they wouldn't be announced for a while. After that came the influx of enrollment at the language lab, as those with skills that had dropped in the last three years decided they didn't want to be isolated and alone in their next Voivode. Finally came the late nights and blurry mornings, as the Voivode took on the feeling of a never-ending leaving party. Members of Draw One would soon be moving to their next Rotation.

On one of those rare perfect days, Carys and Max traveled to visit the site of Carys's first memory in the deepest hills of Voivode 3. With a society-wide inability to talk about where they were "from" or where, realistically, they had grown up, most childhood experiences being transitional and transitory, many of Europia's residents chose to go back to the place of their first memory as a rite of passage.

While the top of Wales's tallest mountain was historically shrouded in cloud and often snow, that day Snowdon was framed by a beautiful blue sky marred only by the smallest white puffs: expelled oxygen from the hybrid trains crawling around the circumference.

Max woke first and crept from the bed to make breakfast, gently placing a tray at her bedside.

"You're waiting on me now? I *have* got you well trained."

He jumped. It was rare for Carys to make jokes before ten, let alone before coffee. "Good sleep?"

"I'm excited to be going back up there." She gestured toward the peaks of the national park visible through the window, sipping the searing coffee and reaching for the toast he'd put by the bed. Her light-brown hair was tied above her head in a huge, looping bun that had come loose in the night and fallen across her forehead. "Shall we get dressed and go?"

"Are you feeling quite well?" He looked down at her, lost in the huge bed, wearing his blue EVSA T-shirt with the sleeves rolled up, and she caught his gaze. She was clutching the mug with both hands to warm them and her face cracked into a huge grin. Suddenly she looked very young, and he laughed. "Come on, then. We'll have to sneak out—I wasn't supposed to use the kitchen. That old lady will beat me with her rolling pin."

"Her what?"

"Never mind."

They piled supplies into rucksacks and crept from the bed-and-breakfast—an aging Georgian mansion held up with steel struts and joists that jutted from the exterior walls but didn't detract from the rising damp and fading sense of grandeur—nestled on the road at the foot of the Welsh valley. The sun lit everything with a crisp brightness but, being early, its warmth felt distant, and around them everything was green. Lime-colored lichen grew over slate rocks that lined grassy slopes, bursts of bracken tickling the paths with fernlike feathers. Carefully Carys stepped outside, found the path, and pulled up the collar of her jacket against the nip in the air. "It's such a perfect day."

"It is," Max agreed.

"Let's turn our chips off and not use our flexes."

"Sure?" he said.

"I can live without technology for a few hours," she teased. "Can you?"

He made a show of turning his chip to sleep. "There. Where to first?"

"Can we go up to the old power station?"

"Sure. You know the way?"

"Roughly. Up the mountain." She scrunched up her face. "Everything's up the mountain from here."

"Good," he said. "You lead, team leader."

A rush of hybrid vehicles whooshed past, pushing them off the path and into the bracken. Carys, overbalanced by her rucksack, promptly fell backward into the scrub.

"What are they doing up here?" she asked, winded but amused. Max offered his hand to help her up. As she took it, he lost his footing on a patch of mud and tumbled down next to her.

"Shit." They collapsed laughing and lay like that for some time, laughing harder as they looked at each other, the joke past being funny but the momentum of their laughter propelling them into tears.

An elderly gentleman, dressed for a day's hike in a hunting jacket and breeches, a beagle trotting obediently at his heels, scowled at them suspiciously.

"Good day," called Max from the ground, and the man tutted as they began laughing again.

"What do you think they were doing here?" mused Carys, as Max dusted her down.

"Locals, darling. The old man and his dog probably live here."

"No, you idiot. The Voivode hybrids." She pointed at Max's jeans, smeared an unfortunate shade of brown.

"Oh, good. I look like I've had an accident. I think they're prepping V3 for Rotation."

Carys nodded. "Right. I keep forgetting the other half have to move soon."

Max looked around as they continued up the incline, but said nothing.

They stopped at the walkers' center for a quick drink, before the path widened into a road and flattened out beside a large lake. Years ago it had been a reservoir, but the man-made details were long gone. Now the water lay stretched out, reflecting the sky and inverting the surrounding hills on its surface—a perfect specimen of Mother Nature, despite its artificial origins.

Carys darted forward and picked up a pebble to skim it across the lake. When she let it fly, it skipped once, twice, three times over the surface.

"Not bad. Not bad," said Max, looking around for a suitable stone. He found one and skipped it four times. "Yeah."

"Hmm." Carys rubbed her thumb over the flat surface of an oval pebble, feeling its weight in her hand. She pulled back her arm but didn't throw the stone. In slow motion she flicked her wrist, practicing the movement.

"In your own time."

"Watch and learn, Maximilian." She whipped her arm around, bending her knees as she released the pebble, watching with satisfaction as it skimmed the water in a straight line, skipping nine, ten, eleven times, before dropping with a *plink.*

Max stood openmouthed. "How did you do that?"

"The knack," she said, as she turned away from the water, hiding her smile, "is to generate spin and forward velocity simultaneously."

"The science of stone skipping." Max was still staring out to where the pebble had sunk, about twenty-five feet from the shore. "My little skipping nerd," he said, pulling her into a hug and speaking into her neck. "You're talking about the science of stone skipping. I can't believe you can do that."

"Five times Tanygrisiau champion I was, growing up," said Carys, her voice taking on more of the lilting accent as she spoke about her childhood. "The final piece of the equation is the angle at which it hits the water. Fifteen degrees is the best pitch."

"Get you. Five times champion." Max dropped the pebble he was holding. "No way I can compete with that."

"Luckily," said Carys, standing on tiptoe to look him almost in the eye, "you don't have to. I can be good enough for both of us."

He guffawed but stepped back, conscious of passersby.

"Oh, relax, will you?" Carys sighed. "I don't think we'll have to maintain the front up here."

"Everywhere, Cari. The rules are in place for a reason."

"I thought they were more like guidelines. How to have a happy life . . . Stay independent and have kids late." She pulled a face.

"Something like that," he said. "Though there is psychology and science behind it, you know." He looked back to the people walking on the other side of the lake. "We should probably move on."

"It's not a police state, Maximilian. Those strangers are not going to ask us to leave the Voivodeship. Or are you worried they're judging you for not holding up the ideal?" She walked back up to the path, knowing she was right—and he knew it, too.

Taking a deep breath, Max grasped her hand, and they climbed the steep, rocky hill toward the old power station.

THE VIEW FROM LLYN Stwlan was astonishing. An enormous dam, carved from stone, stretched out in arches all the way along the mountainside. The dam formed a path across the terrain: on one side, the vast lake of dark water; on the other, a sheer drop down the mountain face. Max and Carys walked along, gazing alternately at the reservoir and the rocky crag, carefully stepping over any greenery that spilled out of the gray stone seams. Above them the clouds puffed across the pale blue sky in a gentle but chilly breeze.

"There used to be a wall here along the top, but it crumbled away ages ago," said Carys, admiring the mountain view. "Bit more dangerous now. And hundreds of years ago there was a steam railway."

"Steam? They were closer than they thought."

She shrugged. "Coal, though—not oxygen."

"If only they'd looked at oxygen a bit harder." Max sat down on the rocky edge of the dam, where the wall used to be, his legs dangling precariously some hundred feet above the water. "How has your day been?"

"Oh, you know, perfect."

"Me, too." He smiled. "And this was your first memory?"

"Close enough." Carys dropped down beside him and he handed her a coronation-chicken sandwich from the rucksack, which she took gladly.

"How old were you?"

She hesitated. "Max—"

"I suppose you were five, like everyone else." He thought about it for a moment. "But then you wouldn't be able to remember so much about the place, like how to get around. And you wouldn't be a five-time pebble-skipping champ." He looked at her. "Carys?"

"My parents . . . Wales had independence, you know, so they opted out of Rotation at first. They stayed here in the mountains. We were some of the last to go."

Max looked at her in amazement. "You grew up outside Rotation?"

"I lived here until I was eighteen."

"Without moving?"

"Without moving. I didn't join Rotation until I was eighteen."

Max sat back. "No Rotation until eighteen. Christ, don't tell my parents, if you ever meet them—they would *not* approve." He took a bite of sandwich, shaking his head. "No wonder . . ."

"No wonder what?" she asked.

"You find Europia—the whole thing—a little inconvenient."

She put the sandwich down. "And you don't?"

"Not really. I mean, it's inconvenient now that I've met you and I'll have to move in two months."

Her mouth made an O but no sound came out.

"Cari?"

"You're moving?"

He had the grace to look down. "I'm in Draw One, Cari."

"I didn't ever ask which draw you were in," she said. It was such a simple question, she hadn't thought to ask. "I just presumed."

"I was waiting for the right time."

"And you picked now?" Her voice twisted with a histrionic twinge, but it couldn't be helped.

"I thought—I thought I'd wait until we had the perfect day."

She mulled it over, then said, "You thought the way to end a perfect day was to tell me you were moving in two months?"

"Yes," he said, but she looked cynical. "No. Maybe. Yes."

"But when we met," she said, "you were looking after the supermarket for your family. You'd just started looking after it for them."

"No, Cari." His voice was gentle. "I'd been there for a while. It's why I was so frustrated. Look, I never expected to meet someone like you, for it to last—it's not supposed to, not yet."

She rubbed her face, staring at the moss on the rocks as she contemplated what to do, and what to say. Finally: "What happens now? Is this it?"

"I don't want it to be." Max was quiet. "I don't want to lose you."

"You're doing a strange job at *keeping* me, Max."

"I don't know what to say. Maybe when we're older . . ." His voice trailed off, and he knew instinctively not to look up.

"Is this it?" Carys repeated.

"I just can't. I can't. How do we justify it? None of my friends are going through this. None of them." She muttered something and Max said, "Please don't push that generation hookup thing at me. That's not what this is about. But the way I was raised . . ."

"What is it, Max?"

He put the remains of his sandwich down. "I told you about my family. They died to found the utopia. My grandparents, their brothers and sisters—my great-aunts and great-uncles—were first generation. I'm from a founding family, Carys. What about that don't you get?"

She was quiet.

"There are a lot of them, sure. But mine . . . We went to language school six days a week. My first fridge artwork was the Europia gold stars on blue. Christ, my first words were probably the pledge." She smiled at that. "My paternal grandparents originally came to the utopia from India and Spain, my mother's side from Switzerland and Italy. My paternal grandmother was a doctor in pediatric genetics— and my mother is, too."

Carys sat still, daunted by the weight of his family's legacy, but fascinated to hear the details she'd craved for so long but had been too scared to ask.

"My grandmother was on the core team that took the outdated statistics about fertility from eighteenth-century France that were still being cited, and commissioned new research. As scientists they explored the limitations of fertility, evolving new techniques and methods, setting new guidelines for parenting. My family finally helped overturn the social stigma of having children later in life."

"So people had to stop saying 'tick-tock' and telling us not to leave it too late," Carys mused.

"Exactly. Which, in turn, led to the instigation of the Couples Rule."

They sat together as Carys took it all in. "So when I tease you for truly believing . . ."

"Do you know how hard it is to go against something you've been told all your life?"

"I don't suppose I do."

"It hurts." His voice was pleading. "If we'd met that little bit later . . ."

"Another decade, almost."

The raw truth hurt them both, and Max wanted to comfort her but didn't know how, so they sat watching the palls of hybrid steam farther down in the valley.

"Where are you moving?" she asked.

"Another EVSA station. I meant it when I said I don't want to lose you."

"But you're the poster boy for the Couples Rule."

"You understand, then."

She nodded. "I guess I do."

He was quiet for a few moments, the cold of the stone edging through their clothes. "I'll miss you video calling on the Wall Rivers to show me every single thing you might possibly wear on a date."

Carys made a face. "That was once."

"And I'll miss the way you tuck your freezing-cold feet between my legs when you sleep."

"Or the way I mess up your tooth-cleansing programs so they spurt water across the glass floor of your bathroom."

"I definitely won't miss that."

"What's wrong with just using a toothbrush? That's what I want to know . . ."

"You're so old-fashioned." Gingerly he put his arm through hers as they sat high above the national park, green mountains laid out around them beneath the bluest spring sky, their legs swinging off the dam above the lake. Max made to say something but stopped himself.

After a moment, Carys said, "Go on."

"I didn't really expect any of this to happen."

She took his arm, leaning against him, and they sat like that for a while.

"Maybe we can visit each other. There are weekends—"

She looked at him. "We're not supposed to, you said it yourself."

"I know." He sounded conflicted; he didn't like this strange role reversal. "But I visit my friends in other Voivodes. You do, too." He chewed it over. "That would be entirely normal. Plus, it wouldn't be fair to send you out into the world before you know how to manage the tooth programs successfully," he said, and she smiled. "I'd be fulfilling a public service."

Carys rested her head on his shoulder, her arm looped through his.

"Don't hate me," Max said. "But I can't quite give up just yet."

"How could I hate you?"

He put the wrappings of their sandwiches back in his bag and made to stand up.

"Perhaps," Carys whispered, her sibilants catching on the breeze, "some rules are designed to be overruled."

eleven

* *Forty-five minutes* *

SKITTERING LIKE PEBBLES across water, Max and Carys sink deeper into the asteroid belt than they ever could have wanted. Circling Earth, the belt creates beautiful shooting-star displays at night and sometimes during the day, but up here—inside the asteroid field—it's perilous.

"It's been forty-five minutes," says Max as they fall, looking nervously around. "We've used half our time. No one's coming, are they?"

"There's no one to come."

"We're totally alone."

"Stop that."

"We may as well give up."

Carys bites her lip. "Give up what?"

"We may as well give up trying to find ways to survive."

She looks at him sharply. "What?"

"What's the point?" He shrugs.

"Please, Max. I don't need to deal with your newfound depression on top of everything else." She gestures around them at the field of meteoroids.

"Maybe we should take our fishbowls off now, embrace the end quickly rather than dragging it out."

She whacks him in the chest. "Stop that. I mean it. Look down." She points toward a fireworks display gearing up over China, as meteors the size of bookcases create trails of fire across Earth's sky as they burn and break up in the atmosphere. "Imagine all the people looking up," she says, "and we're the only ones looking down."

"Hmm," Max says. "That doesn't do much for my terror at us being alone."

"We're not alone," she insists, and they continue to watch the meteors over China. "At least up here we don't have to deal with the Couples Rule, or the Voivodeship Representatives, or the fallout from the decimation of the United States and the Middle East, or those meteors hitting the Earth." She takes a second to recoil at the state of the globe they've left below, a world described as perfect though slowly tearing itself apart.

"But there's no one up here with us. Isn't that somehow worse?"

"The little Russian space dog is probably floating around in her ship somewhere," she says. "Laika."

"Poor little thing," he reflects, a note of desperation creeping in. "Do you think Anna's up here somewhere?"

Surprised, she shakes her head. "No, sweetie."

"She might be."

"I don't think so."

"Somewhere."

Concerned at this radical shift in attitude, Carys hits him in the chest again for good measure, then notices his eyes are a little dilated. "Max? You okay?"

He's still watching the meteors below. "I'm not cut out for this. I'm a chef, Cari." He looks at her, pleading. "I'm just a chef."

"No, you're not. You're a member of the European Voivode Space Agency." She rests her gloved hand on his chest. "I'm scared, too. My physics isn't good enough to save us. We don't know what we're doing. But we're members of the EVSA, and we were trained—albeit briefly—to be here."

"Right."

"Will you please make a joke?"

"Not right now," he says. "I'm saving one for later."

"Good."

"It will probably be about the science of skipping stones."

She wrinkles her nose. "A better joke."

"I'm working on it."

"Good."

"But your physics is sound," Max says, "when it comes to skipping stones."

She laughs. "I guess asteroids are just pebbles skipping around in space. It's simply the setting that's different."

"It would be really hard to skim a stone in zero gravity. Unless you skipped it off this galaxy and into the next."

"That's pretty deep," she says, glad he's beginning to relax a little as they talk nonsense. "You don't think we're alone out here, then?"

He gestures at the purplish tones of the Milky Way. "Come on. We used to think we were the only inhabitable planet in the only galaxy. Now we know we're one of an infinite number of galaxies in an expanding universe. Are we really so lucky that we would get all this to ourselves?"

Carys giggles. "You sound like an estate agent, selling space."

"On sale! Tell all your friends," he singsongs in caricature. "On the left we have a dazzling panoramic view of all the constellations in the cosmos. On the right, an easy 250-mile commute into the center of the Earth, avoiding rush hour. Accommodations cozy, with an authentic glass fishbowl to keep out the elements, but the neighbors are friendly."

She claps her gloves and Max bows. "Thanks," he says. "I feel better."

"I guess that's what we have to do from now on: talk each other off the ledge."

"I wish we had a ledge—this tumbling's exhausting."

Carys looks around. "I know we've always treated Earth as though it's down, but if it helps, in microgravity there is no up or down. It doesn't matter which way we face, it's all the same."

"My brain keeps Earth as a constant below us. Every time it moves, I feel like I'm on a roller coaster."

"Me, too. Maybe we should stop looking at home."

He doesn't say anything about that word—*home*.

"Max? What did you mean earlier, 'roads gone fly'?"

Oh, god. "Oh, god, that."

"What did you mean?"

"Osric told you to ask what you needed to know before we fell out of range. You had time for roughly one more question. Earlier he'd said there were four drones. Drones, Cari. 'Drones offline'?"

She looks at him in shock. "Roads gone fly. Drones offline."

Max shrugs. "I wondered if he could have turned the drone satellites back, got them sent this way."

"You're kidding. Why the hell didn't you say?"

"I did say. But we lost comms," he says, exasperated. "Didn't you notice that Osric could give you answers only to the questions you asked?"

"That whole thing was weird." Don't waste time. What do you need to ask?

"It's too late now. Can't speak to Osric, can't speak to the *Laertes*, can't speak to Earth."

"I'm sorry. I couldn't understand."

"Ah, well. I couldn't guess 'proximity' either, so I guess we're both equally useless." He wipes the glass in front of his face with his sleeve. "What do you want to do?"

"I wouldn't mind a drink."

"I'm serious," he says. "What do you want to do?"

Carys gestures around them. "We don't have a huge amount of time."

* * *

TIME TOGETHER BECAME EVERYTHING while their relationship was long distance, but long distance, it turned out, played havoc with their relationship. Friday evenings were strange, a polite, awkward gateway back into familiarity, one of them always exhausted from traveling, the other tense about hosting. Carys would arrive in Voivode 13 whining and self-conscious, nitpicking about this or that, or an annoying passenger on the hybrid, unable to look Max in the eye. He'd fuss over her, getting her settled, but he didn't have the verbal capacity to put her at ease so they'd go quickly to bed. Afterward they'd lie together, endorphins sating those irritated, self-conscious thoughts, relaxing them.

"Welcome back," Max said, rolling onto his side to look at her. "You're back, right? Why are you always so stressed when you get here?"

Carys turned onto her front and lifted her hair so he could trace his fingers across her back. "I don't know," she said. "I guess when I see you I don't know if anything's changed during the week. I don't know if you're still mine, or still want me—it's like starting all over again. Our relationship has to be reborn each Friday, and it's exhausting. But when you take my clothes off"—she looked at where they lay intertwined—"it's a shortcut back to being us."

He arched an eyebrow. "And it's not a bad shortcut, as shortcuts go." He bit her nose, and she jolted backward, laughing.

"Hey."

Remembering his role, Max switched back to playing host. "Can I get you anything?"

"A glass of water would be amazing." She smiled as he brushed the hair out of her eyes, but when he left the room she jumped up, not yet fully comfortable again in his presence, to check her face in the mirror. As she heard him return she collapsed back onto the bed, gazing up as he closed the door. "Thank you." It would take at least a couple of days for them to remember how to be with each other, by which time they'd be boarding shuttles and hybrids back to their respective Voivodes, kissing good-bye, nothing able to shake that Sunday dread.

"Let's play a game," he said one day, in her apartment near the sea. "Finish this sentence. When the asteroids smash the Earth to pieces, I want to be . . ."

She thought about it. "Far above them, looking down. You?"

"In bed with you." He raised his arm for her to tuck herself into the crevice of his shoulder, laughing as she told him that his answer was a typical male response.

At first they'd found living in different cities quite liberating. Both explored the pure autonomy of weekdays and -nights uncompromised and free, Max staying later and longer at work, Carys retreating into her training in Voivode 6, somewhat relieved that no one was asking her what time she'd be ready to eat and what she might like for dinner. She reveled in minor freedoms: not having to worry about hair on her legs was a plus; abject loneliness at night a distinct minus. She poured herself into her career, flying harder, faster, and for longer, until she garnered a promotion: a license to fly above the Kármán Line, which separates space from Earth's atmosphere. As she took her flawless first flight up, to unanimous praise, adrenaline soaring, Carys simultaneously confirmed to the Voivodeship that here was another young worker able to overachieve when undistracted by love.

The most difficult moments for both were when there were clear indications that one had moved on somewhere the other was unable to follow. In Max's Voivode, Carys struggled to keep up with his acquaintances, meeting them in passing as "Max's friend" on weekends, but never able to achieve true closeness or familiarity. In Carys's Voivode, Max was polite to the people he'd known, but when she dragged them out it gave him the indefinable feeling that he had somehow outgrown his past.

It was the small moments that brought them joy. He'd called her in a faraway city, video calling so his face loomed large on the Wall Rivers in her living room, two other walls given over to the Mind-Share and open media playing the news.

"Hello," she said, gesturing to answer by splaying her hand wide.

"Hi," Max said, smiling. "What are you up to?"

She held up the flight manual from her lap. "Reading. Revising. They're starting to send new pilots up to the asteroid belt, to see if they can break through."

"Yeah?"

"I thought I could get a head start on the reading list. Though"—she dropped the book with disdain—"nobody who's written the manuals has actually *been*, so it's a little sketchy."

"That sucks." He hesitated.

"You okay? What are you doing today?"

"Nothing. Made some food, ate some food. I . . . missed you, I guess," he said, ruffling his hair.

Carys smiled. "Want to hang out with me this afternoon?"

"How?"

"Here." She gestured at the surrounding room, drawing her hands into a wider box so the entire wall was given over to Max's living room. "You do the same," she said, and he did, so each wall in their apartments was given to the other.

"That's . . . cool." Max settled back on his sofa.

"Are you going to sit there and stare at me?"

"What? No." He picked up something in his apartment and she smiled to herself before continuing with the flight manual. They chatted together on and off throughout the afternoon.

After that, they'd often turn the entire MindShare over to the other, their rooms connected across whole Wall Rivers in each of their apartments. Carys liked it when, as she received a delivery from the Rotation restaurants, tucking into folded cardboard food containers, Max would share his kitchen with her, the camera lenses fogging up above steaming pans as he cooked. She watched his knife skills with awe as he chopped and shredded vegetables and meat with minute precision, Carys cheering as he diced an onion; then he held up tiny perfect cubes, blushing at her praise. They'd sit sometimes companionably reading, or napping, the wall a gateway into another living room, in another Voivode, in the other's life.

* * *

"CARYS?" HE ASKS, AS THEY continue to watch the fireworks display over the People's Republic of China.

"Yes, Max?"

"Nothing."

"Are you sure?"

"Yes, Carys."

"I'm glad we had this conversation, Max," she says, deadpan.

"Me, too," he replies, though he's not really listening. Disobeying their own advice about watching Earth issued just moments before, they're staring down at it as they tumble. They are still tethered to each other, and their shuffle through space is less balletic now, more of a misstepped rumba.

"I feel a bit sick," says Max.

"For the love of all we've got left in the world, don't throw up in your helmet."

"Eurgh."

"Look away." She nudges him, not breaking her own gaze from Earth. "Stop looking."

Max turns his head and looks around them at the asteroid belt. The big rocks aren't posing a threat to them yet. The largest is at least a few hundred yards below them in the field. Other sizable asteroids are easily spotted and, on the whole, avoidable. It's the tiny micrometeoroids that could sneak up on them at any time, puncturing their suits and tanks, or cracking their fishbowl glass. Carys is still watching Earth and Max is looking at her with fondness when something clips the corner of his vision beyond her head.

"Was that—"

"What?" she says.

"I thought I saw . . ." He cranes around, trying to see if there is anything behind her, if he had actually seen something move. "Nothing."

"Still feeling sick?"

"Better," he says.

"Good."

He sees it again. "There is something!"

"What?" She turns to him and he points away in the other direction, but when she turns there's nothing there. "Can't see anything."

"I'm sure there was . . ."

"You're not feeling well."

"No—"

"How much air do we have left?" She frowns. "Thirty-nine minutes. You shouldn't be losing your mind yet. What did you see?"

"A light."

"Behind me?" She turns but, again, there's nothing. She gazes back down at China and Tibet, where night is giving way to day.

"I really thought I saw something," he says, shaking his head. But she's staring at the sunrise creeping across the Tibetan borders, lost in sadness and nostalgia that are untouched by Max's current visions.

He sees it again. "A light!"

She swivels so fast she bumps into him and their legs fly up to the side. "Sorry. Where?"

"There." He points above their heads, in a straight line as they lie. "Can you see it?"

Their motion carries them around in a loop and it's a few seconds before Carys can answer. "Is it a light?" She squints.

"Are we saved?"

"Who could it be?"

"I don't know—"

"I see it," she says, and Max's heart tap-dances against his rib cage.

"Yeah?"

"There. But I don't think—"

"What is it?" He strains to get a better view, then slumps with the weight of realization. "Oh."

Her voice is very, very quiet. "I'm sorry, Max."

"It's the comet," he says.

"Yes, I think so."

"It's been heated up by the sun so it's glowing."

"Yes." She's gentle, but then: "Hey, it's traveling exactly this way. Should we be alarmed?"

"I thought it was an actual light."

"Max. Do you reckon it'll hit us?"

He's pragmatic. "That's your field." He swipes away the unintended pun. "Anyway, it won't reach us for ages. We'll be long dead by then."

Carys flinches at his words, unable to challenge them. She turns back toward Earth, and as the sun progresses across its surface, dawn sweeping across Tibet, she feels Max take her hand.

twelve

IT HAD BEEN Max's birthday, and Carys had made plans. She was playing this one old-fashioned: spoiling him with presents before a big night out, all done up in a type of glamour that harked back to an era when a woman dressed only to please a man. She didn't care: it was a role-play for a special day. It was running like clockwork: she left the roast chicken—naturally—to marinate while she soaked herself in lime, basil, and mandarin oils in the bath. Painstakingly she painted her nails the palest blush pink, only stopping in panic to take the rollers from her hair before she became crowned with crazed ringlets. She pulled the curls into luxurious long Hollywood waves, all the while eyeing the dress hanging on her wardrobe door with apprehension. It was a brave choice.

She felt she had to look wildly different so she had chosen the type of body-conscious dress that had been seen for a year on Voivode fashionistas. Carys thought she might need a structural engineer to get her into it. And maybe a hoist: she'd got it stuck around her head when she'd first tried on the damn thing.

The bell rang—Max was late and Carys, nervous, opened the door wearing a kimono, standing on tiptoe to kiss him. She saw him notice the painted nails and styled hair, but all he said was, "You look nice."

"You're late," she said, ruffling her light-brown waves.

"I had a few things to do."

"You keep saying that."

"When?" Max was perplexed.

"Every time you disappear you say you had a few things to do. It doesn't matter. Happy birthday," she said, and led him by the hand to the table where she'd set out a meal for two, the Wall Rivers across the back wall a deep purple. "Sit." She poured him a glass of wine and, with some pride, placed the roasting dish on the table.

"You cooked me dinner?" Max started to laugh.

"Yes!" Carys was indignant. "I've cooked for you before."

"I'm a chef. You cooked dinner for a cook on his birthday?"

She turned away to the counter to pour two tumblers of water, biting her lip. "I thought you'd like it."

He didn't mention he'd dropped in at the Rotation restaurant on the way from the shuttle, which was why he was late. "Of course—why not? Are you going to get dressed for dinner?"

"No." She didn't mention she'd seen it in a film, the woman in a silk kimono and fragranced skin tending to a hot stove—she was too rattled by his attitude. She slid into the seat opposite him. "How was your day?"

"Same old. Spoke to Sayed on the MindShare, which was good."

"How is he?"

"Fine. And I heard from my dad."

"Yeah? Did you mention me?" she teased.

He gave her a strange look. "No. How long did you leave this chicken in? It's dried out."

She pushed back her chair, which made a loud grating noise as she stood. He looked up, startled. "I'm going to get dressed," she said. "We're supposed to be going out in twenty minutes. Sorry to ruin the second surprise."

Carys went into her bedroom, closed the door, and leaned heavily against her dressing table, staring at herself in the mirror. This was stupid. The problem with grand gestures and big plans is that they elevate all expectations to uncompromising levels, which only ever end in disappointment. New Year's Eve, birthdays, graduation: nobody has a good time at an event when they've planned to do exactly that. It can't live up to the hype. She began painting her lips a deep coral when Max opened the door.

"Where are we going?"

"Out." Carefully she traced her Cupid's bow, not looking up.

Catching her tone, he relented and came up behind her, smoothing his hands over the silk of the kimono. "I'm sorry, you've gone to a lot of effort. I'm tired from traveling. Sorry I was rude." He kissed the back of her neck, running his hands over the contours of her body hidden in silk.

"You were quite rude."

"I know. I told you ages ago, I'm an idiot." He slid his hand inside her gown and kissed her cheek, both of them framed perfectly in the mirror. "Forgive me?"

She held the lip pen away from her mouth, looking him in the eye through their reflection. "The chicken wasn't dried out."

"I know. I'm a dick. It's my birthday—forgive me?" He pulled playfully at the sash of her kimono, watching as it fell open to reveal a classic perfume-ad corset. He took an intake of breath. "Wow."

"Shut up," she said.

"Seriously."

"Shut up—you can't be nice to me because you've seen me in my pants."

"Those," he said, "are not pants. You look completely beautiful." He slid the silk down from her shoulders so it fell to the floor. "You look like a painting."

She grimaced. "Really?"

"A movie star, then."

"That's more what I was going for." The Wall Rivers flashed the event reminder, and she hit him. "See? You've made me late. We're going to the fireworks. I'm sure all of your old friends will be there—and some of mine. I'll have to meet you later."

"Is Liljana coming?" he asked.

"No. She's . . . still angry about what happened at the Games."

"About you nearly drowning?" Max was astonished.

"No, dummy—about you and me. She didn't speak to me for months after she clocked what was going on."

"How are things now?"

"I told her we were over, that it was just a fling."

"Probably for the best," Max said, walking to the door, not taking his eyes from her body. "Will you be putting on more clothes tonight?"

She crumpled up the kimono and threw it so it hit him in the face and landed at his feet. "Do yourself a favor and stop being a dick!"

* * *

"AND NOW THE MAN himself, the greatest living astronaut still alive and not yet dead." Liu parodied the familiar intro as Max jogged across the beach opposite Carys's apartment, the ruins of the city reflecting the glow of the bonfires along the night sand. He covered his face, faux miming for Liu to stop. They met and put their hands on each other's shoulders in the traditional greeting, then pulled each other into a back-slapping hug.

"I can't believe you're still reciting that," Max said, drawing back to look at Liu. "I've missed you, man."

"Since it came true, it's my nightly affirmation. I chant it before I go to sleep—it's good for my chakras." Liu put his arm over Max's shoulders, turning to survey the scene in front of them. Crowds of people were gathering on the city beach for the display, some setting up informal bar areas, others starting to boom out music. "How are you getting on—where do you live now?"

"Voivode 13," Max said. "It's freezing, but the views are stunning."

Liu waggled his eyebrows. "And by 'views' do we mean . . . ?"

Max laughed. "You're incorrigible. Yeah, the 'views' aren't bad in V13."

"How come you're back, then?"

"You know. Reasons."

"Reasons." Liu sounded skeptical, his eyes narrowing as he caught sight of someone at the entrance to the beach. "And how's the job?"

"Pretty great, actually. I'm working on the simulation of food from different minerals, to see what we can generate to eat on different planets, eventually."

"Sweet, man. Sounds really good."

"If we ever get out past the asteroid field again, that is." He made a face. "Yeah, it's not bad."

"You wouldn't be considering messing that up for a very *specific view*, now, would you?"

Max looked puzzled. "What do you . . ."

With his arm still across Max's shoulders, Liu turned to where Carys was walking across the sand toward them, and Max tried not to gape. Her hair flowing over one shoulder in loose Hollywood waves, her lips coral, Carys was wearing a bone-crunchingly tight dress, the corset beneath turning her figure into an hourglass. As she walked, her hips led—and all eyes on the beach followed. She came closer and Max and Liu could see that the dress darkened from top to bottom in all the colors of a sunrise.

Liu snapped a short laugh.

"It's not like that—"

"Good," he said to Max. "It'd better not be. Because you can't lose everything for her, no matter how coolly black-sheep you think you're being."

Max didn't meet his friend's eye.

"Do you know what life's like outside Europia?" Liu went on. "Because I do. It's bleak. Aid teams fighting to get water to the refugees left in the United States, the Middle East annihilated. The rest of the world is scrambling to join the utopia, Max. We live in a spectacular place. Don't risk all that for the sake of one girl." He put a hand on Max's chest. "What is it you say in European? 'Toe the line'? That's what they want, Maximilian, people who toe the line. Don't give anyone a reason to ask you to leave."

Max said nothing as Carys stopped to say hi to someone by the nearest bonfire, her profile illuminated by the fiery embers. "I won't. I'm not."

"So there's nothing to worry about?" said Liu.

Max nodded. "I hear what you're saying, Liu."

"Because if there was, my advice would be to lock it up. Knock it off. Now."

"Received loud and clear," Max murmured.

Carys got to where they were standing. "Happy birthday," she said simply.

"You look incredible," said Max.

But he made no move toward her, and she crossed one foot in front of the other, her posture a little awkward. "Hi, Liu."

"Hi, Gary. You look like a Tibetan sunrise."

"Thank god," she said. "That's exactly what I was going for."

Liu laughed. "Let me get you both a drink. I think Maximilian needs to talk to you about something."

Max felt bile rising in his throat and he pulled Carys next to him so they were looking out to sea.

She stood like that for a few moments, wondering what was wrong. "Don't you like my dress?"

"Yes."

"I thought you would—something a bit different."

But it's not different, he wanted to say. It's exactly the same. At the exact moment he thought he should definitely avoid saying so, he found himself saying, "But it's not different. You're dressed like every other girl here." As she reeled back at the insult, as furious with herself for getting the night wrong as she was with him for being so rude, he continued, "Admittedly you're about a hundred times hotter than any of them, which is why every male in the place is staring at you."

Carys was annoyed. You dress for the attention of one man, and he loves it, until he catches other men loving it—then suddenly it's not allowed? That made no sense. "I thought you'd like it." She had nothing else to say.

"I do. But not on my birthday."

She turned to face him. "What?"

"It's starting!" someone called, and everyone on the beach cheered and looked to the sky above the ocean.

"I want to relax, but you're dressed like this when you *know* I can't act on it, when you *know* I can't do anything with you in public. Instead I'll have to see off these predators and try to pay you enough attention to warrant you making all this effort, and I'm bound to fall short, when I didn't ask for any of this in the first place."

Carys said nothing and Max stared out at the darkness of the sea. A wave of upset and rage washed over her, rising from her feet and running up her legs. When it hit her head, she burst. "So you were all over me in the bedroom but *now* I'm inappropriately dressed?"

Liu, who was walking toward them with drinks in hand, diverted and headed for the rest of his group.

Max lowered his voice. "I'm always all over you in the bedroom. It never matters what you do or don't wear," he said. "Has it ever made any difference?"

"No."

The fireworks began in earnest: a shower of meteors burning in the sky above the Voivode, each sparkle refracted in the water beneath. There were *oohs* from the beach and somebody turned up the music.

Max took a breath, then stuck the knife in. "It's always me who instigates stuff between us."

"Stuff?"

"Sex. It's always me who has to make you feel desirable and desired. You never jump on me."

Carys sighed. "Like that first time?"

"That was once. Now I always have to win you over and make you feel loved. But what about me?"

She stared at him. "All this because of a dress?"

"I spend a lot of time making you feel good about yourself, but who's doing that for me?"

"I don't know, Max. Who *is* doing that for you? You never seem to be around when I call."

He rolled his neck, exasperated. "Don't start this, Cari."

"You started it. You told me I look like every girl you've been with."

"No, I didn't."

Against her will her eyes blinked with tears. One cut a path through her makeup, a waterline tinged with black kohl.

"Please don't cry," he said.

"This is awful."

"It's my birthday. Don't cry." Liu was conspicuously marshaling the others to dance, and they watched as he windmilled around, ramping up the party, making them all do the same routine as they laughed, clapping and stomping around the fire, eyes up to the sky.

Carys wiped her cheek with a finger. "I didn't want to fight."

The group disappeared behind the flames, and Max turned to her. "Let's go."

Helpless, Carys said, "But it's your birthday."

"I'm not going to enjoy this. We may as well go back."

"But your friends . . ."

"They won't even notice."

As he walked across the beach beneath the shower of meteors streaking across the sky, turning at the road to wait for her, she noticed he hadn't used the words "we may as well go *home*."

* * *

"DO YOU THINK THEY celebrate the meteor displays in Tibet?" Max says, watching the sunrise draw a line of light across the Earth's surface.

"I don't know," she says. "Maybe they take falling asteroids more seriously than the Voivodeship. We just have full-moon parties."

"I hate thinking about that night," Max says, for once not looking down to Earth or out to space but instead gazing at Carys, her hair plaited inside her helmet away from her face, the small daisy wilting slightly over her ear.

"Me, too."

"We both said some terrible things at the beach."

"Well," she says, "*you* did."

"You basically accused me of cheating on you in my Voivode."

She breathes out hard, fogging the glass of her fishbowl. "I didn't, not really."

"You implied it."

"I didn't really believe it."

"You still said it." He looks down at his boots, then up at her with a grin. "See? We're fighting about it again."

"You drive me crazy."

"I didn't cheat on you, Carys." He considers how he can tell her the most basic truth. "It was difficult when we broke up."

She takes the hand he's proffering and clasps his silver-gloved palm in hers. "Yes."

"I didn't really mean us to. I'd been wound up by Liu . . ."

"I know. We ended up at an ultimatum by mistake."

"Yes."

"We were in a strange situation." She wonders how far she can push him for honesty. "And you didn't want to have to leave Europia, if things became even more serious."

"No. But if I'd known—"

This time Carys actually does look away, down at the flex on her wrist, down through the asteroids to Earth. "It wasn't your fault. Neither of us could've known what was coming."

thirteen

ON A FROSTY autumn morning, Carys was fractured from sleep by the alarm announcing she was more than a little late. Sprinting onto the tram, she felt a deep nausea and leaned hard against the hybrid door.

She was late.

She forced herself to carry on, focusing instead on her second flight up into the thermosphere. She knew to her core it wasn't any part of her own body making her feel this way; it would be something foreign, introducing itself with queasy vengeance. But she made it through the day.

That night, distracted, she ran blood analysis at home. It told her what she suspected, what she'd presumed to be the case all day, though it was meant to be impossible: she was late.

But thinking you might be and knowing you are pregnant are two entirely separate entities. Nothing can prepare you for the tide that hits when you know, categorically, there is a baby. Carys took a seat, her breathing wild, wondering if she should clutch at her stomach like they do in the movies. "Oh dear," she said instead.

'I DON'T UNDERSTAND – DON'T YOU have a triple-A?" Liljana's face appeared larger than life-sized on the Wall Rivers, and for the first time Carys found herself wishing they still used small screens—televisions and tablets—rather than whole walls. Liljana's dark eyes looked down caringly to where Carys had folded herself into a wicker peacock chair.

"I do."

"I didn't think they failed."

"They don't. The contraceptive is perfect," Carys said bleakly. "They never fail. This shouldn't have happened."

"Oh dear. May I ask whose it is?"

"It's mine."

"I mean," said Liljana, "who's the father?"

Carys sighed. "I don't really want to say."

Liljana weighed the situation, then asked calmly, "Is it Max?"

Carys looked up at the Wall Rivers in surprise.

"You're not a good actress," said Liljana, conflicted. "I suspected you were still together."

"I'm sorry."

"Hey, it's your life."

"I know, but you're as passionate about Europia as he is." Carys was apologetic.

"I'm not happy about it, not happy at all. If it gets out . . . No." Liljana made a sign of faith. "We don't need to think about that now. Have you heard from him at all?"

Carys didn't reply.

"Have you told him?"

She was silent.

"I suppose it would be hard to tell him, when you can't keep it."

Carys's head jolted up. "I can't?"

Liljana's face was kind. "You're so young. You'd be the youngest mom in Europia."

"Twenty-five?" Carys snorted. "I don't care about that."

"What, then?"

"I don't know. I don't know how I feel. Everything's . . . strange." She looked down at her belly. *I can't keep you.*

"You should have some green tea. It's supposed to be good." Liljana's wrist could be seen twitching as she flexed, looking up pregnancy facts. "Or maybe it's chamomile. I think green tea has caffeine. You should steer clear of too much caffeine."

"Okay."

"You're killing me like this. Are you heartbroken?"

"No." Carys stood up, spurred into feeling. "I don't know." She paced, tracing the outline of the rug. "On the one hand I'm furious, dismayed, and petrified. I mean, it was meant to be fail-safe, for god's sake. On the other, I'm a bit curious. It's like knowing something momentous has happened but not understanding what it is."

"Are you thinking about keeping it, Cari?" said Liljana. "Sorry, not *it*—him? Or her?"

Anna. But she didn't say it.

"Oh, Lord, it's probably a boy," Liljana went on. "We're always talking about boys. When do we ever have a conversation about the weather?"

"We fail the test."

"One day we need to talk solely about our jobs." Liljana went quiet.

"What—now?"

"Actually, yes. What about your job, Cari?"

"I haven't made this a tangible thing, Lili. I'm trying to process *being pregnant*. I'm not thinking yet about a small child popping out who'll grow a personality. Who will get big and require love, affection, child care, and dentists. That's something entirely different, I think."

"Europia would help you." Liljana's voice was low. "They wouldn't make you do it alone."

"Child care? While I'm at the beginning of my career, with a shot at a space mission, now I've got my license? Years of constant child care?"

"I see what you mean."

"I don't want them to find out—not yet," Carys said. "Not while I make up my mind."

Liljana was firm. "Put me down as your emergency contact, then. So they don't call the EVSA."

"I will."

"What are you going to do?"

I can't keep you.

"I think," said Carys, "it's time to call Max."

"ARE YOU ALL RIGHT?" Liljana leaned forward, her face concerned, the contrast on the Wall Rivers leaping to show her black features as she moved closer and into the light.

Carys's eyes were a little glassy, her face pale. Overall, she seemed thoroughly peaky. "Bit pissed off."

"Why? What's happened?"

"He didn't answer." Carys sank back into her peacock chair, and Liljana immediately softened. "The bastard didn't answer."

"He might be out of range," Liljana said. "Or working. Or asleep. Where is he, anyway?"

Cari blanched. "Voivode 13."

"Time difference?"

"Not much."

"Carys. He's probably asleep. Give him a break."

"Coming from you? That's rich." Carys picked at the wicker armrest. "You're definitely not the captain of his fan club."

"Oh, hush." Liljana leaned back. "I might not understand what you had, and I know I'm certainly annoyed you pursued it, but he's a good guy. He loves Europia. And the man can cook."

Carys was quiet.

"Cari?" Liljana asked. "What is it?"

"Calling him, and him not answering . . . I suppose it's made me realize I wanted him to sweep in and make everything fine. But he's probably moved on." Carys sighed. "I think I'm on my own."

"Except," whispered Liljana, inclining her head a fraction toward Carys's stomach, "you're not." And Carys again felt a wave of nausea.

ON TUESDAY SHE HAD a confidential consultation with the Medical Service. "You had a positive result?" The doctor was clinical in her delivery, a tablet and wall screen lighting up as it ran diagnostics.

"Yes."

"And you have an *Asfalí Apó Astochía*?"

"A what?"

"Triple-A. Greek for 'fail-safe.'"

"Oh. Yes." She cringed at the intimate details.

"It's not meant to fail."

"Not with that name," Carys said, "but here we are."

"You're young."

"Yes."

"Healthy."

"Yes."

"But young."

"I know. It can't be helped."

"Please wait." The doctor tapped some details into the tablet, reading back the results as the system beeped. Carys sat on the orange polypropylene chair, tucking and untucking her ankles around the legs. "There may be a problem."

Carys started. "What?"

"The triple-A should not have failed because you're young."

"Seriously, you can stop saying that."

"It's important," the doctor said. "The younger you are, the stronger the hormone. The hormone from the device may be acting upon the fetus."

"*May* be?"

"That's affirmative."

"Oh."

A pause. "There is also a chance the fetus may become physically conjoined with the triple-A device."

Carys sat back, dazed, and listened as she was told it might be too late, that the damage might already have been done.

Another pause. "Certain hormone levels usually double every forty-eight hours in the first trimester. We'll test your blood each day this week to see if the pregnancy is proceeding as expected, which will be evident if the hormone level rises."

"And if it falls?"

The computer screeched a beep. There was no way a machine could deliver such news with any human nuance.

"Then it is gone."

FINDING OUT THAT THE choice might already have been taken away from her was deeply unsettling. Carys's resolve was fixed: she couldn't be a mother. But would the hormone level rise, or fall?

On Wednesday it rose. She monitored how she felt—was that a small kernel of relief?—with tepid curiosity. She tried Max again to no avail, which she noted with a flaming, angry curiosity. Where was he?

On Thursday, the test showed the hormone level in her blood had risen again. This baby was a fighter, she thought, and caught herself on the word. Was it wrong to think of it as a baby? Everyone seemed to call it a "fetus," minimizing the risk of personal attachment. Carys didn't want to get attached, not when it could change her life forever and risk her chance at a mission.

A mission. A chance to go into space, flying shuttles up to the asteroid belt. A shot at saving the world, in a sense. She couldn't risk it for something that might not even naturally run its course. She had no choice but to pretend everything was normal across the week, piloting simulations with her colleagues before going away to test her blood each evening. Knowing what she wanted, she never allowed herself to rest her hands on her stomach or even to imagine what the baby might be like. Like Max? She shook the thought from her head, the gesture racking her with nausea. She wouldn't miss these feelings.

On Friday her hormone level rose again.

Perhaps it was a little girl with her own eclectic taste in music. A girl who would understand mathematical fractions, whose favorite color would be purple. A raven-haired child called Anna.

Anna.

She saw children playing in the park—brattish, screaming children—and her resolve strengthened: *she could not do this*. But later that night a neighborhood cat curled up next to her on the sofa, its small body tucked against her hip, and she buried her hand in its long, warm fur and pondered that very human need and what it felt like to be needed, particularly by your own blood and kin. After that she felt her resolve fall.

On Saturday, the hormone level rose once more. Oh, god. Where the hell was Max? And did it even matter? Plenty of women had been single mothers, particularly before absolute parity had been introduced. Surely she could raise Anna alone with help from the Voivode members she knew and had met. Her own family would certainly help—particularly her mother, Gwen . . . They'd move around Voivodes together, before her daughter, Anna, would begin her own Rotation, independent from her family. That didn't seem obscurely unachievable . . .

On Sunday, Carys began to bleed.

She didn't wake in the night racked with cramps, or fall to the ground in a pool of blood. The miscarriage crept up on her, light and warm, in an understated manner vastly undermining its significance.

She sat on the toilet, numb, watching Anna leave like a tissue in water.

CARYS HAD ALWAYS NEEDED other people. She grew from their energy, bloomed under their love, and performed better under the gaze of their attention. It was unfortunate, then, that on the one occasion she sought utter independence she'd never needed other people more. On her way to work on Monday morning, having told Liljana she was fine and it had been only "a little bit of blood," Carys doubled over. The tram was packed with commuters, their features hidden by dark oiled coats and capes, waterproof hats and jackets to shield them from the downpour outside. The windows were steamed with condensation, the rain striking the outer glass like penknives. Carys reached for the arm of the nearest person, who muttered an apology at her touch and shuffled over, engrossed in reading something via his chip.

Another jab tore through her as the triple-A device moved inside, trapped, and Carys covered her mouth to stop herself from crying out. *A chance at a mission.* Many of her colleagues traveled this way to work, and she needed to keep quiet. She stretched a hand toward the window and rubbed a small circle clear of steam, peering out to gauge where she was. She looked with blankness at shop fronts and trees, where the tracks veered so close to the buildings that they were practically touching and scraping the doorways, and knew with certainty that the next stop was just past Max's old house.

It was a long shot but it was somewhere she knew and could regroup. She wedged her forearm against her stomach for support and clambered from the busy carriage to the street. She bowed her head against the driving rain, pulling her own oiled hood over her hair and face. She counted the houses by their door colors: black, red, black, yellow. As she walked up to Max's, the gray paint peeling, the facade grand though battered, the door clicked back an inch. She moved closer into the porch to look: the wood was swollen with damp, but the bolt had definitely scraped back against the lock; it still recognized her chip.

She pushed hard. The bloated door scratched across the floor, and she was in the hallway.

"Hello?" she called, uncertain. It was silent and dark, with the type of dank chill that indicated the hybrid heaters hadn't been on for a long time. The hallway lamp was gone but the frames still lined the walls. Typical Max, he hadn't even reset them properly as he'd left. She moaned as a hot poker ripped through her abdomen.

Condensation lined the internal glass box in front of her, but the ancient hallway was freezing as she felt along it to Max's old kitchen, the root of an idea taking hold. She pulled the handle of the cupboard under the stairs, but it, too, had swelled. "No"—she gripped the handle with determination—"you *will* open." She yanked back using her entire body, the door flying open as she bounced into the hall wall behind her, the house creaking with displeasure.

Jackpot: the cupboard was stacked with old supplies from the supermarket, cans and cartons of food, and—what she was looking for—long out-of-date tablet painkillers. She took two dry, then two more. Lying against the wall, slumped in the hallway, she counted fifteen minutes, praying the medication would take effect. It was surreal to be back here, after he'd gone. After fifteen minutes, still in pain, Carys took two more.

Silence. The pain seared and she contemplated how many pain-killers she would need to get her through it. The thought was sober-ing. She summoned a paramedic through her chip and lay back against the wall, staying awake by counting the architraves and mold-ings up the ancient wooden staircase to Max's old bedroom. She thought about how they'd woken in that room together, Max calling up the stairs to summon her for breakfast—

"Carys?"

The voice came from the front door as someone hammered on the wood and pushed it hard across the floor; she hadn't locked the door behind her.

"Hi."

"You called for help?"

"Yes. Thank you."

The paramedic helped her traverse the perilous tram crossing outside the door and climb into the waiting hybrid. She leaned back against the headrest, looking up at Max's house, the gray light of the raining sky too much for her pupils, and began to pass out. Where was he? The medic leaned over to strap her in, momentarily blocking the light, and she zoned back in. He asked about self-medicating and she answered woozily.

"Try to stay awake," he said, as she did the exact opposite.

CARYS CAME TO, HER FACE pressed into the corner of a tiny white room, with pain so acute she briefly wondered if she was in hell.

"She's so young."

Carys turned toward the owner of the voice, which was passing what seemed like the infernal European judgment, but they disappeared as a wail went up from a different room. She curled into the fetal position and clenched her eyes shut.

She felt a figure appear in the doorway, but Carys lay where she was, sore and scared. The pain was getting worse. As she opened her eyes the person disappeared, then moments later returned with another figure in a white coat. Thank goodness.

The doctor examined her, taking her pulse and feeling her forehead to judge her temperature. "Carys? Can you hear me?"

She nodded, her eyes clenched shut again.

"Carys, your body is expelling the triple-A and it's trapped."

She nodded again, slightly opening her eyes.

"It's causing the contractions you're experiencing as a result of your miscarriage."

From the corner of her vision she saw someone behind the doctor start at the word. "Okay."

"We need to remove it now." Carys looked up at the doctor, who began setting up the room, preparing sterile equipment, turning her onto her back. Someone approached, their steps hesitant, then climbed gently onto the bed and moved Carys's head onto his lap.

Carys jolted. "You're here?"

"I'm here." Max smiled down at her, and she beckoned at the doctor.

"Doctor—overdose—hallucinations—"

"I'm *here*," Max said. "Liljana told me to come." She was racked with another agonizing cramp and whimpered. Max put his arms around her, forming a protective cave. "Shh, I'm here."

"You're probably not."

"I am."

"Ready, Carys?" The doctor nodded to Max that he was going to begin and Max took her hands in his, shielding her as best he could.

"Be brave."

She felt it sear across her abdomen, like somebody knitting with her insides. Her face contorted with the pain, internal and external, both cold and hot. "Oh, god."

One last tug, and the doctor stepped back, finished. Max looked up as he placed the intrauterine triple-A device into a gray cardboard bowl, where it lay in a pool of blood. Max turned ashen and looked back down at Carys, his smile a little wonky.

fourteen

SHOULD WE STOP speaking, to conserve our air?" Carys flicks the light of the flashlight intermittently out to space. She jabs the switch with her thumb too forcefully and the flashlight skips out of her hand to float, suspended in the black, tilting up and away from her. She reaches for it, jerking the tether between her and Max so he makes an *oof* sound as she stretches, her fingertips brushing the barrel and clipping the end so it slips out of her reach. "Damn."

Max tries to reach for it but also fails, and they bump for a moment.

"Sorry."

They watch the flashlight float away, the bulb glowing as it rotates to face them, their eyes reflecting the filament. But the beam disappears as it shines out to space, the light dying as it hits the vacuum.

Max shrugs. "What were you saying?"

"About whether we should talk or not. Save air."

"We should," he says. "Of course we should. We can't fall in silence, for god's sake."

"'For god's sake'? Are you turning religious on me now?" asks Carys.

"We need all the help we can get, Cari."

"Help isn't coming, Max. The EVSA—"

"I don't mean them."

"Then who?"

"If there is a God . . ."

"You don't believe that, Max. Not you, not ever. When it comes to Europia you're on the other side of the fence, not sitting in the faith houses praying to an Almighty."

"We're not in Europia."

Stating the obvious, she thinks, but says nothing.

"All I know," says Max, "is out here we need an open mind. Out in the deep. I think we need to try . . . having faith."

"Really?"

He nods. "I need to know we're not alone."

"But you hate religious stuff."

"I don't hate it. I just don't understand it." Max shuffles, thinking how to explain. "I grew up being told that religion divides people, making others fear or hate you. I found it crazy that people believed so strongly in a story, and if another sect believed a version that was in any way different, it was an abomination. So many wars were started that way."

"I know. Faith can be a funny thing to people who don't believe."

"But religion is different from faith. Faith or no faith—it's simple in Europia. And if we were of faith, we'd be praying right now."

"I thought we needed to keep talking to each other," she says, exasperated. "That's what you just said."

"Yes. I don't actually expect us to start praying."

As they twist in perpetual motion among the opaque dusk of stars and rocks, clouds are forming over the Indian Ocean beneath them, stretching a cirrus thread across its rich blue. Carys sighs. "Okay, then. What, pray tell, do we do to show this faith?"

"We should talk," Max says, "for our remaining minutes. We should talk until the end. About all the good things that have happened."

"What about the bad things? Or the sad things?" She falters. "What about when you were gone?"

"I came back."

She's quiet, and more than a few seconds go by.

"Did we need it?" he says.

"Faith?"

"The flashlight." He points to where it is still spinning away from them in the free fall of microgravity.

She laughs. "Oh. No. Not really."

"We could do with a bit of luck." Max sighs.

"Crisis of your newfound faith already?"

"No. But it is time for that intervention," Max says, looking at her air gauge. He looks at his own and feels sick. "Or a miracle."

"Max," she starts hesitantly, "do you believe—I mean, earlier, watching the shooting stars, you mentioned Anna."

He looks at her and waits.

"That she might be up here."

"I did."

"You believe, then, that Anna would have some sort of residual existence?" He thinks about it, while Carys continues, "You've always been so sure religion is something done in the name of others, but here—"

"There's no heaven and hell, Cari. We know that by being up here."

"But when it came down to it, you said . . ."

He nods. "I see what you mean."

"Does this mean you believe in the afterlife?"

"I read somewhere," he says carefully, "that the afterlife is what we leave in others."

Carys ponders this, rotating away from Earth to look through the asteroid field and out at the stars, their pinpricks of light a vast cobweb stretching as far as the eye can see. "Anna didn't live," she says finally. "She didn't get a chance to leave anything behind. Not even a body. Probably not even a brain."

His voice is gentle. "Me and you, out here, we're talking about her. In her short existence she changed our entire future. She's left behind in us."

*　*　*

HE'D MADE CARROT CAKE specially, but as Max rang the doorbell of the apartment across from the seafront he knew the gesture was weak. His voice turned formal and his manners stiff as the door opened. Carys was in her wicker peacock chair, its tall back turned to the room as she sat still, staring from the balconied window out to the sea.

"Hi."

"Hello." She didn't turn to face him.

"I brought you some cake," he said, knowing it was the wrong thing. "Are you all right?"

She turned her head. "You're back."

"Yes."

"In my Voivode."

He thought about what to say and how to say it. "I'm glad Liljana called me. I would've wanted to know."

She retorted, her voice sharp. "*I* tried to call you."

"I'm sorry. I've missed you."

"Sit," was all she said.

Max went all out and served two slices of carrot cake, settling himself gingerly on the sofa in the dark of the room. Carys turned the wicker chair away from the sea and picked up a plate of cake. "I want to clear something up," she said, biting into the creamy sponge. "I was as surprised as I imagine you were to find out I was pregnant."

"Yes," he said carefully.

"And I didn't want a baby, not really. I'm just a bit traumatized by the process."

"I can imagine. Are you . . . ?"

"So I'm grieving, but it's a strange kind of grief."

Max leaned forward. "How do you mean?"

"There's science behind it: hormone levels changing, my body going back to normal. But there's something more—I've lost something I didn't think I wanted, if that makes any sense."

He measured out the words, desperate not to say the wrong thing. "I'm sure you'll get a chance in your life to do this again, Cari. At the right time."

"Maybe. One day." She rested the plate on her leg. "When you're told you can't have something, I think it's human nature to start wanting it."

* * *

"THIS IS WHY I find faith baffling," says Max, trying desperately to find a way to scratch an itch inside his suit, but failing. "You spend so much time waiting and praying. Waiting for a miracle."

"Believers are very patient."

"It's so underwhelming. I don't think I could spend the rest of my life like this, waiting for proof."

"All twenty-five minutes of it, or less?"

Max closes his eyes. "Possibly."

"You're agnostic now?" Carys says, skeptical.

"I suppose so."

"That didn't last long."

"I'm not saying I specifically do or don't believe." Max tugs at the arm of his suit, trying to bend his wrist back inside, double-jointed, to get at the flesh somewhere above his wrist bone. The fabric stretches as he pulls it, much thinner and more versatile than rigid, older versions of the space suit. He can't reach the itch so he scratches through the pliable, scubalike fabric. "Just that I'll need some proof. But I don't want to wait the rest of my life for it. I don't think I've ever had much patience." The itch satisfied, he breathes out, contented. "Apart from when I came to see you every day, trying to convince you to get back together with me—I was pretty patient, then."

"Hmm," says Carys.

* * *

THEY HAD SAT IN the same room, on the same wicker chair and sofa, the faint roar of the ocean audible through the thick glazing of the balcony window. "I've thought about it," she'd said, "and I'm not taking you back."

"What?"

"We're not getting back together."

"Why?"

"I'm not having you bail every time it gets difficult."

"I won't," he said, indignant.

Carys arched an eyebrow. "It got difficult, and you were off. First sign of trouble."

"But I came back the minute I had the faintest clue you were *in* trouble. That's got to count for something?"

She swirled the coffee in her mug, holding the warm porcelain against her chin until all she could smell was Costa Rican beans, the steam creeping up over her features like a mask. "No. I'm sorry. It's a nice gesture, like your carrot cake, but no."

That fucking carrot cake. "What, then?"

"We have such different outlooks, Max," she said. "Clashing outlooks, perhaps. When you ended it you said, 'Maybe it's better this way.' You were relieved."

He nodded slowly.

"You still think we're too young. You still think relationships only work when we're older."

He nodded again.

"You think couples make better parents when they're older."

He hesitated, then nodded a third time.

"You believe," she concluded, "fundamentally in the individual." She made a face.

"It's the way I was raised, Cari," Max said, with desperation. "It's everything I've been raised to believe. That's *my* faith."

"Not me. I know how I feel about you and I was ready to tell the world. But you can't even bring yourself to tell your parents about me."

"They wouldn't understand."

"Okay," she said simply. "Well, I don't understand. And you made your position quite clear on your birthday."

His face was crestfallen. "But . . . I don't want not to be with you. I want to be *with* you."

He looked so upset that Carys avoided being petty and telling him he should have thought about that in the first place, and instead held firm. "No, Max. Anyway, what kind of woman would I be if I let you straight back in right after you dumped me?"

"A happy one?" he said, with hope, but she shook her head ruefully.

"Come on. I don't want to be in a long-distance relationship that's making us both miserable, as well as going against your principles."

"Wait. You said, what kind of woman would you be if you let me *straight back in*. Does that mean you might let me back in eventually?"

"Did I? That's not what I meant—"

"Is this a game? Are you trying to make me feel guilty? Because, believe me, I feel guilty, Carys. Coming back, seeing you in pain . . ."

"It's not a game," she whispered. "But I don't believe you'll go against what you believe, long-term, simply to be with me."

"What would I have to do to make you have faith?"

She thought about it. "I don't know. Something big."

* * *

"CAN'T SEE THE FLASHLIGHT anymore," Carys says. "It's disappeared."

"Probably got hit by a micrometeoroid and smashed."

"There's so much debris out here, it's disgusting."

"Not to mention a great big asteroid field. Remember the panic it caused when it arrived?"

"Yes. Look that way," she says, and he turns his head in the direction she's pointing.

"Saturn." He's surprised.

"With our bare eyes."

"We weren't supposed to see it like that for another thirty years or so," Max says sadly.

"The rings of Saturn. *Focus on the rings.*"

He gives her a brief, regretful smile.

"So you want to use our remaining twenty minutes to talk?" she says.

He looks at her. "Yes. We've tried everything we can. We're waiting for a miracle."

"And we wouldn't want either of us to despair and give up."

"Exactly."

"You know it would be quicker and more painless," she says, "if we took our helmets off now. Stopped breathing and ended it, our choice."

Max looks at her in horror. "Don't talk like that—you sound like me."

"It's true, though."

"Stop it. Come on. *You* don't talk like that. Use our air wisely, with more positive words."

She looks at him expectantly. "We're talking, then."

"There's no better way to spend the last minutes of your life," he says, "than talking to the best person you've ever met."

fifteen

SOMETHING BIG." MAX HAD THOUGHT long and hard about it, knowing "flowers" or "a minibreak" weren't going to cut it.

Something big.

He'd left for Voivode 13, promising he'd find a way to make her believe and would return to prove it. He'd wanted to kiss her, but instead dropped his hand awkwardly on her shoulder when he'd said good-bye, as she sat staring out at the gray sea from the wicker chair, still going through the motions of mourning. She patted his hand, sure that this time was it: they were over.

Something big.

He thought about it as he worked with the team generating foodstuffs out of organic and nonorganic matter, chipping away at the smashed chondrites that fell to Earth during the meteor showers. Max thought about the mistakes he'd made with Carys as he worked with geologists, learning more about asteroids than he ever thought a supermarket manager might.

Each night he went home and stared at the Wall Rivers, blank and empty where Carys refused to answer his calls and connect their living rooms. He found solace in helping people with food queries on the MindShare once more, the interactions removed from real life yet still somehow a human connection. He cherished those moments as he sat inside the cavernous, freezing apartment he'd been given by the Voivodeship, failing once again to decorate because each photograph acted like a skewer through his memory.

Something big.

CARYS PUT HIM OUT of her mind as she crawled out of her seafront hole and returned to city life, back to work at the local EVSA headquarters. She felt the familiar tug when she ordered vegetables from the server, which malfunctioned, and as she glanced around for somebody to laugh with she found nobody amused. She felt a bigger tug as she rode past the secret entry to the observatory, the fleur-de-lis fence dangerously rusted and caving, the hedge grown up and over the gateway.

One evening a message bleeped from Max and, in a moment of weakness, she caved, like the rusted wrought-iron fence.

Hi.

Ciao.

Ça va?

¿Qué tal?

Bene, grazie, she flexed back, and began to smile as something familiar played out, the sound of *pings* bouncing between them like old times. *Et toi?*

Don't make me test your Germanics, he flexed.

Or my newish Greek.

How are you?

She paused, flexing very deliberately and slowly so he could see she was typing. The words were weighted, and she picked a subtly different font that pulsed purple in the wall of blue text before dissolving altogether.

I miss you.

Finally! he replied. *What took you so long?*

Time.

Well, it's about time.

Why?

Because I'm about to do something big.

THEY MET AT THE air terminal, the prickle of uncertainty embarrassing them while, all around, friends and families greeted each other with affection. Max went to kiss her while she went in for a hug, so he ended up brushing his lips against her hair. She pulled back and looked up at him. "Want to try that again?"

"Yes." He dropped his bag on the floor and walked in a large loop around the nearest pillar, coming back toward her with open arms. Gently he pulled her into an embrace, his hand on the back of her neck, and they kissed.

"Better."

"Much more natural," he agreed. "Probably hinted to these people we're old hands at this." But he didn't pull away, she noticed with surprise.

"We are," she said. "Ancient, now. What are we doing here?" she said, flustered but quite happy.

"We're here because you're the only person I can imagine putting up with me," he said. He looked around: they were in an air terminal between their two Voivodes, a neutral middle ground. With no restaurants or shops, it really was somewhere over nowhere. He pointed at Departures. "That way."

"And where are we going next?"

"Voivode 2." They boarded the shuttle, the glass gates clamping down over the jump-jet, smaller than the one they'd taken to the Voivode Games in Australia; this one would be traveling a much shorter distance. Max spread the belt across Carys's lap and locked her in. "It's time you met my parents."

IT WAS A NICE neighborhood in the main city of Voivode 2, with avenues of brick almshouses lined by trees, their roots erupting through the sidewalks. The suburbs were well kept, and less ruinous than the inner cities—entire walls and facades were maintained, often without modern supports. They'd walked across acres of heathland in the north of the city to get there, and Carys had looked around, impressed, admiring the natural ponds.

"How long have your parents been here?" she asked, as they walked through a Georgian village with the original crisscrossed windows, high on a hill, and Max gave her a look.

"They're still on Rotation."

"Of course," she said bleakly. "Less than three years, then. It's a nice area."

"My little brother has a respiratory disorder, so they have special dispensation to live in the low-pollution Voivodes to help him breathe."

"Would it not be better for them to live outside the cities?"

Max looked around at the green and pretty village. "This is the compromise. They live here because it's near the hospital."

They took a left and Carys hitched her rucksack up on her back, trudging down the hill. Far at the bottom sat the glowing white cube of the district hospital, modern and clean next to the red and yellow period bricks. Max turned into a neat front garden some way before the cube, waiting for her to catch up before he knocked on the door.

"Ready?" he said.

"Too late to say no."

A tiny replica of Max opened the glossy red door and, before Carys could gape at the similarity, Max had pulled the younger boy into a bear hug.

"Mac!"

"It's me." Max laughed, then added, "You've grown. How old are you these days?"

"Seven." He beamed, great toothless gaps in his smile as Max picked him up and swung him through his legs. The boy wriggled with joy. "How old are *you*?"

"Four times older than you . . . You've lost some teeth, buddy."

"Diego knocked me off the spaceship."

"Spaceship?"

"The climbing frame in the junior jungle."

"The junior jungle?" Max couldn't keep up.

"Diego knocked me off the spaceship in the junior jungle and my bottom teeth fell out."

"Right." Max set the child on his feet and he stood there, curious.

"This is my best friend, Carys. Carys, this is my best brother, Kent."

"Hello, Kent," she said solemnly, and Kent looked at Max, baffled. "A girl?"

"A girl," Max intoned.

Kent ducked out of Max's grasp and ran into the house, calling, "Mom, Dad, Mac's at the front door. Mom? Dad? Mac's here. Guess what? He's brought a *girl*."

Carys walked into the cottage behind the boys as Max grabbed the little one once more, tipping him up and over his shoulders into a fireman's lift. "Why's he so surprised?" she whispered.

"Seven-year-old boys are just realizing girls are 'different,' " Max whispered back. "The idea that you're my best friend is *mind-blowing*." He put Kent down, still smiling, as a man walked toward them, his arm outstretched. "Hi, Dad." They each rested a hand on the other's shoulder in a formal version of the favored greeting, and Max gestured to Carys. "Carys, this is my father."

She noted he'd introduced his father to her and not the other way around, but made nothing of it. "Nice to meet you, sir."

"Pranay, please." Max's father put his arm up for the greeting, the type of man whose intellect made him appear distracted or standoffish. "Carys—Welsh origin?"

"Yes, exactly."

"And what do you do?"

She smiled at his obvious cut to the chase. "I'm a pilot."

"Very good," he said. "Commercial? Military? Charity?"

"Space Agency."

"*Very* good." His approval thawed him a fraction. "That's very good indeed. I'm in logistics myself. Feeding the Voivodeship. I run the Rotation restaurants and supermarkets."

"Gosh. All of them?"

"Many of the restaurant chains, yes. And the smaller supermarkets, too."

"Wow. I think I met Max at one."

"Voivode 6? I believe Maximilian turned that outlet fashionably retro."

Carys nodded, trying to figure out why a man who ran all of the Rotation restaurants wouldn't place his aspiring chef son in one, while Kent encircled the older man's legs, showing off in the way kids do before they visibly slump with faux boredom when the spotlight moves away from them.

"Do you fly planes?" Kent asked her. Up close she noticed he had a transparent oxygen pinch across the bridge of his nose helping him breathe.

"Shuttles, mainly," she replied.

"Awesome."

Max reached over and ruffled his hair, and Kent whizzed off, his energy ignited again by the touch of attention.

"Come on through," said Pranay, leading them into the kitchen, the cottage reinforced with Europia's customary glass and steel interiors. "Let's get this pilot a cup of tea."

"I should've known he'd like that," whispered Max, resting his hand on her lower back to guide her toward the rear of the modest house. "My father only admires hard work and success, and I mean *only*."

In the kitchen, a tiny woman sat knitting at the table. "Hi, Aunty Priya," Max greeted her.

She looked up at him in dazed delight. "Maximilian. What a pleasure."

They sat down at the table and Max's father, a big, physical man, moved around the kitchen counter, dipping teabags and pouring milk with the formality of tradition. "Sugar?" he asked, and Carys shook her head. "Good," he replied. "Sweetness is a sign of weakness."

She breathed out with relief at seemingly passing some unspoken test, and accepted the mug with thanks.

"Any for you, son?"

Max balked at being called "son." His dad always made him feel small. He declined the tea.

"You haven't changed. Still no stomach for hot drinks, I see."

Max wondered why such an immaterial judgment should feel like failure and shrugged. "I'll take some water if it's going. Where's the Professor?"

"Alina will be down soon." He sat at the table, his frame overwhelming the farmhouse chair and making it creak under the strain. "So."

"So," said Max, sipping water.

"What brings you out here?"

"I wanted you to meet Carys," he said, his gaze not moving from the water tumbler. "I wanted you both to meet Carys."

Max's father said nothing, but Carys saw his wrist twitch as he flexed something.

A second later they heard a door open upstairs. A formidable woman, her streaked hair pinned in a neat chignon, came into the kitchen and dropped a hand formally on Max's shoulder, then moved to the counter. "Coffee." Spotting Carys, she continued, "You must forgive me—I'm on nights at the moment and was catching some rest upstairs." Kent bumped into Alina as he bounced off the kitchen cupboards, and as she steadied him, Carys was struck again by how like Max he was. "Your father said I should come down."

Max picked up his glass from the table. "I wanted you both to meet Carys."

His parents' eyes met. "She's a pilot," said Max's father as Kent said "She flies space shuttles" with evident admiration.

"Ah," said his mother. "Hello, Carys. I see you've won all of my boys' approval."

"I—" Carys stalled, and Max looked at the table with a grin. This was deliciously awkward.

"How long have you worked together?" Pranay took a sip of tea.

"Since my Rotation in V6," Max said deliberately, "and we've been together as a couple since then, too."

There was silence in the kitchen.

"A couple?"

Kent slipped out of the room and turned on the open media in the small living room with an eruption of sound.

"You're very young," said his mother carefully.

"Not that young." Max took Carys's hand in his. "Old enough to know."

"To know?"

"I tried being without her, and it didn't work." Max sat back, only the slightest shake betraying his nerves. "So we're going to continue to be together."

Max's father said nothing, sipping his tea. His mother played with a silver bangle on her wrist, eyeing Aunt Priya's knitting as the needles clacked together, underlining the tension. "Shall we go into the living room? It's more comfortable in there."

"Sure," said Max, keeping his hand over Carys's. "Whatever you'd prefer." His mother led the way through to the front room, swiftly negotiating with Kent, who turned off the games and thundered up the stairs, two new coins clinking in his pocket. Max's father left the kitchen without a word, and as Carys pushed her chair back Max shepherded her into the living room, smiling genially as they sat down together on the plump sofa.

"Comfortable," Max said, bouncing a little on the feathers. "I like your new sofa."

His mother deigned to smile at her son, then took a breath and turned her attention to Carys. "You met in Voivode 6?"

Carys nodded.

"And you're still there?" she said. "Max has moved."

Again, Carys nodded. "I'm in Draw Two."

"Why would you even think you could stay together until you can move on Rotation as a family?" She looked from Carys to Max. "You can't apply for a decade. That's a long time."

"It is," said Carys quietly, "but we thought we might try."

"You can't. It's against the rules."

Something big.

"Carys doesn't know this yet," said Max, "but we're actually on our way to the central Voivode. I'm going to request a repeal of the Couples Rule."

THE ROOM EXPLODED WITH the aftershock, and Carys rocked back in surprise. Max's revelation had hit her square in the face: until seconds before, she'd thought bringing her here, standing up to his family, was his gesture, his something big. She'd never imagined he'd do that, let alone question the Voivodeship—that was something different entirely.

Max's father, having been silent throughout, looked apoplectic.

"Dad?"

On cue, he erupted: "Why do you have to challenge everything?" Max tried to speak but Pranay interrupted: "What gives you the right? What makes you think you know best? Why would you push against rules that are intended to protect you?"

"But, Dad"—Max held up his hand—"the rules are changed if enough people want them to be. I have to speak up. The system works because—"

"The system works because people like me and your mother obey the rules." Max's father stood, his colossal frame looming over Carys and Max on the sofa. "Just because something isn't going your way doesn't mean it's wrong, Max. People with much more experience than you set the guidelines. Stop acting like a child."

"Dad, it's—"

"Stupid boy." His father's voice dropped a hundred decibels. "Thousands of people died so you could live this charmed life."

"*Charmed?* Those people were first generation. You're second. Don't you think life might be different for me, for my generation? Do you truly believe the world is still the same as when you were a kid?"

"Don't you dare call your grandparents 'those people.' " His father's hand went to his forehead. "Your grandmother—highly esteemed—changed the social dynamic forever. Your great-uncle— killed in action. Your great-aunt—my aunt—permanently injured, mentally scarred, while tending the sick in an aid hospital off the coast of Florida. They dropped bombs using drones, not even real people—nobody brave enough to do it in their own name . . ."

Max stayed quiet, as he did every time his father talked of their relatives. "I'm sorry. I'm not challenging the whole system, Dad. I'm not challenging the Voivodeship."

Pranay raised his arms, exasperated.

In shock, Carys stared at the floor.

Max clambered to his feet. "You always taught me there was great value in being individual," he said, as he stood opposite the man who had raised him. "You told me to do everything in my own name—doesn't that include obeying rules? Shouldn't I evaluate each rule and work out if it's right for me? The people who blindly do what they're told without ever wondering why—I can't imagine they're happy."

"Of course they are. We live in a perfect world, and somehow you're still not content." His words were so forceful that Max took a step backward.

"I am—"

"If you don't like the rules, you should leave." His father pushed him toward the door. "You should leave Europia."

"That's not fair. I believe in every aspect of what we're doing. Everything except"—he clasped his hands together—"the Couples Rule."

Pranay opened the door to the porch, gesturing for Max to leave. "You don't get it."

"Mom—"

"No, Maximilian," she said.

"I love her, Mom."

Carys blushed at the words she had rarely heard, but his mother didn't stop. "This will pass. Lust always does, and then you can move on, like everybody else. When you're established you'll meet someone you'll actually want to spend the rest of your life with. You can have intelligent, healthy children. But if you don't stay strong, and if you don't think this through, you won't be able to undo it. You can't take back the mistakes of your youth—you should trust your elders on that, at least. Are you really going to ignore our advice?"

"You're not listening—"

"I'm sorry, Max, you won't find any supporters here. Not unless you do the right thing." She looked at him expectantly.

After a pause, he shook his head, and Alina stood with her husband by the porch, gesturing for the younger couple to leave. As Max and Carys stepped out onto the sidewalk, she pushed the front door until the lock closed with a firm click.

CARYS DROPPED HER HAND onto Max's shoulder as he sat down by the curb, clearly surprised by how badly their visit had gone. Thrust out of the family home, defeated . . .

Was he really going to do this? Max wondered whether to knock and reengage or leave it for today.

He watched the evening darkness creep across the white cube of the hospital, the light failing fast. Twilight. His aunt appeared alone in the bay window, her face somber, and he stepped toward her. Silently she put a finger to her lips, then splayed her palm against the glass.

Max lifted his hand and rested it against hers, the gesture in her wrist activating the chip in the room behind her. Photographs Max had never seen filled the wall frames, and he studied them, confused, moving from frame to frame, image to image. His aunt and her brother—Max's father—looking overjoyed but exhausted holding the stars of Europia, a sea of blue and gold flags behind them. His grandfather joined them in another, the three of them beaming in front of a lit-up red sign that read "Fox Supermarkets." His aunt and a man he'd not seen before, sitting together in a hybrid truck piled high with freshly cut vegetables. His aunt at an early Voivode Games, the image capturing the joyful moment she had cheered, the same man by her side.

The images dissolved and a final photo of Aunty Priya appeared, unhappiness marking her out like a smudge on the print. She shrugged and dropped her hand.

"I don't understand—"

She gestured behind her at the walls without turning, her voice a whisper through the glass. "Obeying the rules is in our blood. But it doesn't always make us happy."

sixteen

CARYS SHIVERS. 'I'M COLD.' The temperature varies wildly in space and their silver suits are programmed to detect and continually adjust the heat.

Max looks at his thermometer. "Turn up your thermostat. It should've done it automatically, but that's a big drop. Turn it up now."

"Okay. Done. You?"

"Mine did it by itself," he says.

"Huh." She looks at her own thermometer, tapping the screen as if that will make a difference. "I hope my suit isn't going to malfunction on top of everything else."

Max grimaces, thinking about his failed experiment with the expelled oxygen from her pack. "I hope it wasn't my fault."

"I'm sure it wasn't. It will just be my luck." Carys shivers again. "I'm still cold."

"You'll warm up now the thermostat's right. And we'll fall back into the line of the sun shortly."

"You'd think when I have a space suit custom-made for me"—she points at her name, embroidered beneath the blue EVSA badge—"I'd finally be warm."

Max rubs his hands over her arms in an effort to warm her, moving from her wrists to her shoulders and back, although the insulated suit makes the gesture fruitless. "You're always freezing. Remember the training sessions? You used to shake with cold." He doesn't mention how terrifying he found watching Carys train in the EVSA's pools, reliving the incident at the Voivode Games every time she stayed underwater for a second too long.

"Hours submerged, wearing a wet suit?" She gestures around her. "Actually the perfect training ground for being in space. Who knew?"

"You've probably got bad circulation." He circles back. "Your hands and feet are always chilly."

Carys smiles, ignoring the jibe. "The asteroid field is probably interfering with the temperature gauge, as the rocks keep throwing me into shadow." They look around at the fractured gray asteroids, some abruptly smashed and ruptured where they've collided. "Not to mention the interplanetary dust clogging up my system."

"And mine," he murmurs, checking her thermostat again. "How long do we have left?"

"Thirteen minutes," she says, trying to keep the dread from her voice. "Unlucky for some."

"I'm not sure luck has much to do with it," Max muses as a micrometeoroid moves past them, heading toward Earth. "Unless you think, with our choices, we made our own luck . . ."

* * *

MAX'S PARENTS WOULDN'T BACK DOWN. Despite their son's calls, messages, and further visits, his father refused to come to the door. His mother disappeared into her work. Desperate to see Kent one last time before they left, Max had hatched a plan to steal some time with the little boy.

"He spends half his life at the hospital," Max had told Carys, as they'd sat at the local Rotation restaurant. "My mother's working on a cure. She feels guilty because his disorder became worse when they moved to Macedonia for her work—the pollution there nearly killed him. Voivode 19," he added as an afterthought.

"Is that why he hasn't started Rotation?"

"Exactly. They said he'd move when he's better, when he's a little bigger," Max told her. Then his voice turned wistful: "By the time I was his age, I was already living on my own."

He arrived at the white cube at the end of visiting hours, sliding through the doorway as the last stragglers left, pitching left into the staff room as the guard disappeared around the corner. He'd momentarily considered picking up a white lab coat, like a proper intruder would, impersonating a doctor reading patient notes, then remembered how futile a piece of sterile white cotton would be in getting him past the medical staff's biometric chips and check-ins. He ran his eyes down the unit's MindShare, looking for queries directed at his mother, praying for a geotag in her replies. There were none.

Hearing a group in the hallway, Max swung around toward the lockers, leaning against one as though he was about to scan his chip. Five nurses came in, off duty and exhausted, but still in high spirits. As the last appeared, talking nineteen to the dozen, Max swiveled around, keeping his back to the group, at the final second catching the door and slipping through to the other side. Directly opposite the staff room entrance there was an old-fashioned whiteboard, covered with marker pen, wobbly lines marking out a hand-drawn grid. As he stood staring at it, he found what he was looking for: his mother's name (and rank), and a list of her patients in clinic "AR." As more medics came around the corner Max dashed toward the elevator, scanning the hospital map. He headed to the apex.

It was quiet and Max relaxed a little as he walked through the corridors of private rooms and wards, colorful images playing on the Wall Rivers. A teddy bear bounced along the wall next to him. When he came to Kent's room, the bear catapulted itself around the door-frame. He swiped it away and pushed open the door. "Hi, buddy."

Kent opened his eyes groggily and smiled. "Hi, Mac."

"How are you feeling?"

"I get a coin for every night I stay," he said.

"That's pretty good. How much did you get for that front tooth?"

"Chocolate."

"Nice negotiation skills." Max slid into the room and sat down on the armchair next to his brother. "I wanted to see you before I skip town."

Kent looked solemn. "With the girl?"

"With the girl," Max agreed.

"Mom and Dad have been shouty."

Max bit his lip. "I'm sorry."

"I wish I could see you more."

"Me, too. I've been working for the Space Agency."

"You're the only one who hugs me."

"I'll come more often, buddy—I promise." Max's heart hurt and he stroked Kent's fluffy hair off his forehead, the little boy struggling against sleep and presumably a hefty dose of medication. Max sat forward to lean on the bed, still gently stroking his hair as Kent snuffled back into deep sleep . . .

"How did you get in here?"

Max snapped awake as his mother loomed over the bed, annoyed. "More rule breaking," she said. "What are you doing?"

"I came to see Kent," he said simply, adjusting himself in the chair and looking up at her.

She splayed her fingers to open the projection of the boy's notes at the end of the bed. "He's been through enough. He doesn't need to know what you're planning."

"Maybe he should."

"No."

"It's not your decision."

"I don't want him tarred with your dirty brush," she snapped, and Max looked down, bitten. "He'll be a pariah when people find out what you've done."

Emboldened, Max said, "You should hug him more."

She clicked off the projection. "Thank you, Maximilian. I don't need advice from someone like you."

Max flinched. "Why? Because I'm young? It's that sort of closed mind that will ruin the Voivodeship."

"No, *you're* the one ruining the Voivodeship."

He stroked the little boy's cowlick down on his forehead without waking him and kept his voice low as he said, "It's a social democracy, Professor. Maybe we'll find people agree with us, and not with you."

She narrowed her eyes. "I very much doubt it. Europia has been honed by an *experienced* central government of experts setting the rules, based on what works for *the majority*."

Max sat forward. "But what if you're wrong and it needs 'honing' further? You can't foist out-of-date rules on everyone—Europia works because people *choose* to follow the rules. We weigh the different ways of life and choose this one. Don't you think that's the true meaning of *utopia*? Europia would be a very sour place indeed if people like me lost their curiosity and didn't ask why we have certain rules. It would be better to be dead than not be curious."

She laughed. "How lightly you skip out quasiphilosophical platitudes about death and choice. You'll have no choice soon. How long, do you think, until you're forced to do things in her name rather than your own? *In whose name*, Max?"

He gathered Kent's slumbering little body into a hug and kissed the side of his face, breathing in the smell of chalky talcum powder. "I'd better get going."

"Yes, you should. I look forward to picking this up when you've come to your senses—hopefully before you're dismissed by the Representatives in the Grand Central Hall for petty dissension."

He took one last look at his brother, then walked straight past his mother without a word.

THE STATION WAS CROWDED with commuters, the Wall Rivers sliding with continuous information of arrivals and departures. Max was looking around for Carys, worried, when a pair of cold hands snaked around his face and covered his eyes. "I'm either being robbed by a twelve-year-old," he said, "or those are the skinny wrists of a girl I once knew." He whirled round to face his assailant. "She's dead now. Murdered in cold blood, after a failed mugging in a station. Very sad."

"How awful." Carys reached up and kissed his cheek. "Criminals take on all kinds of appearances these days. Children, beautiful women"—she flicked her hair—"all sorts."

"Beautiful, hey?" He picked up their bags. "Come on, we're going to miss our hybrid."

"Did you see Kent?"

"Yes."

"Was it okay?"

"Yes."

Carys suspected the monosyllables indicated otherwise but didn't push.

"Hey," he said. "We managed to have a little joke, then."

"We did." She turned to face him. "But if you're going to point it out every time we do, we'll never move on."

"What do you mean?"

"Let's not look at every single interaction to see if we've still got it, if we still love each other, whether we'll ever recover from the breakup. If we do that, we'll kill it. We'll die."

Max said nothing.

"So let's get back to making jokes, keeping it light, and going to do this teeny-tiny thing that just might change the lives of everyone our age."

"I see what you mean," said Max, picking up their bags. "The perfect scenario to keep it lighthearted."

They walked to the platform, the humming of engines pouring a haze of oxygen onto the carriages and over the passengers, creating the atmosphere of a nineteenth-century steam train preparing to leave a rural town. The city here was anything but: the sun flared behind the station's sheet glass as it set, the pale blue overhead fighting with the red fires of the sky to the west.

The train was busy and Carys and Max climbed to their allocated seats, settling into the pale gray upholstery and locking themselves down.

"Ready?" she said, and he felt she didn't mean the journey.

"Ready." Then: "Are you sure?"

"Of course." She settled in as the train pulled away, feeling the kick in her stomach as the hybrid picked up rapid pace, the g-force pushing her back in her seat. Soon the city fell away and a ragged patchwork of farming fields filled the windows: browns, greens, and the startling yellow of rapeseed. "I hate that color."

He laughed. "Curious thing to hate."

"I hate its name, too. 'Rape.' I hope, if anything, the utopia will fix social issues like that one day." She watched the farmland pour past.

"There will always be broken people, no matter how well society works."

They were quiet for a while as the train headed under the Channel. Then Carys asked, "Max? Why did you do it?"

"Do what—this?"

She nodded.

"Would it have been enough if I'd simply told my family about us?" Max said.

"Yes," Carys said. "It would have been enough."

He shook his head. "It would have been enough *for now*."

They went quiet again, watching the landscape evolve into the vivid greens of fields on the continent.

"Do you think we're selfish?" she asked.

"Why?"

"Asking to change the rules based simply on how we feel."

He thought about it. "If we feel like this, then it's likely others do, or would, if they were allowed the opportunity."

"Even if at the moment, everyone just wants to sleep around—like you did?"

"Hey." He rubbed his hands in his hair. "That hurt."

"I'm sorry. But you're our ultimate case study."

"I think we need to give everyone the chance to feel like we do."

It wasn't long before the hybrid plowed into the central Voivode, and Carys looked on in awe. "They have an aqueduct like mine," she said, "but not old and crumbly. In the middle of the city."

"It powers the central buildings—they're self-sufficient."

"Wow." Modern dam walls rose high above their heads, the looping arches of the aqueduct like a defense system, the reservoirs outside them a medieval moat. "It's incredible."

As they walked through squares lined by neat coffee shops and language labs, the fluttering digital flags reminded Carys of the Voivode Games. "Do we simply turn up?" she asked.

"No," he said, guiding her across tram lines. "I booked us a slot."

"With whom?"

He stopped. "With the Representatives, Cari. We're speaking at the Grand Central Hall."

"Really? I thought we'd have a meeting in a side room."

"They're interested in what we have to say."

Surreptitiously, she smoothed down her hair, noticing that Max was dressed more smartly than usual in a pale blue shirt. "Better not keep them waiting."

On the far side of the largest square lay an imposing white building, colossal in scale, fronted by ten elegant white pillars supporting a large portico overhead. The entire structure was encased in reinforced glass, a reverse of the Voivodeship's usual architecture, encased and protected for posterity. Inlaid in the triangular portico, dating all the way back to the European Union in the year 2000, was the official motto of Europia: *United in diversity*.

Together they made their way through to the huge entrance chamber, the footsteps of every person—and there were hundreds—echoing off the marble. "Look." He pointed up into the corners. "Chip scanners."

"Not surprised—safety must be paramount."

"After America."

"Yeah."

"A war of terror led to the annihilation of two nations. I guess we can't be too careful."

The acoustics boomed in their ears as they walked to the front desk and registered, holding out their wrists for the chip readers and fixed flexes to verify their identities. When Carys's turned green, the greeter beeped and the turnstile opened.

"Welcome to Wonderland," Carys said, walking through the elaborate security gate.

"Huh?"

"Did you *ever* read?"

Max made a face. "I like stories on screens."

She began to laugh. "So every time I reference a book, you just pretend to get it?"

"Yes." He walked through behind her, the gate lighting up as it scanned his full frame. "Patronize me all you want, little girl, but you're the one watching cartoons when I'm trying to share our living rooms on the Wall Rivers."

"They're very comforting," Carys whispered, as the elevator

crackled and rattled at deafening volume. There it was again: the utopia motto, pulsing in blue text on the three sides.

" 'United in diversity,' " Max muttered. "Come on, then. Let's give them some diversity to talk about." He took her hand as the doors opened, and a steward stepped forward to greet them.

"You must be Maximilian and Carys." They nodded and he gestured for them to follow. They fell in behind him, noticing how silently his feet moved across the plush royal blue carpet. They walked into a large, circular vestibule lined with ornate cornicing. The ceiling was painted like the sky and sloped down every twenty paces to a set of carved double doors, behind which they presumed was the Grand Central Hall. The steward stopped at a pair of old-fashioned wooden church chairs. "You may wait here."

"Thank you." Carys sat down and Max followed. She nudged his foot and pointed with her toe toward the doors, above which a squat, naked cherub was painted, holding a flute. They both suppressed a giggle.

After fifteen or so minutes, Max leaned over to the steward and spoke softly, his voice still echoing in the round chamber: "What are they discussing before us?"

"The safety of the aid teams in the former United States."

"Right," Max said, awed.

"Christ," Carys whispered, daunted, "there's a bit of perspective. What are we even doing here?"

He took her hand but continued to speak to the steward. "Can we go in and listen?"

"I'm sure you can. Let me ask." The steward bowed and walked away. Carys and Max eyed each other at the formality. He returned and beckoned to them. "You may go in. Your session will start in a few minutes."

"Thanks." Max wondered if he needed to bow, too.

Carys and Max walked in and gaped. The vestibule had given away nothing about the size of the Grand Central Hall. From their position beside the entrance at the back, the Hall soared down in circular tiers, a futuristic round Camelot crossed with a majestic period theater. Gold stars adorned the ceiling above clusters of huge blue and white balconies, stacked on top of each other up to the roof, laid out in a vast ring, the full circumference of the room.

There must have been at least two thousand Representatives there, seated inside the balconies by Voivode, and Carys knew from her school days that most of the Representatives were experts in their fields. She gasped as she realized each balcony moved forward when that particular Voivode had the floor. She looked up to the top balconies and felt dizzy—they were so high.

In the middle of the Hall, on a round platform, stood the Speakers, watching and moderating the balconies like hawks. The Hall was voting on the best course of action for the aid teams.

"The Representatives of Voivode 12 agree we should mobilize the teams to focus on the people most in need in what's left of the South. We need to get the survivors to the coastal region and establish camps with food and water. But extra security should be provided."

Carys looked at Max and subtly indicated the visors and screens around the room, knowing not only were these Representatives making decisions but tens of thousands back in the Voivodes were wired in, also able to vote and pass comment, democracy on a scale not previously experienced. Carys had no doubt Max's parents were tuned in for today's sessions.

"The Representatives of Voivode 7 would like to point out the surviving children in Georgia are most at risk." The room shuffled. "Along with the additional security we should send extra supplies into Savannah, particularly clothing, medication, and child vaccinations, and we should review again in a week."

Each balcony lit up green, and the Voivode Speaker looked pleased. "Motion carried."

"This is great," whispered Max, and Carys nodded.

Voivode 7's Representative called for the floor once more. "May I also suggest"—he cleared his throat—"an education program for the refugee children about the asteroid field? They must be frightened." The Hall was filled with the sounds of debate before some of the balconies turned red.

"No clear majority." The Speaker was kind. "We'll review again once the key basics for survival are in place."

The steward indicated to Max and Carys that they should make their way down the stairs to the center of the Hall.

"Shall we?" Max started walking, looking back to where she was still standing at the top, sensing she was scared. "Come on. They're not going to sentence us to death."

They walked down through the tiers, and the balcony members gazed at them with open curiosity. The room reverberated as the Speaker announced: "Next, we have two young citizens who would like to talk to us about the Couples Rule."

The noise in the room grew clamorous, and by the time Max and Carys reached the center they were wide-eyed. She held out her wrist and as Max grasped it, the room, seeing that small gesture, hushed. Max looked at the Speaker, who nodded.

"Hello. My name is Max. I currently live in Voivode 13, and I work for the EVSA." He paused. "This is Carys. She lives in Voivode 6 and also works for the EVSA." Whispers bounced around the circle and some of the balconies shifted in height. "Like most modern love stories, we met online. We've been together for a while now, and though we're only in our twenties, we would like to ask you to revisit the rules and recommended guidelines for couple Rotation."

The sound in the room had ebbed and swelled as they'd run through the key beats of Carys and Max's courtship. A screen displayed Carys's near-fatal swim at the Voivode Games, Max distraught at her side. She scowled, finding it mawkish, and Max was apologetic. "Good PR," he'd whispered.

A Representative from a Voivode in which neither had ever lived leaned forward. "In whose name do you act?"

"Not God, not king, or country," Max replied, while Carys clutched his hand.

"In whose name?"

"My own. And, I suppose," he added, "in hers."

The Representative gave a terse smile. "And you think these feelings between you are sustainable, that you'd last all the trials of a relationship?" She steepled her hands and rested her chin briefly against her fingers. "You can't tell if your feelings will wane. That's the point. You can't tell if you'd be able to support each other through difficult times."

"With respect"—Carys stepped forward—"we already have. We suffered a miscarriage, and we got through it together."

The Representative raised her eyebrows, but not without sympathy. "Were you planning a child? Is that the next rule you want us to review?"

"No. I don't think the guidelines on parenting should change," said Carys. "But surely *choice* is at the heart of a people's utopia."

The Representative again leaned forward. "Do you think that we ban love, or that we 'excommunicate' younger parents? Because we don't. Don't labor under a misinterpretation." She gestured around the room. "Every citizen living in Europia is free to love whom they want. The only thing we ask is they live alone, on Rotation, until they're established."

Carys spoke again, her voice very quiet: "What if we are established? What if we're ready?"

"Professionally, or emotionally?"

"Both," she countered. "We're ready. What does *being established* have to do with it?"

"It means everybody doing their best and giving their all, undistracted. It means success for individuals, and a better society for us all. You know, the Couples Rule is not entirely random," said the Representative, leaning on one hand. "A lot of psychological research was undertaken on the significance of those first failed adult relationships on the psyche. A much higher success rate was found when those adults were established on all fronts. Age, career, outlook. All reaped the benefits."

"We're established," repeated Carys.

"You certainly have a lot of opinions," the Representative said. "Do you know of anyone else in a similar situation, who feels like you do?"

Carys looked toward Max, and he tried to explain it. "Not exactly.

But I do know a lot of people the same age as me who are going the other way. They're not bothering to form real connections at all." Max paused. "If I might be so cheeky as to say so, you could probably do with a few younger people in this Hall—life for us third-generation Europeans is quite different. I don't know if you spend much time outside, or if you spend much time with people in their twenties, but it's becoming a little soulless out there. They think that you, in this room, *don't let them* be with anyone they love, so the relationships they're experiencing are empty, and a lot of that is due to these restrictions."

One of the balconies moved forward. "We don't want that. We should commission a study across the Voivodeship to see how people are feeling."

"Just like that, on the say-so of one kid?" The call came from the higher tier.

"The boy is right. That's what I've seen in Voivode 9," said a Representative on the left.

"It's been that way for years, since the advent of the Internet," shouted a voice, and the room guffawed.

"They're not the first to come and ask for this," said another.

Max looked sharply at Carys, who, shocked, stared back at him.

"Everything we do is in the best interest of the Voivodeship," the Speaker said. "Society values competent government above ideology. We don't want people to turn against the whole structure of our democracy because one rule by which we're living has become outdated. We should commission the study."

The balconies lit up green, and the Speaker nodded. "Motion carried."

Max squeezed Carys's hand with relief.

The Representative with interlocked fingers hadn't leaned back and again motioned to speak. "And what about these two? What do they do, while we study their peers?" She smiled kindly.

The Hall buzzed.

"They both work for the EVSA," said the same voice that had called Max a "kid."

"Two thousand miles apart," Max reminded the Hall.

"It begs the question," said a stern-faced Speaker: "Did you come here to repeal the rule for yourselves, or to appeal for the greater good?"

Carys bit her lip as Max spoke. "For everyone." His voice shook, betraying his nervousness.

"Perhaps"—the Representative who'd smiled kindly looked around the room—"they could be something of a test. Every sociological study needs a control group. Ours could be away from the Voivodeship."

Max and Carys looked at each other, dismayed.

"You can't send us away," Max said with panic. "That's not what we were asking." No, no, no: anything but this. Anything but being booted out of Europia. He'd wanted freedom and, if he was honest, a victory over his parents and their archaic beliefs—not banishment.

"America?" called one of the Representatives, and Max blanched.

The female Representative from Voivode 23 didn't falter as she addressed the Hall. "We've all been worrying about the impact of the asteroid belt on our development. Our human development," she corrected, before anyone could interrupt, "bigger than Europia or the sum of our parts. We've debated what to do in this Hall many times. More times than I can count.

"We're hemmed in," she said, looking around the Hall, paying particular attention to the screens. "We can't leave Earth to explore or to look for new planets to spread the utopian message. We can't even leave Earth simply to look down. Space-based research has stopped. The Space Station is abandoned. The lunar missions have ceased. Everything we were trying to learn about the universe has come to a halt.

"Now, the very best of our thinkers have always claimed our future lies above us. Human development depends on it. It's agreed, I think, that we have to find a way to get out beyond the asteroid belt." There was silence in the Hall as the gaze of the Representative came to rest on Max and Carys. "When we were presented with this case, we were told the girl had recently gained her license and was ready for an EVSA mission. The boy has been working on minerals and meteoroids, albeit in different ways. The timing would be . . . optimal."

The irritated Representative from the upper balcony spoke: "That would be highly unusual."

"We would speak to the EVSA," she said soothingly. "I'm sure they would consider it. They've already undertaken anthropological studies into whether established couples make the best team, and the most efficient unit."

"Yes, but *older* couples."

"We should give them a chance. We're a meritocracy, after all, and they are most likely the best suited."

"Excuse me," Max said. "Space?"

She nodded. "We need to find a path through the asteroid belt. Perhaps you can do that." She looked at Carys, then Max. "And you can continue your studies on board."

"Space," Max repeated.

"In space, yes. The perfect control group, in an uncontaminated petri dish, if you like."

"It's not a petri dish," said Max. "It's a deathly vacuum."

The Speaker looked down at him. "The optimum condition for a laboratory test."

"But nothing grows in a vacuum."

"Love does." The Representative leaned forward. "Love loves the unknown. Away from the pressure of society and your peers, you can focus on your relationship, and we can really tell if the bonds formed at your age truly warrant a complete rethink of the system. Because we want to be sure everyone has the chance to be happy."

The balconies again lit up green, and the rest of the discussion passed in a blur. Motions were carried, the balcony tiers a wave of movement in Carys's and Max's dazed eyes as they tried to take it all in, but all they could see were the looping golden stars on the ceiling of the Hall before they were ushered to take a seat or go back out to the square.

As they exited the Hall, Carys turned to Max, her excitement itching around the edges. "I can't believe it. We're going to space."

He looked at her, her excitement bubbling, but all he felt was immense dread. "I guess we are," he said.

seventeen

* *Ten minutes* *

FROM DOWN ON EARTH, the stars above blink with fire, "twin-kling" as the light bends and refracts through many layers of atmo-sphere. But up in space, the stars lie flat like static dots, surrounding Max and Carys as far as the eye can see. A fuzz of dust and rock chips frame them more closely, as do the larger gray meteoroids, gently spinning while they're tugged by gravity toward Earth.

"It's amazing to see the colors of the planets with our own eyes," says Carys, looking far out to the left where they can see the blue of Venus. "Most people don't realize the first images captured from Mars's surface were transmitted back to Earth in black and white, and colored red by NASA."

"Funny."

"And Saturn looked like it was in grayscale when we saw it from home."

"True."

"Max? You're turning monosyllabic on me."

He fidgets in his suit. "Am I? Sorry. I was thinking about how we got here." They're quiet for a moment, thinking about all the ways they were brought together—and kept together—in this moment. "Do you remember in the Grand Central Hall that Representative said something about couples making the best teams?"

"A research study," Carys says. "I don't think they'd got past it on paper."

"Do you think we've effectively proved the theory?"

"We haven't murdered each other up here," she says. "And I haven't killed you yet for getting us into this with no propellant."

"But you said after couples have been through so much together, it's hard to be lighthearted."

"Did I?" She thinks for a moment. "That's not what I meant. And it's been easy for us to be lighthearted today. What do they call it—gallows humor?"

He nods, a twisting nod, because his body is still moving in slow, perpetual motion, falling and turning in balletic slow-mo. "I thought we'd get a break at some point," he says. "I thought we'd get an easy patch, where we could coast along—but everything's been so hard."

She blinks at the sudden depth of thought and leans to comfort him. "I think it's human nature to struggle, even in a perfect world. Cavemen struggled to find food and shelter. More recently men struggled in wars. But us? We get depressed if we say something stupid on the MindShare. We've got enough, so we have nothing to fight for. And it makes us unhappy."

"We've been fighting for the past"—he checks the gauge on his oxygen tank and the time on his chip—"eighty minutes. So we can assuredly say that having something to fight for is exhausting. I wish we were home." There—he'd said it. For the first time in the aftermath of what he'd done by taking them to the Grand Central Hall, which in turn had pushed them into months of training at the Agency, undertaking powerful simulations and trips above the stratosphere in reduced gravity, plus their crash course in advanced meteor studies, plus survival; after all of that, he'd finally admitted it.

"Me, too." Carys looks down toward Earth, then at Max's air gauge.

Max catches her line of sight. "Do you think it'll hurt?"

"What?"

"Running out of air."

Yes. But she doesn't say it. "They say it's painless, like falling asleep."

Carys knows drowning is anything but, that it hurts like someone pulling your lungs out from your body through your nose, your entire respiratory system being tugged—no, tugging itself—panting, pleading for oxygen, but she doesn't say so. "Probably. We'll just drift off."

"Good."

Another micrometeoroid fizzles past and pops soundlessly next to them, its expiry a timely punctuation mark. Carys stretches her silver-covered fingers, accidentally activating her flex. "Oops."

With proximity switched on, random characters appear across her and Max's helmets, dissolving into question marks as her dictionary fails to form words. He laughs at the suddenness and the silliness.

She switches off the flex so it no longer appears on Max's screen. "You know, I tried writing you letters," she says, "when we were in different Voivodes. But they didn't really take, with you."

"No—sorry. I guess long form's gone out the window now that we've got Wall Rivers."

"That's fair enough. I just thought it would be fun to have a pen pal."

"I've been called many things in my life," Max says, "but 'pen pal' is a new one."

"Did you not get one during your studies? I was given a pen pal in a very far-flung Voivode."

Max makes a careful face. "That's probably because you were being eased into the Rotation system a little late."

"Oh. That's weird. Most of my experiences are probably different from yours and everyone else's. I never thought about that before."

"It's what makes you unique."

She furrows her eyebrows. "Unique in a good way?"

"Uniquely bonkers." Their energy sapped, the conversation is dispensed with a quarter of their usual verve, the delivery of his teasing indolent and lethargic. "Carys, what would you do, if you made it home after this?"

"Give public talks about the perils of the asteroid field. You?"

"No, seriously."

"Seriously?" she asks. "I don't think we're going to make it home. We've got nine minutes of air remaining."

"But if we did . . ."

Carys swallows. "I'm thirsty. Are you? We used one of the straws but we've got one left. I'm sure we've got time to share."

* * *

THEY HAD LAIN ON the sand in a different climate, in what felt like a different life. Grounded from training for a week by excessive meteor activity, they'd finished prepping the living quarters of their new ship—the *Laertes*—and headed northeast to the beach.

"How come you've stopped using your last name?" Carys asked, eyes closed, the sun dappling and dancing across her eyelids.

"Huh?"

"I saw it in the flight manuals after last week's trip up." They had recently graduated from simulation training to real space shuttles, and for the first time Carys had flown them above the ozone layer. She'd watched Max nervously, the harness pushing him down into the seat, as she'd lifted the shuttle off the ground in a vertical take-off, the throb of the engines loud in their ears.

"I'm surprised you noticed that and not my knuckles turning white."

"Ha," she said. "You were holding on pretty tight."

The patchwork of green fields around them had become smaller as they'd lifted higher and higher, and Max had groaned as she'd rolled the shuttle around and accelerated up toward the darkness, the light disappearing behind them. He looked down at Earth, which was beginning to curve into a globe, and muttered, "What have we done?" But then he looked at Carys, guiding the shuttle confidently through the stratos, and bit his lip, proud through his terror.

"I stopped using my surname . . . for some distance from my family," Max said quietly, down on the beach. "Plus, everyone knows me simply as Max now. Rule-breaking Max."

"You could reinvent yourself as a superhero," she suggested. "Add it to the list alongside chef and astronaut."

"Or spy." He pulled a silly face. "The name's Fox, Max Fox."

"Max Fox. Two *x*s—that's got to be pretty unusual."

"I'd get a good Scrabble score." He turned to face her. "Why did you ask?"

"I was thinking . . . maybe I'll use the name Fox, too."

"Really? People don't do that anymore."

She propped herself up on one elbow, resting her head on her hand. "I think we should."

"'Carys Fox.' It does have a nice ring to it. Do you think there would be repercussions?"

"From whom? We don't live in a police state. They could've kicked us out already, but they didn't."

He looked out to sea. "They've given us a get-out clause, Cari, but until the rules are formally changed we probably shouldn't do anything to rile them."

Along the shore, sunbathers splashed in the ocean or lay stretched out on the sand. A few older couples strolled on the board-walk with their arms linked, checking the contents of their buggies, like penguins mollycoddling their offspring.

"We're leaving the Voivodeship," said Carys. "We can still see each other, be together. Isn't that what we wanted?"

"You think it's going to be that easy, up in space?"

"First flight up with me that bad, was it?"

"No," he said, "a textbook takeoff and landing. Seriously, Cari, it was perfect. It's just . . . Aren't you daunted at all?"

"Anything will be easier than Rotation." She leaned over to kiss his face—a gentle, brushing kiss—then at the last minute poured a carton of water over his head. Max yelled and lifted her from the beach, ran to the nearest flotation device hovering in the shallows, and dropped her inside it. Water flew up and the airbags bounced and inflated, throwing Carys into the air.

"I said 'Rotation,' you bastard," she said, breathless, "not 'flotation.'"

"We've just got to get through the mission in space," he said. "Then we'll be fine." He looked down at her as she dug sand with her hands from the seabed to throw at him. "We'll be fine."

* * *

CARYS CLOSES HER EYES once more, feeling the sun's strength against her flimsy eyelids, but the glass of her helmet shields her, protecting them. "It's not glass, is it?" she says, reaching up to thump her fishbowl with her hand. "It's Perspex."

"It's probably all manner of things."

"How much air do we have left?"

He checks. "About eight minutes."

"Not long." He doesn't tell her that she has eight and he has twelve—not now. He'll find a way to make them the same.

"I guess this is it, then? Nearly." No. He won't let it be. There has to be a way out of this.

"Do you remember that day on the beach?" she says. "During training? You spent the day playing games on your chip and got sun-burned on the soles of your feet."

The day when Carys had asked to take his name. "I should've let you."

"What?"

"I should have let you change your name. I'm sorry."

As far as she can in space, she shrugs. "It's fine. You didn't want me to, I get it."

"It wasn't that! It's just—you were pushing me to challenge even more than we already were."

"*Me*?" Her voice is disbelieving. "You did most of it yourself."

"I'd challenged as much as I felt I could, Carys. We were too young to feel the way we did."

She's quiet. "And yet . . . we did."

"Yes, but it didn't work out that great for us, did it? I mean"—he gestures around him at the vast expanse of nothing—"we're here." He wraps his hand around her wrist, looking down again at her gauge.

"I can't believe we're going to die," she says quietly.

"We should do it."

"Do what?"

"We should have the same name."

She looks surprised. "Really?"

"Definitely."

"If we get rescued, we can both be Foxes back on Earth—"

"Nobody's coming, Cari." His voice cracks. "We're not going to be rescued, and we're running out of time. We should have the same name right now, before it's too late."

"Oh, fuck." She starts crying. "There goes my brave face." They fall, together, in horrified silence. They're tethered to each other by rope; Max still clasps Carys's wrist. "I wish we could touch," she says.

Despair draws its own path over the laughter lines of Max's face. "I wish I could hold you." He reaches out a hand to touch her, but it rests only against the glass. He starts to claw at the glove of his suit.

"What are you doing?" she asks.

"I want to feel you, actually you."

"You can't! Don't break the vacuum, Max—you'll die!"

"We've only got a few minutes left, Cari." He has nine. "We may as well go out with a bang, together. At least that way we choose it. We choose death."

"No!" But it's too late: Max rips off the glove and they stare in horror at his hand, waiting for it to shrivel, turn bulbous, or blue— but nothing happens. Instead his suit seals itself at the wrist, and he calmly wiggles his bare fingers against the particles of space.

They look at each other in surprise.

"I guess we don't know everything we think we know," Carys observes.

"Another space myth." He interlocks his fingers with her gloved hand, and she continues to look at his hand.

"What's it like? Hot? Cold?"

"Neither." He turns his hand over, palm up, and beckons her. "Technology's come a long way. I've been taking those pills. Plus we're shaded, behind the *Laertes*—and there's no way it's absolute zero out here. Come on. I'm not dead yet."

"But in direct sunlight you'll burn to a crisp."

"Not likely in the next few minutes. Go on, Carys," he pleads. "Choose to do this with me."

She nods, then slowly takes hold of the silvery scuba fabric holding her hand captive and pulls. She expects to hear it tear, a ripping sound, as she feels the fabric fracture beneath her touch, but outside their audio comms there's only silence. She tucks the torn glove into her pocket and holds out her naked hand to Max, who, instead of taking it in his, quickly ties a loose thread around her fourth finger.

"What's that?" she asks.

"Now we have the same name, we should be joined in the same family."

"How quaint." She laughs, but she's touched.

"I've always been fond of a grand gesture," he says. "I should've done this ages ago." They link their bare hands and gently touch their glass helmets to each other. "In the old days I would've given you a diamond."

"Christ. Imagine having that kind of power on your knuckle. Did they not know?"

"They thought it was a carbon allotrope, which sparkled."

"If I wanted something that sparkled, I couldn't be anywhere better, could I?" Carys points at the stars around them. "We're surrounded by sparkles."

"We're in a damn asteroid field. We're surrounded by sparkles, frozen water, ammonia, carbon dioxide. Look over there—more heading toward Earth." They watch the asteroids for a moment, working up the momentum to burn through the atmosphere and light up the night sky.

"Down there, they look like shooting stars, don't they?" says Carys. "Up here they're just burning rocks."

"There's a shooting star." Max points into the darkness. "Want to make a wish?"

Carys is silent.

"It's not a bad way to go, wishing on a star. Cari?"

She stays quiet, watching the arc of the shooting star moving slowly through the field.

"Carys."

She counts under her breath, still watching. "It just arced down below that big rock. How did it know to do that? It should've smashed straight into it."

"Pull of the Earth, maybe?"

"I don't think so." They're both staring at the light. "It's mirroring Earth's curvature."

"Gravity?"

"No. Look at it. That's definitely an orbital plane—"

"Does that mean . . . ?"

"It's on an elliptical orbit," Carys shouts. "It's a satellite! Max, it's a bloody satellite."

eighteen

THE LIGHT COMES toward them slowly, a phantasm of hope. "We're not going mental, are we?" says Max. "It's not a mirage?"

"How do we get to it?" Carys is jigging with renewed vitality, stretching her arms and kicking, trying everything to make her body travel toward the light rather than fall through the dark. "Will it pass nearby?"

"We might be hallucinating," Max says. "Lack of air."

"How can we calculate its trajectory? It looks like it's coming this way—"

"They probably programmed our oxygen to release more slowly at the very end. We're breathing thin air."

She reaches out and strikes him. "Max, will you get a grip?" He reels away from her before the tethering rope yanks him back. "This is happening. This is real. We need to act on it before it's too late."

"It is too late, Cari. We don't have time—"

"Max Fox." She looks him square in the eye, rock steady and certain. "This is our last chance."

He swallows, a dry, rasping breath, and gives her what she wants. "Okay."

"We can do this."

"Okay," he repeats.

"The huge asteroid below us, to the left. Reckon it has a sizable mass?"

"It's bigger than you," he says, and she glares at him. "It looks pretty hefty," he amends.

"See how it's totally static. It must be, what, a hundred yards in length? All this dust flying around, yet this big one is still. Why is that?"

"I can't believe you're talking about interplanetary dust right now."

"Shut up, will you? My physics may be limited but I'm trying to work out if that asteroid is at the Lagrange point out here."

"Tell me again what that means?"

"The five points where gravity has no pull—there's no time for this," says Carys. "Let's hope it's at Lagrange. Otherwise we'll carry on falling and that satellite is going to pass right above our heads."

"Let's find out. Coming up in five, four, three, two . . ." Instinctively they bend their legs, like ballet dancers landing on the floorboards of a stage, and as they level with the stony asteroid, for the first time in nearly ninety minutes, they stop tumbling. "I don't believe it." Max is incredulous. "Physics, eh? Always right."

"Apart from when they thought the Earth was flat," Carys says absently, scanning the sky. She grips his bare hand in hers. "Do you reckon it's manned?"

He squeezes back. "Who knows? Try and communicate. Flex to them. They've been sending ships helmed by animals into space since Laika in 1957. Give it a shot, have a chat with a space dog."

"Space skeleton, more like." She checks the mesh is in place, looped over her knuckles, and begins to flex. *Help, this is Carys . . . Fox, from the* Laertes, *requesting immediate assistance. Do you read me?*

She waits.

I repeat: this is Carys Fox from the Laertes *requesting immediate assistance. Do you read me, over?*

"I'm not getting anything," she tells Max.

"Keep trying."

Please help us. If you don't, we're going to die out here.

Her audio crackles to life with a clangorous *ping*. Hello, Carys. This is Osric.

"Osric!" she shouts, as the blue text fills the side of her glass.

I am communicating directly with the satellite's computer to patch this to you, Carys.

We missed you, Osric. Is anyone on board?

I'm afraid not, Carys. This is one of our own drones.

"Crap." She turns to Max. "No one's on board—it's one of ours."

"Can it carry anyone? Can Osric send it to our location?"

Osric, can you redirect the sat to us?

It will be with you in six minutes.

"Cari?" asks Max. "What's happening? I can't see your conversation anymore. I think you turned it off."

"The sat is coming straight to us in six minutes."

"Six?" Max falters. Six minutes: the time it takes to boil the perfect dippy egg; the average duration of most couples having sex; the total time it took to decimate New York City.

Carys falters, too. "How long do we have? We haven't got six minutes, have we?" She slumps, deflated. "We haven't got enough air. Oh, god."

"Wait—"

"Can we hold our breath? Is that possible? I suppose we'll have passed out by the time it gets near and we won't be able to work the air lock—"

"I've got enough air."

She recoils. "What?"

"Just about. I've got six, and you've got two," Max says. "Cari, I'm so sorry, when we were trying earlier, when we used your pack to try a makeshift propellant—"

"I've been reading your gauge, not mine. Yours was right there in front of me." She stares, dully. "But mine was on my side. Christ." She holds back a choking sob. "At least you can make it."

"Don't be stupid. We can split the air between us," says Max. "We'll each have roughly four minutes, and we'll hold our breath for two. We'll both make it to the satellite air lock, then traverse the sat back to the *Laertes*. We can make this work."

"Really?"

"Easy." Max squeezes her hand once more. "Let's get ready." He scoots around behind her and makes a show of tapping her pack and adjusting the shoulder straps and cables. "There." Very gently, he lifts off his pack, still connected to his suit, and places it on Carys. She doesn't notice: the pack has no weight out there. "Won't be long now."

"I can't believe we're going to be all right." She turns her head toward him, smiling. Below them the world pours past, a weather system brewing over Africa. "Everything is going to be okay. We're going to make it home."

He keeps himself behind her, and she raises her bare hand to her shoulder and he clasps it, perhaps for the last time.

"Listen to me, Carys. You're going to have to change tubes briefly when your air supply runs out. I loosened it earlier—you just have to switch and screw the thread into the other air pack, all right? Turn it until it locks." He's still holding her hand. "Do you understand?"

"Why do I—"

"You can't hold your breath, Cari. Remember the Games."

The image flashes up in Max's mind of Carys laid out by the turquoise pool, her body twisted unnaturally, her skin an icy white as the medics worked hard to bring her back. "You've never been able to hold your breath."

"But—"

It had never occurred to him that it might be possible to drown in space. After the last time, he'd sworn he would protect her. "Carys. I can't risk that you won't make it. Change the tube." Max lets go of her hand and begins to loosen their tether rope.

"No, please, Max—"

"I'm sorry. It's the only way."

"Stop it, I can't—"

"No, *I* can't, don't you see?" They float freely, and Max puts his hand up to his helmet. Carys's air supply is falling dangerously low, and breathing carbon dioxide begins to make her faint.

"Please—"

Max unscrews his air supply, holding it in place while he looks at her for the last time. "You see? I saved you when we met"—he smiles wonkily—"and I'm saving you now."

With a terrible final gesture, he pulls out his tube and pushes Carys as hard as he can toward the approaching satellite. As she spirals away from him into the dark, she sees him mouth the words "I love you."

"No! Max!"

part three

part three

nineteen

CARYS, CAN YOU hear me?"

"You don't have to talk about it, Carys. You don't have to talk about it." The warm female voice hesitates. "You don't have to talk about"—she breaks off and consults quietly with an insistent doctor—"Max."

SHE'S STARING AT THE WALL. A crack in the paint, a magnolia fleck, has held her attention—or, more honestly, not lost her empty gaze—for the past twenty-eight minutes.

All time is measured in minutes now.

IF ONLY SHE COULD get her nail under it. Really scratch around beneath it and flick it off. Perhaps grow the fleck into a black hole. A magnolia nebula.

They keep telling her she doesn't have to talk about it, so she doesn't, which is exactly the opposite of what they want. People who say you don't have to talk about something are usually dying to extract it from you.

THE NEXT DAY SHE CLIMBS up the wall into the black hole and disappears for a few hours. Carys watches from behind her magnolia fleck as doctors and nurses come in and look down at the sleeping body lying in her bed.

"How long has she been out of it?"

"About three hours. The morphine's knocked her out cold."

Osric?

CARYS WAKES IN THE NIGHT as she does every dawn: screaming as the skeletal canine corpse lurches toward her in zero gravity.

"Laika!"

Heart racing, she reaches for the light, but the mongrel dissolves, dissipating as the light particles touch its very bones.

"CARYS, DO YOU THINK today you ought to try—"

"Please don't tell me that I need to brush my hair." She doesn't lift her head from the bed or attempt to turn toward her mother's voice. All voices are the same here. All the same in that all of them are here, but not one of them is his. "I know. I can't."

She lies beached on her side, back to the door in the dark.

"I really think we need to change the sheets, at least. You've been in them for days." Carys doesn't reply. "Please?"

"I like them this way." The bed smells earthy. Salty, human—comforting smells, like sweat and panic.

Gwen walks from the doorway, playing with the room chip, and the Wall Rivers spring to life with photos from a trip to the sea, flowing from frame to frame around the room. "There. Isn't that better?"

A different climate, in what felt like a different life. She remembers the heat on her face, the warmth of him next to her on the sand. She doesn't look up but pulls the duvet over her head. "Please, Mom. Not today."

"I'M GOING TO STAY with you for a while, Cari," her mother says. "Just until you've recovered."

Recovered? How do you recover from something so cataclysmic? But she only nods.

"I thought it would be nice for you to have some company."

Dragged out of bed and urged to head into the sunshine, Carys ignores the offer of company and instead stalks through Voivode 6, heading to the small city beach and staring out at the waves, avoiding the crowds.

Infamy is grief's worst enemy and Carys shakes it off like an unwanted hand grasping at her shoulder, a layer of sympathy and a symphony of whispers she neither cares for nor wants. Notoriety has made her angry, cutting through her untouchable lethargy. She knows people look at her in reverence, wanting to ask what happened and how she's feeling, but she walks wild-eyed and wild-haired through the streets of the Voivode in Max's old fisherman's sweater without stopping or meeting their gaze. Lethargy keeps her numb. It means she doesn't have to grieve. Anger rouses her, and she doesn't want that.

She visits the Voivode's dog rescue center, searching for the face haunting her dreams. She finds him in the features of a small terrier cross and, anemically, inquires about adopting him.

"You can't take him home today," says the administrator. "You can visit for a few weeks to acclimatize, and we'll have to do a home visit to check it's suitable for a dog."

Carys says nothing, staring into the mongrel's eyes—a haunted shade of green—trying to gauge the pup's soul.

"Will you be calling him Fudge?" the lady asks kindly.

"Sorry?"

"His name. He's Fudge here, but you don't have to keep it. Though we recommend names that sound similar to avoid confusion."

"Laika." Carys reaches out to stroke him and he shudders under her touch, quaking at two hundred beats per minute as he cowers. "He's called Laika."

"You'll be good for little Laika, I'm sure. He's had a tough time."

"Him and me both," says Carys, though the administrator presumes she's misheard.

"Lovely." She shuts down the screen and looks up at Carys. "Oh, gosh, you're not—are you? You poor thing."

SHE VISITS LAIKA DAILY, taking the stringy terrier treats. At first he doesn't trust her, but damaged creatures have a way of sensing a kindred spirit and slowly she coaxes him toward her, the puppy fearing no threat from the woman who crawls into his room on all fours and lies next to him. After two weeks he is gangling out of his kennel to see her, and together they sit quite contentedly in the center's garden until visiting hours are over.

"He's ready to go home with you now," the administrator says, and Carys nods. "You two look like soul mates."

Soul mates. The idea fractures her, and she retreats again into wordlessness.

"YOU HAVE TO JOIN the world again, Carys. You can't lock everyone out."

She has installed herself once more in the wicker peacock chair facing out to sea, Laika snoring on her lap, but people won't let her *be*. They won't let her not talk. "I've let Laika in." Her voice has lost all its modulation. Now it's flat, like the ocean when the tide is out.

"That's a dog." Her mother, Gwen, tries a different tack. "You can't let everything pass you by as if it's happening to someone else."

If Carys had the energy, she'd explain that it *had* happened to someone else; it had happened to Max, turning Carys into a bystander in her own life.

"It's the memorial tomorrow."

She stares at a buoy in the water, floating gently. She's never seen the water so still.

"Carys? You really must go."

"I will."

"You'll be there? Professor Alina was asking."

It takes a moment to place the name, and she flinches. His mother. Tomorrow she'll face everyone who ever loved him and come up short. "I'll be there."

Sensing a flux in her, Laika unfurls and reaches to lick her gently on the nose, which soothes Carys in welcome distraction. He's still tiny, but filling out daily.

Tomorrow: twenty-four hours. One thousand four hundred and forty minutes—sixteen times more than they had together at the end.

"YOU CAN'T BRING THAT mutt in here." The usher is insistent but Carys takes no notice, walking past with Laika clutched to her chest, his growing limbs sprawling out from her arms. "Please, miss, this is—" He stops short when she turns to look at him, taking the dark sunglasses from her face. "You can sit in the second row," he finishes, somewhat lamely.

She nods, not noticing how he eyeballs her outfit. She's pulled Max's ancient fisherman's sweater over the only black dress she owns, her hair dragged high into a looping bun on her head. Laika chews at the fraying sleeve.

"Carys." Max's father receives her in the aisle. "We didn't know if you'd be able to join us." He doesn't say more but simply places his hand on her shoulder in the formal greeting, and she implies significance in the touch, even if it's only his respect for her rank.

"Thank you, Pranay." What she's thanking him for she isn't quite sure, but she's aware she uses his first name to put them on an equal footing. She takes a seat, laying the dog on her lap, and sits quietly. Max's family has pulled out all the stops, and Carys thinks calmly how he would have hated it.

Music starts playing, the type he'd laugh at, and his mother and Kent enter, the Professor in a neat black veil. Carys rolls her eyes at the dramatics. They're expressing all the aesthetics of grief, but there's no evidence they're actually grieving.

Kent stops by her aisle. "Wow, cool dog."

"Thank you."

"Can I sit with you?"

"Sure."

Professor Alina pulls him away. "Come, Kent, you sit in the front with the family." The words burn straight through Carys, and she recoils as her insides are torched by the untruth, looking down at the broken strand of cotton knotted around her finger. *Family.* His mother inclines her head at Carys, and Carys, wary, nods. As Kent looks back at Laika longingly, Carys surreptitiously shifts along the bench until she's sitting behind the small boy and Laika paws at his back. He smiles, and she smiles back. She cannot begin to think about how much like Max he looks.

Somebody slides into the pew next to her and she smiles half-heartedly when she sees it's Liu, looking at her with curiosity. "You came" is all she says.

He strokes Laika's nose. "Is this your surrogate?"

"I'm sorry?"

"It's common to get a dog." His face is not unkind.

"Oh." Feeling she might have to say more at some point, she takes the plunge and adds, "I didn't realize I was such a cliché."

He takes her hand and squeezes it, and in that gesture she sees the root of his sorrow, a hollowness etched around his eyes and mouth at the loss of his friend.

"I'm sorry," she murmurs. "I'm so, so sorry."

"Whatever for? It wasn't your fault."

"I should've saved him . . ."

His father throws a glance over his shoulder, and Liu hushes her discreetly. "Let's not take the blame while unimaginative family are within hearing distance." He hands her a tissue but her eyes are dry, as they have been since she returned to Earth.

"He saved me, and sacrificed himself," she whispers, and finally it feels good to talk to somebody who knew the Max she knew.

"Of course he did. Would you have expected him to do anything else?" Liu wraps Carys's fingers around Laika's front leg for comfort, and she grasps it, stroking the fur to his paw. "Well, then."

They hush as Pranay signals for the service to begin, and Carys listens with curiosity as he recites stories from Max's childhood she's not heard. His tone is flat but not dispassionate and she senses that of them all, he may be struggling the most, though they are so put together it's almost impossible to tell.

"Our son always had to know how everything worked," he is saying. "He was always questioning how, or feeling around the edges to test why. I remember taking him to the beach when he was very small. 'Why can't I ride my bike along this fenced-off bit of seaside, Dad?' he asked, over and over again, and it was only after a long and detailed explanation of what it actually was that my son would take my word for it and not try to ride his bicycle with stabilizers up the North Atlantic quarantine."

Carys smiles at this sketch of a younger Max, the first moment of the ceremony in which she can identify him. His father closes his notes with a splay of his fingers. "The last time we saw Max, it wasn't good, and I wish it had been different."

Carys sits forward, suddenly curious.

"But it wasn't, and we have to live with that. He made his choice.

Max would want us to carry on living and not resent him for anything that has happened."

She slumps back, defeated, as Pranay once more takes his seat. That had been the moment when his father could have acknowledged that it might have been different with their son. By accepting no blame and conceding no sense of guilt, they retain their porcelain veneer, and Carys begins to feel sick.

The esteemed doctor rises and begins to ruminate on her son's life, the words impassive. Her presentation is faultless, the Professor clearly accustomed to public speaking, and Carys hates her for it.

"The Voivodeship lost an important citizen, and I'd like to thank the members of the EVSA for coming to honor him today." Carys looks up—many of the support crew and admin team that they got to know during training line the back rows. "Max was a talented young man at the forefront of his field. He found his place in Europia and was rewarded with an exciting opportunity." Carys looks on in disbelief as the woman carries on speaking words, words, words, about a boy she is starting to feel she didn't know at all.

Kent joins the Professor to talk about "my Mac," though the frame of childhood memory is painfully narrow. He stumbles over the words, snuffling a little, before coming to a stop. "Mac told me that the girl was his best friend."

The room looks up from its bowed-head position and a shocked Carys smiles, as Max's mother turns rigid in front. Carys lifts Laika's paw and waves it weakly at Kent, who waves back. The people in the room look at the shabby girl in the second row.

"Mac told me nothing matters as much as your best friend," says the little boy, bigger now than when Carys and Kent had first met. "And he was mine."

The room murmurs in response, heart strings pulled, and the Professor gazes stonily at Carys.

"That's put the cat among the pigeons," murmurs Liu, looking at her properly for the first time, noting how drawn her face is, how enlarged her features are becoming. "When was the last time you had a proper meal?" Carys shrugs. "Come on. Let's get out of here and find something to eat."

"We're blowing off the ceremony?"

"It's what he'd want. Do you see Max in any of this?"

"No." Only in the face of his younger brother up front.

"He's not here, Carys. There is nothing of him here."

She hesitates.

"They're wrapping up anyway. We'll give him our own memorial. One worthy of him."

She waits a second before sliding out of the pew and walking to the exit at the back of the room, her head low, Laika in her arms. As she leaves, a man near the back lifts a hand, trying to catch her attention, but she doesn't want it to be caught, not now, not ever.

Not now that he's gone.

twenty

LIU'S CHARM GETS them a table at the Rotation restaurant even with the dog. He magics a bowl and some scraps from one of the waitresses and puts it down on the floor, where Laika eats hungrily.

"Make sure you feed him," he says gently, and Carys's temper flares.

"I can look after my own dog."

"I'm not sure you're looking after yourself, darl, that's all I'm saying. Even if you're not hungry, the dog still needs to eat."

She watches Laika lapping water, desperately thirsty, and feels a flood of guilt. "Oh, god. I can't look after anyone. I kill everything I love."

"Shhh," Liu says, taking her wrists and putting a menu in her hands.

"I'm suffocating him."

"He's a rescue dog. He loves it and he needs you."

"I can't . . ." She stares at the menu without reading.

"You know," Liu says, "it's really hard to be logical and deal with big feelings when you haven't eaten. Come on—order."

She complies and orders a bowl of spaghetti, holding out her arm for the chip scanner, having to scrape back Max's battered old sweater to reveal her wrist.

"She'll have some garlic bread, too." Carys makes to protest but Liu waves away her objection. "Carbs help. That's science. Now," he says, "tell me your favorite Max memory. Your defining anecdote of that fine chap."

She looks up, surprised.

"Did you think I was going to let you mope?" He shakes his head. "What happened up there is done with. We need to get on with honoring him, not you killing yourself with the guilt and sadness at what might've been."

"That's easy for you to say," she whispers.

"It's not what he'd want. He'd want you to draw a line under this. And at some point get blind drunk." She grimaces, but she understands. "So tell me your favorite memory."

"I didn't think you approved," she says.

"Of you two? I don't—or, rather, I didn't. But then I'd not long left an oppressive culture, so I know what it can feel like to go against the social grain."

Carys closes her eyes.

"Tell me your favorite Max memory."

"I don't know," Carys says, thinking about Max for the first time, her mind wavering around the edge of his spotlight, refusing to step fully into the beam where those emotions may have to be confronted. "There were so many things about him—so many stories."

"Here's mine. I'll give you the abridged version." Liu pours water and lays out the cutlery and condiments. "When we met, he helped me with some food queries, as you probably know. Such a beautiful boy—what a waste. I went back to the supermarket every day, but he wasn't to be charmed. I convinced him to help me learn to cook— me, the RR's number one patron." He lifts his glass in a toast. "He offered to give me a lesson in his kitchen, as I didn't have one. After that, I turned up at his house most evenings, and he'd let me in. We'd sit watching films in companionable silence."

"That's your defining memory of Max?" she asks, confused, as Liu ends the anecdote there.

"Yes." Liu pushes a glass toward her. "Because it was so exactly him. He didn't actively seek out my friendship, he just let it happen. I wanted it, and he let my feelings carry it into existence."

Carys thinks how entirely opposite to Liu's experience hers with Max had been. True, after they'd met he hadn't sought her out either, letting a sort-of-chance meeting bring them back together. But he'd wanted to. And in front of the Representatives . . . with her, was that the first time Max had actively chosen a path for himself? "I suppose he did the same with me," she says, thinking otherwise.

"No way," Liu scoffs, breaking the newly arrived garlic bread with his fingers and offering her half. "He was different with you, and that was why you were the real deal."

She's surprised. "Thank you."

"Eat that, then tell me yours."

She nibbles at the edge of the buttery bread, feeling the tang of garlic hitting her deprived taste buds. "I really don't know."

"Dammit, Carys, tell me a nice Max story."

"Okay." She wipes her mouth with a napkin. "When we were on board the *Laertes*—our ship—we'd sometimes have hours to kill.

Max had his greenhouse and the geology center, but there were processes and experiments to sit through. One day Max wanted to find out where the name 'Laertes' came from, and he used the ship's computer to research it. He was absolutely delighted—*delighted*—when he discovered not only that 'Laertes' was taken from *Hamlet*, but the name of the ship's computer, 'Osric,' was, too. He thought he was unraveling an EVSA in-joke. He was so excited.

"The next thing I know, he's called up the script and projected the whole thing around the ship. He's insisting I read the play with him, that we 'better ourselves' while we're up there alone. For a while I thought he was trying to suss out if any of the other names were also from Shakespeare. The man who never reads books decided we must enact one of the great plays. It was crazy.

"He began learning Hamlet's speeches whenever he had a down moment. It got to the point where I'd wake up," she says, now smiling, "hearing 'To be or not to be,' and fall asleep to Max practicing his reaction at seeing a ghost.

"On our last day, I was flying the ship manually when he gave me a daisy from the greenhouse. I was trying to concentrate, but Max leaned over and tucked the flower into my hair. He was reading a scene between Hamlet and Ophelia, begging me to put the ship on auto and read it aloud with him." She falters, remembering. "But I thought I saw—I thought I could see . . ."

Liu takes her hand, gently urging her to continue.

"The alarms sounded. The *Laertes*'s hull had been ruptured by a meteoroid, and oxygen blasted through the flight deck in great jets. We grabbed our suits and ran to the air lock, heading outside to fix the breach . . ."

Still holding her hand in one of his, Liu, with the other, puts a slab of garlic bread on her plate.

"There were micrometeoroids everywhere. We were trying to get to the breach when we were hit ourselves . . ."

She struggles to go any further. "I never found out what Hamlet said to Ophelia. Max was wearing a red T-shirt with a Space Invader on the front, rumpled like he'd just climbed out of bed, his hair a mess, proudly reciting *Hamlet*—"

"I never had Max down as a theater buff," Liu says kindly. "It must be true what they say: space does change you."

Carys looks down at Laika, named after a piece of space mythology so potent she can't bring herself to answer. *Space does change you*. She daren't look at herself through that lens.

"So what's next for you?" he asks as their main course arrives.

She shrugs. "The EVSA will look after me for life, after what we—I—went through."

"But surely you'll be bored. You can't do nothing for the rest of your life."

"My Rotation is up soon," she says. "I'll find out where I'm going and see what's there, I suppose."

"Carys. You've got to get a grip." He's firm. "You've got to work."

"Yeah?"

"You're one of the most focused people I've met. Infuriatingly so. You've got to get back at it."

"I will, eventually."

"I'll expect progress reports."

She looks at him in surprise. She's never imagined he'll want to keep in touch. "Really?"

"Yes. You'll write to me, and I'll write to you. I can be your pen pal . . . Carys, what did I say? Is there something wrong with that word? Carys?" Liu didn't expect, with that simple platitude, he'd have to pick Carys out of her spaghetti bowl and mop up her flood of tears.

THEY MEET A FEW more times before Carys's move, ostensibly to take Laika out. During one of their final walks before Rotation, Liu finally manages to make her laugh.

"Are you moving soon, too?" she asks.

"Yes. V17." He makes a face. "Nothing to write home about. No home to write to, in fact. No one left in the Middle Kingdom to receive those letters."

"That's sad." She whistles for Laika, who's going bananas beneath a sprawling dwarf lemon shrub.

"What about you? Where's home?"

"Given 'home' and the location of our families are totally separate entities," she says, "my mom and dad live in Voivode 14. My brother is in the former United States, and my sister's living it up in the sun. And home," she says, "was in the mountains, where I lived for half my life."

"So Gary from Wales has a home. You really are rare. Has your family been around during all this?"

"Yes," she says quietly. "My mom moved in with me. I don't think she expected to have to spoon-feed me and brush my hair."

"Babyhood reborn. It's every mother's dream," Liu says. "I wouldn't worry. You're looking much better—skeletal chic wasn't really you."

"I didn't take that sweater off for days," she says. "I thought hollow and gaunt was quite becoming."

"No."

She looks at him closely. "Liu, are you . . . wearing eyeliner?"

He tosses his head. "Maybe."

"Is it for my benefit?" She's uncertain, and a trifle concerned.

"No. While you're wonderful, you've never been my type. Not even in your Tibetan sunrise heyday. I'm actually going out tonight." He smooths down his hair. "Want to come?" he adds, knowing she won't.

"Yes."

"Pardon?"

"I'd like to come, please."

"Christ."

"Oh, thanks. Now I know you didn't mean it." She extends a lead for Laika and snaps it on his collar as the dog goes berserk, straining on the lead to befriend another dog sniffing nearby. Carys pulls him back, petting him.

"I did mean it. I'm just surprised." She doesn't say anything, and he adds, "Of course you should come."

"Can I borrow some eyeliner?"

"Yes."

"Will you do my makeup, plait my hair and stuff?"

"Maybe."

She smiles. "Sounds great. Where are we going?"

He hesitates, but only for a millisecond. "The Dormer."

"Fine. It will be good to get out, make some fresh memories. Pick me up at eight?"

"Eight," he scoffs. "Old-age pensioner. I'm heading out at

eleven—you can come and get ready at my house at ten. Bring wine."

THEY'VE BEEN AT THE CLUB for only half an hour when Carys knows she's made a horrible mistake. The place is indelibly touched by Max's shadow. This was where she'd first talked to Liu, the night she'd seen Max but he hadn't seen her. *And now the man himself, the greatest living astronaut still alive and not yet dead* . . . Why is it you can find resonance in anything after someone's death, even an inane pickup line?

She sits on the crumbling chesterfield sofas, looking around. The doorman lets in gaggles of excitable girls and louche, too-cool guys; she sees underage teenagers make it in and high-five. The group Liu has pulled together are painfully hip, and everyone makes great efforts to be nice and include her in their chat. But Carys bears an outsider's mark of grief and, though she tries, they gradually drift away from her. She stares at the bar, where she'd first heard Liu ramp up Max's entrance. *A man so out of this world he'll take you to the moon and back* . . . A few of the group head over and wait to be served by the repurposed altar, and Carys wonders why Europia is so obsessed with fetishizing old structures and original features. Maybe the American fixation with new buildings led to Europe closing ranks and worshipping the old? Perhaps there was something anticorporate about sitting inside a ruin, modern glass interiors providing a new lease on life, not masking the original structure but celebrating the heritage. The only aesthetic crime, if any, is that it's too deliberate.

The group at the bar laugh and walk back to the sofas, carrying old wooden test-tube holders filled with glass eyedroppers. When one girl in oversized spectacles hands her one, Carys takes it and, after a slight hesitation, drips the sticky fluid onto her cornea. After a few moments the group starts laughing as the effects plow into their bodies, and Carys notices that everyone in the club is joyful and wonders how she missed that detail before.

"It's better for you than drinking," Liu yells in her ear, hugging her, and she hugs him back.

"What does it do?"

"Momentarily excites your nervous system," he shouts. "Totally safe. And now," he says, "*dancing*." He takes her hand and she follows him, and suddenly they're lurching, lurching, flying up the staircase of glass steps toward the dance floor, and a giggle erupts from her chest as if it's been torn from her rib cage. Liu shouts, making everyone look his way before he flings himself onto the dance floor in a knee slide, the cubes of color lighting up, like a piano glissando, beneath him as he glides across the floor. The crowd cheers and he throws up his arms, triumphant, spinning back on his knees to face where he came from. He welcomes the rest of their group, who run toward him with glee. They start dancing and Carys watches the floor below her feet, hypnotized, as she twists and turns, taking steps onto different color cubes.

A different girl—Maisie? Marcy?—holds out another eyedropper and Carys dutifully bends her head back, letting the girl drip another spool of fluid onto her eye. She blinks it in, some sliding into her mascara, which draws a line down her cheek like a mime artist's. With her dark leotard outfit and taut, lean figure, she looks menacing in the darkness.

Her heart begins to pound as the second dose of liquid reacts with her nervous system and she dances furiously, jabbing out her limbs with a sharpness that forces the group nearby to move away, laughing. "A man so out-of-this-world he'll take you to the moon and back," she chants, over and over, and she's moving and cutting and tearing and dancing before she realizes she's stumbling, stumbling, every misstep illuminated by the glass floor beneath her feet. She looks around for a familiar face but Liu's busy dancing with a beautiful Hispanic man on the other side of the room and she's falling and her heart might jump out of her chest when she sees a face—a face—

"What?" Maisie or Marcy is leaning toward her.

"Did you see that face?"

"Face?"

"That man?"

"What man?"

"Over there." Carys points, but her arm is unsteady and Maisie or Marcy reaches out to steady her. "He was staring at me."

"Probably because you're gorgeous," the girl says, pulling Carys back on to the dance floor, but she disentangles herself.

"No. It wasn't—"

"You're gorgeous," she repeats.

"No . . . that man . . ."

Losing interest, Maisie or Marcy turns away and joins in with the oversized-glasses girl, and Carys crawls to the staircase, looking for the owner of the face that had looked at her so speculatively, she'd felt embarrassed at the state of herself. He was nowhere to be seen.

twenty-one

CARYS MOVES ON Rotation to Voivode 18 with little of the fuss she'd made on previous transfers: no crying and hugging her friends, second cousins, or neighbors, with promises to keep in touch, visit, and all the rest of it. This time she packs her bags and moves by jump-jet to the northern reaches of Europia, Laika wrapped up against the chill in his new fur-lined coat.

She steps off the hybrid and takes an icy breath, each inhalation forming icicles on the lining of her throat and lungs. Hell, it's cold. She'd better learn some local swearwords. She moves into her new apartment, a cavernous white space inside the ruins of a former factory, with chip frames from floor to ceiling, which, for once, she leaves unfilled. She ships her wicker peacock chair to the north, and when it arrives, she positions it in front of the wood burner in the middle of the living room.

Every morning she takes Laika for a walk and each night feeds him a scrambled egg with a touch of gravy. When he's full, he stretches out next to her by the wood burner. He's so much bigger, with his thin waist becoming round—and even rounder after dinner. She no longer tries to cook for herself, happy to take meals from the Rotation restaurants, particularly the ones that deliver.

For the first time Carys has moved without learning the local language. She has arrived in the dark and realizes, with the regret of hindsight, that she'd better schedule some catch-up classes. Belatedly she delights in the similar heritage of Scandinavian languages, discovering she could easily learn all three, then maybe the other North Germanic languages, too. She remembers the sign in the previous Voivode's language lab: "Learning five languages lets you talk to 78 percent of Earth's population." She spends hours at the lab, her only real sanctuary aside from her apartment. Like most across the Voivodeship, the lab serves overroasted coffee that everyone could quite easily make at home, were it not for the frothy milk. Frothy milk, Carys decides, is the secret of a national coffee obsession, the addictive fuel powering society. Every day she pays somebody a number of coins to froth her milk. As she waits, she notices with chagrin that the paper cups require a separate piece of corrugated cardboard to be slid over their middle, and casually puts an integrated-cup suggestion into the MindShare. Some months later she's pleased when it's accepted and begins to roll out across the Voivode.

Leaving the lab early one evening, Carys spots a man across the street and stops, surprised. She's sure he was sitting by the door at the memorial, trying to grab her attention when it couldn't be flagged, and she thinks now that his might be the face she'd seen when she stumbled that night at the Dormer, his features illuminated by the flashing color cubes of the floor. But she can see now that she doesn't know him. Disappointed, she understands that, in the bottom of her heart, she'd wanted it to be . . . Well. Never mind.

The man walks toward her, hesitant, and she tenses in reflex at the unwanted recognition. She'd hoped that might have stopped by now. He pauses, clearly thinking better of it, then walks toward her once more. He's tall and lean, like a tree bowing in the wind. He moves to speak and his voice is more forthright than she would have expected from someone so . . . willowy.

"Excuse me. Are you Carys Fox?"

She's startled at the surname. "How did you—"

"You are, aren't you?"

"No one calls me that." She's wary now. "How did you know?"

"I'm sorry, I didn't mean to offend you. I wanted to call you by your last known name." He brushes his fair hair to one side. "I work for the EVSA."

"Of course, I'm sorry." She holds out her hand. "You're probably one of the many people to whom I owe my life."

He smiles. "No, please—"

"Or with whom I should have a stern word about safety protocols, perhaps."

"I mean, I wanted to call you"—she's about to interrupt again so he gabbles the end of his sentence—"the last name I knew you by."

She pauses. "Have we met?"

"Not strictly. Can we get a coffee?"

"I'm sorry, I'm—" She gestures apologetically in the direction of home.

"Carys, my name is Richard—Ric. I looked after comms systems aboard the *Laertes* for you . . . and for Max."

She blinks at the name. "Comms?"

"I communicated with you via my operating handle, Carys. Osric."

"I'm sorry?"

"My name is—I'm Osric, Carys."

"ARE YOU ALL RIGHT?" His concerned face looms above her and he takes her arm, supporting her. "I didn't mean to shock you."

She blinks, the impact of what he's said washing over her again. "Osric? The computer?"

"I was about to chicken out and tell you my name was Ric, and no more," he says, talking more to himself than to her. "I should've worked up to it."

"Osric?"

"Let me help." He takes a step but Carys remains in the same place. He lets go of her arm.

"Seriously, what the hell?" She looks at him, furiously surprised, and he looks back at her with remorse. "You're not a computer."

"No."

"You're not AI."

He glances around. "Can we go somewhere and talk?" The light's failing, the darkness coming up fast, and with it the chilly stalactites of the Voivode's wind. A few people are hurrying, heads down, into the warmth of their homes, and the roads are becoming deserted as the light disappears. "The lab?"

She nods. "Okay." As they walk back toward the language lab, she adds, "But I'm confused."

"Sorry about that, Carys."

"Ah," she says, hearing the familiar cadence, "there it is." She sits down in an old leather armchair, waving away his offer of coffee. "Why are the labs always coffee shops?"

"The Voivodeship decreed years ago that freelancers working in the cloud felt most at home in coffee shops," he says, and Carys rolls her eyes. He goes to the counter and orders a coffee and a cold drink, returning with her favorite, which she gazes at curiously.

"How did you know?"

He shrugs. "On the ship I knew a lot of the ins and outs, your likes and dislikes, allergies and preferences."

She blushes, then is furious. "Could you hear everything?"

"No," he says quickly. "It doesn't work like that. Let me explain. Please."

Suddenly Carys feels very wary of this stranger speaking of her likes and dislikes. "You'd better start at the beginning, because I feel like I've been punched in the face. And by *beginning* I mean Osric not actually being or having artificial intelligence."

Ric takes a long sip of his drink and settles the mug between his hands, looking at her. "I'm not supposed to talk about this," he says. "The EVSA are incredibly secretive. But I wanted to meet you . . . I wanted you to know that you're not alone, that there is someone who understands your experience, firsthand. I'm so very, very sorry about what happened up there, Carys."

"Thank you. The EVSA are secretive?"

"I hope you don't mind me coming out from hiding. You really want to know this?"

"Yes."

"Good," he says, settling into his chair. "I didn't want to put too much on you." She sighs, and he hurries to explain. "I'm sure you know that the space race has always been defined by who can do what first. Who can get a rocket into space, a man onto the moon, a Rover across Mars. Strategically the first nation to do this always wins. You agree?"

Carys nods.

"During the mutual destruction of the United States and the Middle East, it became clear that every nation in the world was looking for a way to automate war. Fighting with drones was becoming commonplace. Artificial intelligence was obviously going to be the next evolutionary step. To go from remotely detonating a bomb carried by a drone, to a machine deciding to detonate the bomb on our behalf—as humans we would be entirely absolved from the actions of war. Not only that: the first country to demonstrate the practical use of artificial intelligence would send a message to all the nations in the world."

"Like the atomic bomb," Carys says slowly.

"Yes. Dropping the atomic bomb displayed a terrifying technological superiority, but also the will to deploy it. There was no going back from that."

She leans forward. "So AI . . ."

"When the European Union closed ranks to protect itself from the cataclysm happening on the other continents, Europe made an important decision not to be an aggressor."

"You're talking about the election of Kent." She forces herself to ignore the name of Max's younger brother and focus on his namesake: the politician who advocated peace and not war.

"Exactly," he says, clearly pleased. "We would neither appease the United States nor attack it. We simply defended our borders. An important choice." He stops to take a sip, and Carys drinks from the glass of cloudy apple juice, enjoying the taste.

"Have you been following me?" she asks, playing with her straw.

"Yes. But not in a creepy way. I really wanted to explain and, if I can, to help. But you're a tricky person to track down."

"I don't get out much."

"I understand. But I guessed from your developed language skills that you might surface at the lab in your new Voivode, eventually."

"That *is* creepy," she says.

"Is it? I'm sorry. I thought it was logical."

"Oh." She sighs. "You really *are* Osric. Tell me more about AI."

He nods. "The warring continents mistook our nonaggressive stance for rolling over—attack was the only form of defense admired in modern warfare. They were eyeing up our territories, and we had to act. But the majority of the European Union was against us entering the war, and we knew we'd never be able to coordinate an offensive with multiple separate countries. So instead . . . we revealed a technological advantage in a simple, innocuous way."

"The space race?" Carys says.

"Yes. We introduced artificial intelligence on our current missions at the time, with little fuss but key media coverage. Cosmonauts orbiting the globe began flexing with their ship's computers, which would run comms and perform basic system functions aboard the shuttles."

She sits back, and he glances at her. "But it was fake," she says.

"It had to be. And it worked. Our would-be attackers looked elsewhere for weaker targets, and in the aftermath of world war, Europe became Europia, and the early stages of the Voivodeship were put into motion."

"How can it be fake when so much in the Voivodeship is open source? How could you fake artificial intelligence?"

"The data is ring-fenced. We couldn't simply hand it to our competitors. Anything that gives Europia a strategic advantage is protected."

"But if we've 'had AI' since the founding of the Voivodeship," Carys says, thinking it through, "we've been unable to create it in actual fact since then?"

"What can I say? It's really hard."

She looks at him, waiting. "That's it?"

"I was being deadpan."

"A deadpan Osric—the mind boggles." He smiles, but she looks stern. "I'm still angry."

"I know. I'm sorry." His hands are crossed in his lap, his fair hair combed neatly to one side—though a strand of hair at the front is rebelling and wisping in the wrong direction. She looks at his long legs in jeans, shirt carefully buttoned, his beard glinting with blond. Not unattractive, but Richard "Osric" Ric is more what you'd describe as "neat" or "thoughtful."

"Tell me then," she says, "why couldn't *we* know, at least? Why did they let us hinge our lives up there on something so flimsy?"

"PR, maybe? I don't know. They couldn't risk that anyone so often in the public eye would slip. Plausible deniability, I think they call it. You can't confirm or deny what you don't know." He wipes his hands with a napkin.

Neat, she concludes. "So you've come all the way to V18 to tell me you were there while we were dying."

He flinches. "I tried to help you, Carys. I really tried."

"Oh?" She tries to remember, in the asteroid field, when they were falling out of range. Don't waste time. What do you need to ask?

"If there was anything else I could have done, I would've done it. If there was anything I could've told you that would've saved you . . . but you were quite brilliant. You tried everything remotely possible, even if it was unfeasible." They sit together for a moment, both separately recalling her dalliance with black oxygen. "It was a shame nothing took."

"You're telling me." She stares at the table, the unwelcome remnant of leftover apple pulp sticking to the sides of her glass.

"I tried everything when you fell out of range. In fact . . ." His voice trails off and she looks up.

"What?"

"I tried everything," he finishes, and she looks down again. From the other side of the room the barista begins to clean the machines for the end of the day, and the whoosh of steam through the nozzles fills the room with an uncomfortably loud noise and the smell of scalded milk.

"I should go," she says, reaching for her bag. "I've got to get back to my dog."

"Right," he says lamely. "The one from the memorial?"

"Laika. A rescue," she says. "Are you staying in the region long?"

"Yes. I can work from anywhere."

She's surprised. "I had visions of you cooped up in a bunker on lockdown."

"No, we work flexibly. I have a primary ship, then I look after comms on three or four other missions at any one time."

"What if they all ask questions at the same time?"

"You mark it immediately for one of the support team to pick up. The delay is imperceptible."

"Why are you telling me this?"

"You deserve to know," Ric says.

"Was I your primary . . . ?" she asks, and he nods. "Did I ever talk to other Osrics?"

"No," Ric says, smiling. "You weren't very demanding, I could always manage the volume of your queries. Max asked more questions, particularly at night."

"Oh?"

"We talked a lot—I came to think of him as a friend."

"I didn't know that." She reaches down to gather up her things. "Will I see you again?"

"That depends on you," he says.

"What do you mean?" She stops rummaging for her belongings.

"Europia doesn't make me move because, on paper, I don't really exist."

"You don't have to move because you're in the EVSA?" Carys is staggered. "Now *there's* an irony."

Ric shrugs apologetically.

"If only I'd joined a different part of the program." And Max, she thinks, but doesn't say. If they hadn't had to move—no long-distance relationship in far-flung Voivodes, no requesting a repeal . . .

"I'd really like to talk again," Ric says, "if you're free. I have something I'd like to run through with you."

She looks at the door, unsure. He knows her but he doesn't, not really.

"Carys." His voice is gentle. "Couldn't you use a friend?"

After a beat, then three more, she breaks her gaze. "Yes, I suppose I could." She reaches out to shake his hand. "Richard. Ric. It's been a baffling surprise to meet you."

"Nice to meet you, too, Carys Fox." As they leave, he holds open the door for her, letting it close softly behind them.

twenty-two

CARYS AND RIC sit on dark rocks overlooking a sheer-sided inlet gouged out by glaciers, as Laika chases a crow halfheartedly in the way dogs do, knowing they'll never catch their quarry but will often be rewarded (by their owners) for the effort.

"So," Carys says, " 'Osric.' Not named after *Hamlet*, then."

"Yes and no," says Ric. "Yes, it's a character name taken from *Hamlet*, like the ship's, but also 'OS Ric.' Probably a happy coincidence." He shifts. "The world was used to 'OS' being short for 'Operating System' so it sounded suitably AI."

Carys starts laughing. "If I was a comms specialist, my ship's computer would be called Oscar?"

"Yes. And your ship's name would probably be a nod to Oscar Wilde, or something." He throws a stone down into the fjord and Laika follows it, rushing toward the water before making an emergency stop at the edge. The poor dog is terrified. "Sorry, Laika," Ric says softly.

"You shouldn't tease him." They've been walking this way every day for the past few weeks; Carys has given up asking Ric when he might head back to an EVSA outpost or the central Voivode. He doesn't seem to have a place to head back to, or the desire to do so, and, frankly, she's glad of the company. She finds him curiously easy for somebody so neat and thoughtful. She'd taken those traits for mildness when they'd met, but he is surprisingly opinionated as they argue at length about ideology and the Voivodeship, yet so *polite* with it.

"Carys, I have an idea I want to talk to you about." She raises her eyebrows but doesn't say anything, so he carries on, cautiously: "I'm so sorry to bring this up but . . . you're the only pilot who's made it through and out the other side of the asteroid field."

She's silent.

"I know you have. You know you have. In any other circumstance, you'd be proud of your achievement—the Voivodeship would be celebrating you widely. Maybe even the whole world. But they don't know, in the chaos of what happened, and the aftermath."

She doesn't say anything.

"And you've not told them—I understand why. But with the *Laertes* completely lost, you're the only one who knows how and where. Your first-hand experience is invaluable—actually, it's vital. I know you don't want to remember," he says, "but if I helped you . . ."

"Oh," she says, her tone bleak.

"I'd do anything not to ask."

"But I'm the only person who can get us off this planet."

"Sort of, actually," he says. "Yes."

They gaze together at the water. "I don't suppose you can do it if I transcribe some logs or recall the maneuvers, or something?" she says.

"The EVSA logs just show a huge stream of parameters. You're the only person on Earth who *knows* what you did," he says apologetically, and she sighs. "Think about it. I'll help any way I can."

HER MOTHER, AN INTERMITTENT VISITOR, joins them on one of their walks to the fjord with Laika, huddling against the bitter wind inside down-filled jackets and fur-lined hoods. On a bleak winter day, tinged the same gray as the rocks around the inlet, Gwen and Ric spar over the Voivodeship's new sanctions in the former United States. Carys stays quiet, aware that the smallest veer in conversation could take it toward a sensitive place.

"With respect, Gwen—"

"You should know, Richard, that people who start a riposte 'with respect' usually intend no respect."

He blushes. "Sorry."

"Start that one again." Slightly enamored, she bosses him around like this, and he lets her.

"Gwen," he says. "Surely it's the responsibility of Europia, China, and Africa to step in and help the nations that have been fractured by war?"

"Yes," she agrees, "if *help* was all we were doing. But you can't trust the motives of any nation that thinks it's better than the one it's imposing itself upon."

"We're in the strongest position to provide aid. It's the humane response." Ric throws a stick for Laika across the craggy rocks around the glacier and the dog belts off, his paws clattering on the stones. "Perhaps you feel this way because you raised your family outside the utopia—"

"Don't you dare, Mr. Imperialism. I don't need to be part of some club to analyze the value of said club, thank you very much."

"A low blow," says Ric, holding up his hand in apology as Laika belts back with his prize. "Sorry."

"Regardless of where my children were raised, my son is there right now, *helping*."

"Of course," says Ric. "Perhaps it's us three who are a little outside the system, up here."

Gwen sniffs. "We may not have a system much longer, if all the repeals are passed."

"Repeals?" Carys asks, speaking for the first time. "What repeals?"

Gwen and Ric exchange glances. "A few residents are raising questions over some of the rules. Nothing to worry about," Gwen says calmly.

"Nothing to worry about," Ric repeats. He meets Carys's eye and winks, a subtle blink that makes her smile. She reaches down to ruffle Laika's fur, tugging the stick from his mouth.

'YOU SEEM HAPPIER.' CARYS'S MOTHER is washing up at the sink, rattling pans and plates in a basin of soapy water.

"Happier?" Carys asks, her voice a little dulled.

"Not so destroyed emotionally." Gwen puts two side plates into the drying rack. "A little more content."

"Content."

Her mother stops what she's doing and looks at her. "Are you going to repeat the last word I say all day?"

"All day."

Gwen smiles indulgently. "Good."

"Good." Carys snaps out of it, laughing this time. "Sorry—that last one was accidental. I wasn't thinking."

Gwen lowers herself into the kitchen chair, pushing a mug of tea with lemon in front of Carys. "Seriously, though, you seem much happier. I'm pleased. You have to get on with living."

"Get busy living," Carys muses, "or get busy dying."

"Well, quite. You're working again?"

Carys has been reluctant to commit to it, but nods. "Sort of. They've asked me."

"Via Ric? What will he have you doing?"

And there was the thing. A program based on her unique experience in the asteroid field, when she knew she wasn't ready. Blocking out the period was fast becoming the easiest way to move on from it. "Writing training programs, drawing maps."

Gwen nods. "Think you'll ever go up there again?"

"Up where—space? I don't think so."

"At least you're contributing down here." Gwen dabs at the table with a dishcloth and smiles at her daughter. "That's what matters. Apparently we all have to do our bit."

THE DAYS TURN COLDER, far colder than they ever could have imagined the temperature would possibly drop. On the coldest afternoon to date, the sky dark at only two o'clock, Ric explores rock formations with Laika when Carys, hanging back, says quietly, "I'll do it. I'll write a flight simulation of the asteroid field."

Ric turns to look at her, his hands ruffling and tugging at Laika's tufty muzzle. "Great."

"Do you think I can get the mission transcript?"

"Yes—it's a matter of public record."

"What?" Carys is surprised.

"In the event of a catastrophe in space . . ." They stare at where Laika is trying to excavate a sheet of slate that he hasn't a hope of dislodging. "I'm afraid Max's passing made it rather public for the EVSA."

"Oh."

He tugs at Laika and throws a stone for him, and the dog tears off. "What made you decide?"

"My mother said something about everyone doing their bit." Carys gazes at the waterfall in the distance, dainty strands of white rapids tumbling into the glacial waters beneath. After a moment, she adds, "I'll build the framework for the simulation. But I can't quite bring myself to recall all the individual maneuvers."

"I'll help with that."

Carys makes a noise.

"Do you want to talk about it?"

She kicks mud off the rocks with her toe. "Not really."

"Okay. Race you to the fall?" He starts jogging and she can't help but laugh at his gangly head start and runs after him to catch up, the mud cracking beneath their feet where it has frozen solid.

"IT'S TIME," SAYS GWEN during her next visit, when she and Carys are sitting in front of the wood burner one day.

"You're going home already?" Carys says.

"It's time," Gwen repeats. "You ought to think about settling down."

Carys makes a pained face. "The guidelines say I have to wait."

"Forget the guidelines. When have I ever cared about those? You're the right age, whatever they say."

"I'd need to meet someone first, surely." Her mother raises one eyebrow. "What?"

"Oh, nothing."

"I live in the middle of nowhere. Besides—"

"Yes?"

"There's no one who—I mean, I can't, because—"

"Max."

Carys jolts at the directness. Most people still tiptoe around his name. "Please don't talk about him."

"Why not?" says Gwen. "He played a big role in your life. It's not disrespectful to say his name."

"Mom, I can't."

"I understand why you asked for the rule change, Carys. I know what it's like to love someone more than is acceptable. In my case, it was my children. I couldn't let you go."

Carys says nothing, unwilling to have this conversation.

"You could've talked to me about your decision to ask for a repeal."

"He caught me a bit by surprise with it," Carys says. "There wasn't much time."

Gwen weighs up this new information. "The repeal wasn't your choice?"

I tried being without her, and it didn't work. So we're going to continue to be together. She shakes free of the memory. "Not really. I mean, I probably would've . . ." She trails off, unable to talk in any depth about—

"Speak about him, Cari. You still love Max."

"Of course I do."

"Of course you do. Max was your first love."

"Max *is* my first love," Carys corrects gently, "and I don't think I'll ever get over that."

"You will."

Carys is indignant. "I don't think so."

"It's your right to have a partner, and a family, and to be loved in the present." Gwen gets up and kisses her head, then walks from the room. "Don't make yourself a prisoner of the past."

CARYS STARTS WITH THE BLANKS. The simulation is difficult and she takes longer than strictly necessary on the basic maneuvers, because recalling them brings back snippets of conversations and fractures of time that hurt like paper cuts: insidious at first, with a lingering ache. Ric helps as he said he would, working the logs, looking up the days as she needs them, but sometimes he asks too many questions and she wants to run away with Laika and hide.

"Anna?" he repeats, questioning.

She shakes her head. No. The name had popped into her head, unbidden, and her mouth forms an O of surprise as Ric looks at her—she hadn't meant to say it aloud. "Sorry," she says. "I'm not sure where my head's at today."

"Don't worry. You're doing great."

"I don't think I could do this alone," she says, grateful for his companionship, even if sometimes he's too inquisitive. Ric shuffles uncomfortably and dread rises in her. "What is it?"

"I have to go back to the continent for a few months," he says. "There's a big launch at the Space Agency."

"Oh," she says.

"I'll be back in the spring."

"Right."

"I have to go," he says. "I'm sorry."

"It's fine."

"Can you look at me?" Ric asks, and lifts her chin. Carys jolts at his touch. "I have to go, but I don't want to."

"Why?"

"Because I'm worried Laika will pine for me," Ric says, letting his hand fall from her face, with a shade of embarrassment.

"He'll be all right," she says. "I'll distract him with chews. I don't know what my mom will do with you gone, though."

"And you? Will you carry on with the flight plan? Go out walking every day?" She nods. "And let me know when the daylight breaks?"

"Yes."

"Will you water my snowdrop when it arrives?"

She smiles. "You have such misplaced faith in my black fingers."

"They'll be green by the time I return, I'm sure. Perhaps spring can be a new start for all of us." As he says it, her heart fills with guilt that threatens to spill out and quadruple the chill of winter in Voivode 18.

CARYS CONTINUES TO PLOT the framework of the asteroid belt, working from the mission logs retrieved from the EVSA. Thankfully Ric has removed anything personal, simply leaving sets of coordinates taken from the *Laertes* logs. She writes lines of simulation code and reams of best-practice advice for pilots.

Gwen still visits often. She makes spaghetti and it's disgusting, so they revert to ordering from the RR.

Laika gets bigger—even bigger by the time he eats an entire plate of discarded spaghetti.

"Why do you keep coming to visit, Mom?" Carys asks one day. "I mean, I like it, but surely you want to be at home?"

Gwen weighs her answer as she sits on the floor, cleaning the frets of the acoustic guitar with a cloth, a pile of replacement strings at its side. "I didn't think you should be alone too much in the year following your ordeal."

"What about Dad?"

"Oh, he's fine. We talk on the MindShare when I'm here."

"Good." Carys pauses. "The thing is, Mom, it's been a year."

"And are you better? You're still alone. I'll keep visiting until Ric comes back, then perhaps—"

"Mom," Carys says, "I don't think Ric is coming back."

"Of course he is. He left you his snowdrop to care for. He's coming back."

"Gwen, listen to me. I don't think Ric is coming back."

"Don't *Gwen* me." She puts down the guitar as, again, she weighs how to reply, thinking through her words to cause minimum offense and maximum cut-through. "Has it occurred to you, darling, that he might want you to *ask* him to come back?"

"I can't—he wouldn't . . ." She trails off. "He's not manipulative like that."

"It's true that that man has no agenda whatsoever. He's a saint, plainly loyal. And perhaps it's time you showed him some loyalty in return."

Carys is horrified. "Not like that."

"Why not like that?"

"I don't feel . . ." Her sentence has no end. "No, that's just it. I don't have any more words. *I don't feel.*"

HOW COULD SHE FEEL anything again? The thought is alien, and Carys ponders her mother's suggestion obsessively, mulling over the inference that there could be feelings on Ric's side, then hating herself when she finds, after some time, that she's curious. Damn. She'd thought she'd insulated herself against all of that.

She sits with Laika on her lap and the flight simulation at her workstation, questioning whether she's really about to do this, before switching on the Wall Rivers, her hand raised and hovering. She's about to flex to Ric when—

Help, this is Carys Fox, requesting assistance. Osric, do you read me?

Carys. There's a lot of interference, and you're falling out of range.

The thought fractures her mind, her mental blocks dropping like stones. Bile rises in her throat as her wall disappears and Ric's face appears, larger than life, concern etched at the corners of his mouth. "Are you all right?" he asks.

"Did I call you?" She's startled, still thrown by the memory. "I was going to flex, but . . ."

"When?"

"Just now." In the background she can see aisles of blue workstations, all empty, with tables and chairs stretching into the distance. She breathes, calming down. "I wanted to say hello."

"Oh." He sits back. "Hello."

"Are you free to talk?"

"Sure," he says. "It's a ghost town around here."

"You look well," she says, recovering, though it's not true: pale and gaunt, with his blond cowlick wisping free, he looks as if he's been sleeping at his desk.

"Liar."

"Somebody once told me it's polite to be polite."

He smiles. "You, on the other hand, actually do look quite well. How's the dog?"

Carys reaches for Laika and pulls him into the frame. In return he collapses, his full tummy sprawled toward the camera. "Hi, buddy," Ric says. "Hasn't he grown?"

She nods. "I've made progress with the simulation."

"Yeah?"

"I think I've cracked it, in fact."

He beams at her, and she feels herself warm to his happiness. "You'll be the savior of Europia."

"*We'll* be. Both of us . . . I could do with a little bit of help, if you're available?" she says.

"Cari, I'm always available for you."

RIC UNDERSTANDS WHAT SHE'S been through and how she feels. Devastated himself at the loss of Max, he never trespasses into her memories or Max's presence in her life. He understands. In a small way, Carys's loss is Ric's loss, too. Leaving Max sacrosanct is his own mark of respect, and driven by that respect, Ric decides not to tell Carys how he'd reprogrammed the satellite drones to go back for them, breaking every part of EVSA protocol on artificial intelligence to do so. He doesn't tell her how he'd had to cover up the coding changes, or why he now works remotely to stay away from the far-reaching gaze of the AI program. To claim credit in her survival, but Max's demise, would take ownership over something she feels is resolutely and heartbreakingly hers.

Also, in the depths of his subconscious, he fears reprimand and blame: he'd managed to save one but not the other.

RIC WILL NEVER TELL Carys anything that would hurt her, but Gwen feels it's a mother's duty. Gwen takes a deep breath and pats the space next to her on the floor—she's sanding the boards: DIY is a long haul, and she's been working on Carys's apartment during each visit through the winter.

Carys dutifully drops down beside her mother and begins to play with a piece of sandpaper. They sit together, the great floor-to-ceiling glass windows towering above them, Carys's empty frames on the other walls.

"I want to talk to you, Cari, about Max."

This feels familiar. A woman's voice, soft, hovering somewhere above her. *You don't have to talk about Max.*

"Carys." Gwen looks concerned.

Carys snaps back to the room. "Are you going to talk about me moving on? Because I hear what you're saying, I do," she says. "But what if I don't feel like that again?"

"You might never get the flight of butterflies again, but you will get stability. Or you might get the flight, but not the crippling insecurity about where he is, or what you look like."

"You mean," says Carys, "settle for less?"

"Settling," scoffs Gwen. "We all *settle*. There isn't a person alive who matches every element of the fantasy we wish for. Every person in a relationship has *settled*. What you choose to compromise on is up to you."

"You're telling me to settle for someone I don't love as much as I have in the past."

"No, that's not what I'm saying," says Gwen, "but, like I said, most people don't feel the burn of first love again. Don't sacrifice happiness searching for it."

You see? I saved you when we met, and I'm saving you now.

Carys throws down the sandpaper and gets up. "I know what this is about, Mom. You're talking about Ric."

"Think about it. Try it. He's a good man, Cari, and there's no shame in loving a good friend."

'I HAVE A TERRIBLE CONFESSION.' Carys reaches behind her chair and brings up a flowerpot cracking under hard ice.

"Oh, no. What have you done?" Ric leans forward, squinting down from the Wall Rivers. "Is that ice?"

"I killed it. I'm so sorry."

As he looks at Carys holding his snowdrop, his face breaks open with a warm smile. "Cari, snowdrops flower in winter by shattering the ice with their hardened leaves."

She falters. "It's not dead?"

"Not at all. It's thriving beneath its harsh exterior."

"I didn't murder it with my black fingers?"

"Give it another few days and it'll probably break through the frozen soil. It will soon bloom again."

"Of all the metaphors," she mumbles, but he misses it. "Are you finishing down there soon?"

He pauses. "I can do."

"Really?"

"I can be there next week, if you like," Ric says. And though she would usually put up platitudes of resistance, this time she nods, the guilt in her heart coy.

"He's coming back," she tells Gwen, holding the icy flowerpot, and she begins to cry.

"Oh, Cari." Her mother takes the snowdrop and sits her down, while Laika zips across the room and curls into Carys's lap, licking a salty tear as it drips from her chin. "Are these happy tears, or sad?"

"I don't know," Carys says. "I don't know what to feel. Max once told me the afterlife is what we leave behind in others. But what if the only thing that's left in me is sadness?"

"It's not." Gwen strokes her hair.

"I've got nothing left, Mom. I have nothing left to give."

Gwen tries to find the words. "I've been thinking about how to discuss this with you for over a year. You have to make Max a positive, *cariad*. Don't be destroyed by feelings for a person you can't move forward with."

Carys shakes as her tears run dry.

"If your first love ends badly, then your self-esteem and confidence, how you trust and love—all of these are affected in your future by the shadow of how you loved, or were loved, in the past. You never get over your first, Carys. Your body doesn't know how. But if you make it a positive, you can use the feelings and experiences you've known to grow and, in some ways, to make the next chapter of your life even better." Carys says nothing, so Gwen continues. "The thing about first love, Cari, is that it breaks you. It changes everything about who you are for the next person."

"That's just it, Mom. I *am* broken." Carys cries again, knowing she's at a crossroads where she must move back or forward in life, and in time. She has been frozen since that moment in space, since that moment when—

twenty-three

THE LIGHT COMES toward them slowly, a phantasm of hope. Surrounded by sparkles, frozen water, ammonia, and carbon dioxide, the satellite moves slowly through the asteroid field, mirroring Earth's curvature on an elliptical orbit.

"We're not going mental, are we?" says Max. "It's not a mirage?" They watch what they thought was a shooting star travel on a steady orbital plane. "We might be hallucinating," he goes on. "Lack of air."

"Will you get a grip?" Carys speaks quickly, her voice urgent. "This is happening. This is real. We need to act on it before it's too late."

"It is too late, Cari. We don't have time—"

"Max Fox." She looks him square in the eye, rock steady and certain. "This is our last chance."

He swallows, a dry, rasping breath. "Okay."

"We can do this."

"Okay," he repeats.

"The huge asteroid below us, to the left. It's at a Lagrange point."

"What's that?"

Carys stops everything and looks at him, her face somber. "That asteroid is at a Lagrange point, where the gravitational pull of the moon and Earth will be canceled out. I'm certain of it. In five seconds, as we draw level with it, we'll stop falling."

"Let's find out. Coming up in five, four, three, two . . ." Instinctively they both bend their legs, like ballet dancers landing on the floorboards of a stage, and as they level with the stony asteroid, for the first time in nearly ninety minutes, they stop tumbling.

"I don't believe it." Max is incredulous. "Physics, eh? Always right."

"Apart from when they thought the Earth was flat," Carys says, scanning the sky. She grips his bare hand in hers. "I'm going to try to flex to the satellite."

He looks down at her hand. "Good idea. See if it's manned?"

"It won't be."

"You're very sure of everything all of a sudden."

"Like I said," she says, "it's our last chance. Let's take it." She checks the mesh is in place, looped over her knuckles, and begins to flex. *Help, this is Carys Fox from the* Laertes *requesting immediate assistance. Do you read me?*

She waits.

I repeat: this is Carys Fox from the Laertes *requesting immediate assistance. Do you read me, over?*

Nothing.

Please help us. If you don't, we're going to die out here.

Her audio crackles to life with a clangorous *ping*. Hello, Carys. This is Osric.

"There you are," she says with audible relief, as the blue text fills the side of her glass.

I am communicating directly with the satellite's computer to patch this to you, Carys.

Thanks, Osric. Is the drone fully functional?

Yes, Carys.

Have you redirected it to us?

It . . . will be with you in six minutes.

Thank you.

"Carys?" asks Max. "What's happening?"

"Osric is sending the satellite straight to us in six minutes."

"Six?" Max falters, and Carys nods. "Cari, we don't have six minutes. We don't have the same amount of air. I'm so sorry—when we were trying earlier, when I was experimenting with your pack as a makeshift propellant—"

"That's fine."

He looks at her. "It is?"

"Sure."

"But I'm saying I have more air than you."

"I understand. Please don't worry. So you have . . ."

"Six," Max says, "and you have two. I'm so sorry." His face crumples slightly on that last word.

"Right. If I've got two minutes of air, you're going to have to tow me in. And after I pass out you'll work the air lock and throw me through, then resuscitate me."

He thinks about it. "That's quite a risk."

"It will only be a few minutes, and the air in my suit will probably cover me for another minute or so." It won't.

"But you'll go unconscious. I don't think . . ." He trails off, unable to confront the horror of Carys almost dying at the Voivode Games all these many moons later. "You've never been able to hold your breath, Cari."

"I've been practicing." She smiles, a gentle raising of her lips that's higher on one side than the other, and puts her hand on his arm, the ragged thread tied around her bare finger. "Come on." She knows she mustn't let him get behind her, or allow him to do anything with her pack, so she focuses his attention instead on securing the tether rope one final time.

She can't say with any certainty how she knows all this, how she's so strongly guided by what to do and what feels right. But she knows in her heart that she can't let Max sacrifice himself for her. She knows what her own life will be without him: it's grief. It's a grief she'll push down through the years and believe to have passed, but nobody gets over the loss of love in that way and it will change her. She won't love again in the same unbridled way; she'll never feel the sharp brightness of her own personality when he gazes upon her, when he draws a spotlight over her and she responds, fully illuminated.

She looks at him, impulsively throwing her arms around him, and he stops to let her hug him.

"Hey, you. We're going to be okay." Max squeezes her hand once more. "Let's get ready." It had never occurred to him that it might be possible to drown in space. After the last time, he'd sworn he would protect her.

He makes to scoot around behind her, and Carys says quickly, "Let me do it." She makes a point of tapping his pack and adjusting the shoulder straps and cables. "There."

"I'd better check—"

"Max, I've checked everything. You should focus on how you're going to tow my unconscious ass across space."

Anxious, he fiddles with the tether. "Are you sure this will work? I'm a little concerned—"

"Yes."

"Yes, you're sure, or yes, I'm right to be concerned?"

She swings around to face him. Below them the world pours past, a weather system brewing over Africa. "We'll be fine. This way we can both live."

"What?" he queries, but she's gone, checking the cabling and squinting at the satellite, heading their way on its elliptical orbit through the field.

Carys's suit starts beeping, a shrill alert in her left ear, which she dismisses. "Get ready," she says, as the light gets brighter.

"I'm ready." Max steels himself.

"It's time for me. I'm running empty."

Max's face is anguished. "Are you sure?"

"Yes." A red alarm light flashes on and off in the center of her fishbowl glass and she swipes it away with her flex. "You know the plan. Be ready to grab the satellite however you can." Max nods. "You know where the emergency hatches are?"

"Think so."

"Get in there and connect me to the oxygen system fast."

Max blinks. "What if this drone doesn't have one?"

"It does." Carys's head begins to feel light as the recycled air in her system becomes less fresh.

"Right."

"Oof." She feels woozy and her head lolls, the dark night of the sky with its spray of stars, like strands of LEDs, stretching out above her.

"Carys?"

"Concentrate."

"Bossy," Max says, and smiles when he hears her whispered retort: "Assertive."

He rubs his hands together, one bare against the cold of space, the other encased in silver and warmth. He's got to do this, and get it right, for both of their sakes. As the satellite gets closer, he scans its sides for the entrance hatch and, when he can see it, sucks in a breath.

"What's wrong?" Carys asks, sounding very far away.

"It's going to be tight."

"Make sure you don't run out of air, too." Her voice is quiet, the words now taking a long time to form.

"Mmm," he replies, noncommittal, his mind racing with plans and ideas.

"It will get here after your suit has started beeping, Max."

"Mmm," he repeats, once again rubbing his hands together, one covered and one bare. She knows what that means, and she can't let him. Not this time. She knows that if Max lives, he will be all right: his belief system and structure will help him recover; he'll return to the way his life was before she bent it out of shape.

No. She will not let him.

As her head rolls back once again, and consciousness starts to ebb, Carys urges her hand to move, feeling dull relief when her nerve endings respond. She drags her bare hand into the pocket across her thigh, tapping her fingers against the items stored, feeling for what she knows is there.

She finds it and closes her palm around it, calling for one final burst of strength to do what is necessary.

"Max," she breathes, and he turns to look at her. "You don't have to make the big gesture to save me."

"What?"

"Please."

He moves, but—

"Live well," she says, "for me."

With one final motion she pushes Max with her feet so he jerks away from her, at the same time sliding her arm from the pocket on her thigh and up to the tether. As Max is jolted toward the approaching drone and Carys away from it, the small knife carried in the patch kit of every EVSA crew member slices through the tether rope. They're left tumbling, each on their own, the blade falling out of her bare hand as she drops away from him into the dark.

"Carys!" As the satellite approaches, Max emits a guttural animal cry, reaching one arm up for the drone and the other out into space, but she is gone.

twenty-four

MAX STIRS ON THE SOFA, blinking awake against the harsh light. He cricks his neck from where it's been bent into the arm of the furniture and reaches to turn down the volume on the Wall Rivers. The news is playing on an endless loop, seeping into his subconscious. He's had bad dreams again; dreams of nothing. For a while there was only nothing—no air, no sound . . . no her. He changes his mind and turns up the volume of the news.

The same faces appear on open media in public and private buildings, in Rotation restaurants and language labs, as well as in living rooms across the Voivodeship. Experts are called in again and again to muse, illustrate, and remonstrate about the top story. Max tunes in, finding solace in others' misery.

"Europia has today tripled aid to the former United States. Experts have categorized the survivors in the South most at risk, as known rebel groups operating in the area are engaging aid workers in combat and making it difficult for the teams to provide food and water to those most in need . . ."

Max pulls a cardboard food box from under his hips and throws it on the floor, feeling where the grease has sunk through to the back of his T-shirt. Great. The anchor interviews an expert and Max watches, impassive, his face filled with signs of a restless sleep.

"It's going to be difficult, Sven, for Europia to resource these new teams. They're being sent to unreachable places, deep in the wetlands, where living conditions are impossible and the survivors are desperate. They are under attack from rebel groups—it's not an appealing sell. The utopia will need a strong recruiting drive, or we may have to consider conscription. When you add the constant overhead presence of the asteroid field to the desperate situation in the United States . . ."

Max clicks off, not wanting to hear about the damn asteroid field—he doesn't want to be reminded. He dedicates his slight attention only to situations unrelated to his predicament, to crises not of his making, watching the world turn and the news churn and knowing somehow he has no place in it—that nothing he ever did or will ever do again will affect the world in any significant way.

He'd been numb when he'd got back, listening to the EVSA's debrief; numb, too, when they'd offered him "compassionate leave of absence." But the numbness had moved toward anger when they'd held up, rather apologetically, the health and safety waiver he and Carys had signed to fast-track them into space, absolving Europia of any and all liability.

Compassionate leave of absence, Max thinks. What an oxymoron. "A dishonorable discharge," his mother calls it. Max failing to return immediately to Rotation or any semblance of a normal life underscored, to his parents, how far he'd fallen from the ideal.

Max has only to think about his parents and his father appears, looming in the kitchen doorway, holding a French press. "Coffee?" he asks.

"Please."

"Make up the sofa before you come through. And get that grease off the carpet," he says, "before your mother sees it."

Max starts to pack away his bed. He's angry, and it's only eight o'clock in the morning. He grabs at the takeout carton, annoyed that his parents have already got to him with their criticisms, but annoyed most of all that, after everything, he's here. How he ended up with them he's not sure: nobody wanted him there, including Max, but with the EVSA medics citing post-traumatic stress disorder, there really was no choice.

"What are you doing today?" his father calls from the kitchen, looking up as Max walks through, eyeing the grease stain on his T-shirt.

"I thought I'd work in the shop for a bit," he says, wincing as the coffee scalds his throat. He's not acclimatized to hot drinks, though the caffeine gives his system the kick it desperately needs after nights full of terrors. He suffocates in his sleep, the oxygen sucked out of the room as he watches Carys's hand slip out of his into the darkness over and over. No air, and no her. "Then I thought I'd visit Kent at the hospital."

Max's father looks grave. "That will upset your mother."

"It's not meant to."

"Hmm."

Max throws the mug into the sink and the clatter is loud in the small room. "Is she ever going to forgive me?"

"I'm sure she will." Pranay runs a hand through his thinning hair. "Give her time."

"Time is something I've got," he says, blinking away a vision of an air gauge continuously counting down from ninety to zero.

He heads into work, cycling furiously, pounding the bike's pedals toward the ground as though they will thump it, instead of turning a full revolution and coming back up toward him. He gets his heart rate going and feels it slamming in his rib cage with a burn. The pain feels good, and if he can't beat the road he'll beat his own body into submission. Live well, Carys had said, for her. But how to do that *without* her? How could she expect him to do that, how could she have overlooked the obvious—

Max kicks the brick wall of a low-lying ruin and it crumbles onto the sidewalk in a pile of yellow dust and chalk. "Don't desecrate the past," says another cyclist, liquid-locking his bike next to Max's.

"I'm trying," Max mutters, but holds up his hand in apology.

Technically they have programmed servers to stack shelves all day, but Max prefers the mindless labor to working the tills and having to be polite to the few customers who venture into the supermarket. It's not the same shop, as he's living with his parents in Voivode 2, but it's similar enough to hurt.

From shop boy to chef to astronaut and back to shop boy. He puts on an apron and walks to the stockroom.

He trundles out a cart full of kidney beans and begins to stack replacements on the shelf. He finds a rhythm: left one, right one, left two, right two. A couple of hours pass unnoticed. He pushes the cart back, filling it this time with cans of pineapple. He traverses to a different aisle—desserts—and stacks them: left one, right one, left two, right two.

As he lifts the third variety of cans into his cart he notices the label. He stares at it for a moment. He lifts one can up to his face, reading every word, then tosses it unceremoniously into the trash. He hulks the entire cardboard carton of cans and dumps them, too, the noise deafening.

"What's up with those?"

Max turns to see Lindi, a worker in a faded red-and-green-striped grocer's apron, and grunts. "Past their sell-by date."

"Right." Lindi nods. She doesn't point out that most of this stuff is past the sell-by date. It's part of the genius of canned food.

Max bends to collect an escaped can from the floor. He glances back to find Lindi still watching from the doorway.

"Tea?" she offers, not moving.

"Right." After a minute he gets up and follows her to the melamine kitchen, a work counter balanced between two skeletons of remaining brick walls. She puts on the kettle, resting against the wall, pink brick dust rubbing off on the back of her legs. Max doesn't point it out.

"So," Lindi says.

"So."

"How's your day going?"

"Fine."

She regards him, her gaze light. "Not a man of many words, are you?"

"Not really."

"That's nice, sometimes." She drums her fingers against the brick, and he gazes at the kitchen counter. "Watched kettle."

"I'm sorry?"

"Never boils."

"I suppose not."

She pours out two steaming mugs of watery tea, honorably handing him the least chipped one.

He takes it and decides he must make an effort. "Have you worked here long?"

"Since I moved—I'm a member of Draw Two," she says, and he notices she speaks as though modulating her cadences would be too much effort, like she's tired all the time. "Your dad had made me the manager until you came along."

"Sorry."

"No bother," she says. He doesn't push. "We'd better get back to it, then."

He nods. "Thanks for the tea."

"Anytime." She reaches down and brushes her legs. "Damn."

He moves to stack more cans, returning to his rhythm: left one, right one, left two, right two. He's reaching back into the cart when he sees more of the same cans he'd trashed earlier. Distracted, he pulls his hand out sharply—a damaged can with a jagged edge of razored metal has torn into his thumb. A stream of red gushes out and runs down his hand. Angrily he watches his blood trickle in rivulets across his wrist and down his arm; the pain cuts through and his temper snaps. He hurls the offending can across the room.

The goose fat explodes against the plate-glass front window and slops across the floor. "For fuck's sake, as if I want to be *reminded*—"

"Maximilian."

"Aunty Priya," Max says as the small woman puts her hand up against his chest.

"Your father said I'd find you here," she says into his torso, before holding him tight. He moves to pull away but she holds him in place, whispering, "It's only food."

"But—"

"It's not her. It's just a can."

"Yes," Max says, patting her hair. "I suppose it is."

"Come," she says, pulling back and holding him at arm's length as though to examine him. "Let's talk for a minute."

"I need to clear up the mess." He gestures to the window but stops when he sees Lindi with a mop, cleaning the puddle of fat. She nods, and after a second he nods back in thanks.

"We need to talk. I have something to tell you, something I should've told you already." Priya takes his arm and looks closely at the blood clotting around Max's thumb and congealing down to his elbow. She gestures a scrubbing motion above the arm and they walk back to the basic kitchen unit, where she turns on the tap for a few moments and makes to lean against the wall.

"Careful," says Max, his manners finally returning. "The brick dust stains." He holds his arm under the flow and watches his watered-down blood drain away. "How have you been?" he asks.

She waves away the question. "The same."

"Me, too."

"The one thing you're not, my dear," she says kindly, "is the same."

"No—I suppose not."

She points for him to sit down, so he balances on a stepladder and Priya takes the only fold-up chair.

"I wanted to explain the last time we saw each other, before you came back."

"Oh?" says Max, distracted by his bleeding hand.

"When you came to tell your parents about your plans to request a repeal, I showed you some photos through the blinds. Do you remember?"

"Yes." Max is determined not to remember Carys standing next to him, the feel of her breath against his arm, the touch of her cold hands as she'd snaked them up over his eyes.

"They were taken thirty years ago. Photographs of me with Francesco, my first love"—she smiles—"and, like you, we decided we wanted to be together long-term." Max is surprised but doesn't interrupt. "I met him when your father and I were helping our own father set up restaurants in each Voivode. The food system at the time was shoddy, and our father had an idea to centralize restaurants and take-out places so residents could eat together, to make mealtimes more social for people on their new Rotations.

"Francesco delivered fresh produce. He was a farmer of sorts, and he'd deliver fruit and vegetables in the morning between six and eight. I'd run to meet his hybrid," she says fondly. "I'd always make sure I got there first. After a while, he would come back when he'd finished in the afternoons, and we would take walks." She gazes at Max, who is looking cynical. "Much more chaste than your 'generation hookup,'" she says. "I know, I know—not you, not now.

"We'd take walks and hold hands, and we began to make plans. I was due to set up a restaurant in Voivode 10 and Francesco had made the decision to follow me. We wanted to be together. We didn't want to wait until we could move as a couple under the guidelines. We didn't want to wait until we were old."

Max sits forward, fascinated. "What happened?"

"What do you think?" Priya says gently. "I was twenty. My father and brother were furious. My mother, the esteemed genetic scientist, was so disappointed—they wanted me to observe the Couples Rule. There were confrontations, arguments . . . A little familiar, I think?"

"So when I turned up with Carys it was like history repeating itself."

"Yes, but we never made the bold step to try to get the rule changed. That was brave."

"Or stupid."

"Brave. But there is something else you need to know, something that is misunderstood in your generation." She stands up from the wobbly chair, walks toward him, and attempts to take his hand. "What you need to know is there are no secret police to sweep in on an 'illegal' relationship. You will not be reported and excommunicated for breaking the rule. The biggest truth about Europia is that it's almost impossible to live here if you can't live by the utopian guidelines. Do you see?"

"What do you mean?"

"Francesco couldn't stand it. He couldn't bear to be forced to live in a certain way against his wishes, so he left the Voivodeship. Nobody made him leave—he went of his own free will."

Max rubs his temples. "He didn't have to leave because he broke the rule, with you?"

Priya shrugs. "Like I say, there are no secret police, no excommunication. They won't punish you. People who can't live by the rules of a utopia tend to find it's not really a utopia for them. They're the ones who go looking for something else."

The stepladder under Max trembles. "I thought the rules were gospel."

"Your parents want them to be. We live as if they are. But being individual also means knowing what's right for yourself."

"That's what I kept trying to tell them," he says.

"You have to opt in to Europia. Europia won't opt you out."

"Jesus. Why didn't you tell me?"

"You were so plucky, asking to change the rules. I believed it was for the *greater good*—I thought you would succeed. I didn't know . . ." She trails off.

"No," Max says bleakly, "I guess none of us knew how it would turn out." In space. With ninety minutes of air remaining.

Her voice is sad. "I don't know where Francesco is now."

Max puts his hand on her shoulder. "It's unfair, Aunty Priya. For all of us."

"It is. It was. But he wasn't brave like you. He didn't want to challenge the system. Instead he became disillusioned and left."

"I was so frightened when I was with her," he says. "I couldn't have lived like that for another decade. Always scared we were going to be caught and kicked out."

"Only you could've made that decision."

Max kicks the folding chair and it collapses. She watches the short fuse of his anger catch alight, her face showing only a pitying sadness. "Did you go to your girl's memorial?"

"Yes."

"I'm sorry for you. I know what it's like to lose somebody you love."

Max nods, his face bleak.

"She was special to you. The memorial must have been hard."

"Her family isn't into that. It was a 'life celebration.'"

"Good lord."

"I know." He smiles properly for the first time, though his face is pinched. Her memorial had been painful. It tore him into jagged lines, cutting through his torso until his ribs were hanging off, revealing his battered heart beating, slowly, but still beating. Because that's what seems to happen, despite what grief tells us: our own hearts continue to beat, though we may beg otherwise. Life goes on.

"Thanks, Aunty Priya." On impulse he reaches over and hugs his aunt.

She pats him on the back. "I just thought you should know," she says. "You need an opportunity to talk about your feelings."

He sucks in a sigh. "I guess."

"You have to address it sometime, Maximilian. Otherwise it will rip at your insides. They'll cut you open and her name will be written in the scars."

"That's precisely how it feels." He looks at her in grudging admiration.

She smiles. "They'll never understand, you know."

"Maybe not," he says. "But at least I know you do." He leans over to drop a kiss on the top of her head, and she gestures him away.

"Have you thought about talking to someone?"

Max shrugs. "They gave me a course of therapy. Me, sitting in a corner, talking to an automated service on the Wall Rivers. The perfect way to feel sane."

"PTSD is serious, Maxi. You need to look after yourself."

He flicks his hair off his forehead with his hand, the blood congealing from his earlier fight with the goose fat. "Sometimes sitting still doesn't feel like the best way to move on."

"I don't disagree. But you have to make sure you're *emotionally* strong, as well as physically." She gestures at his lean body. "Don't throw yourself into anything too intense."

"I'll never be an astronaut again, Aunty Priya. That's probably the most intense thing I'll ever do."

"Probably. But you can't spend your life on your mom and dad's sofa—it's not what she'd want."

He doesn't say anything, though he acknowledges her point.

"What are you going to do?" Priya looks at her blue-eyed nephew somewhat expectantly.

"I don't know," he says, as they walk back toward the shop floor, gazing around at the supermarket, "but I don't think what's left of my future is here."

twenty-five

MAX HEADS TO the gleaming white cube of the hospital, the wards exactly the same as the last time he visited, only with different names on the walls and different children in the beds. An infinite churn of patients requiring the skills of the doctors, or an infinite churn of doctors requiring the illnesses of the patients. He feels mean at the thought, but more and more his mother prompts such ideas. Their anger consistently rubs them the wrong way, putting a personal sharpness into every exchange, forcing them apart when they should be attempting a truce.

He goes straight to Kent's room in the apex, meeting his mother in the corridor, her face wearing the same disdain as it had at their last confrontation in this place. "You came" is all she says.

"I want to see my brother."

"Oh, *now* it suits you. You never cared before."

And so it goes, thinks Max. How easy to overlook the truth when it suits an argument. "I'm here now."

She takes a digi-clipboard from next to Kent's door as the animated teddy bear on the hallway's Wall Rivers begins its jolly bounce toward them. "You weren't here for him."

"For him, or for you?" For the first time Max wonders what she might have gone through when he went up to the asteroid belt. He had so wanted them to acknowledge *his* pain that he hadn't considered theirs. He'd presumed they didn't have any.

"For Kent," she says curtly. "He's innocent in all this."

"I know." Max closes his eyes, unable not to fan the flames. "Are you ever going to ask me about what I went through up there?"

"You went. You failed. I'm not sure it needs discussion."

"She died, Mom. She died to save me. You can't dismiss that."

"And I'm sorry for you, Max, but that doesn't excuse you breaking the rules."

"We didn't break the rules, we asked to change them. And they were listening to us," he says. *Unlike you.*

"Yes," she says, leaning forward in the claustrophobic corridor so she's extremely close to his face, so near he can taste the tang of coffee in the air when she breathes. "And haven't you noticed things have been . . . *a little different* since you came back?"

"What do you mean?"

"All of the repeals, the introspection, the dissension?"

"Repeals?"

"You haven't noticed," she says, her voice flat.

"No. What do you mean?"

"That's typical." She takes a step away, turning back toward Kent's door. "Challenging the rules of a utopia, then not even noticing what happens after you have."

"But—"

"I don't know what's worse: challenging the rules, or providing the worst possible outcome for the very few people to whom you gave hope."

"Oh," Max says, his face bleak.

"This is what happens," she concludes, "when you let a child run around doing whatever he wants."

Knowing it will tip her over the edge, he says very quietly, "I'm not a child."

The Professor slams down the digi-clipboard and the noise is deafening as the tablet hits the floor. "You keep acting like a child so we keep treating you like one." The animated bear catapults itself around the doorway, and she swipes it away furiously. "Why won't you listen to me? I'm trying to help you. I don't know if you're ever going to learn."

He says nothing, his hands and muscles taut.

"Maximilian, I know we're tough on you, but the Voivodeship was built for the people by the people. You can still make up for what you've done."

Max is quiet, thinking on her words. "Dad liked Carys when he met her."

His mother is confused. "What?"

"You thought she was great, until you found out I loved her."

"I don't know where you're going with this."

He sighs. "You liked me, too, when I was living as you wanted me to."

"Maximilian. Are you listening to me? You need to make up for what you've done. You have to show people that you were wrong and that you'll live in the right way."

The language strikes a chord in Max. *Live well*, she had said, *for me*. Against his better judgment his mother's insidious words creep in, mingling with Carys's until he can no longer take the pressure inside his head and shouts to drown them out.

His mother stares in surprise.

Max struggles through his feelings, his anger pushed out with the scream until he is empty. "I can't do this anymore."

"Pardon?"

Max closes his eyes. "How do I fix this, Mom?"

"Really?"

"Truly."

Her face is skeptical as she looks at her son. "You really want my advice?"

"What should I do? Tell me."

"You could start by helping people, rather than helping yourself."

Max doesn't have a retort, knowing in the back of his mind he has begun to fix things rather than inflame them. He says gently, "I'm more than you think I am."

"We all hope so, Max."

"I'll prove it."

"Hallelujah," she says. "At last."

"I might need your help," he says, all fight in him broken, and she nods.

"Whatever you need to make it right."

"Fine," Max says. "Now can I please see my brother?"

She acquiesces by opening the door and letting him through, but she stands watching her two sons from the doorway.

Kent looks up from the bed, groggy, and beams a gap-toothed smile. "Hi, Mac."

"Whoa. Have you lost some more teeth?"

"All of the baby ones have gone now." Kent is so proud that Max's heart aches for the little boy in the big bed, proud of reaching a milestone. Max hopes Kent will reach all of the milestones, that he'll have a chance to overcome his illness and live a long, full life. *Unlike Carys.*

Her absence hits him like a punch in the stomach. The mind trick of grief twinges and he thinks, again, how unfair it is that the brain can forget all that's happened for a second, only for it to strike again as new. How could he forget, even for a moment, that she was gone?

"Are you sleeping in my room?" Kent asks, and Max shakes his head.

"No, buddy. It didn't seem right, not when you're coming home so much. I've been sleeping on the sofa." The boy's eyes are round as he imagines such a rebellion, and Max ruffles his hair. "But I don't think I'm going to stick around for much longer."

"Is it the girl again?"

Ouch. "Kinda. You remember she was a pilot?"

"She flew shuttles."

"That's right. And she got me a job at the EVSA, the Space Agency."

Kent nods. "Dad told me."

Surprised, Max glances at his mother, then back at Kent. "She thought I could be an astronaut . . ."

"Cool!"

". . . but I can't. She was wrong about me—I'm a chef." He looks at his brother, wondering why he's confiding his life choices to a nine-year-old. Well, he realizes, there's no one else. "I'm just a chef. I'm good at cooking. And there are a lot of people who need help with food."

"Like here? In the hospital?"

"Like here," Max says, again glancing at his mother, "but abroad. Where there are starving people, and soldiers, and a lot of people scared about the asteroid field."

Kent rubs his eyes, trying to keep up. "You're leaving?"

"I'm leaving, but I'm going to call you every day." He holds out his wrist so his chip syncs with Kent's and takes his brother's hand. "I'm going to send you a message every day, because you're my best friend."

Kent leans against Max in the bed, resting his head against his shoulder. "And Carys is your second-best friend."

"You're my best friend," Max repeats, "and Carys is my always."

MAX GOES DIRECTLY TO the Voivode's recruitment center to see if they'll take him. He answers all of their questions, then submits to a physical. He winces as the recruiter tells him his lung capacity is excellent—if only he'd known before—and shakes his head as they run through his medical history.

"Any eye disorders, musculoskeletal disorders, infections?"

"None."

"Any psychiatric disorders?"

He hesitates only for a second. "None."

"Great. You're in good physical condition. You should have no trouble."

"Thank you."

She swipes her notes to one side, a long list of volunteers and recruits appearing on her screen, all needing to be checked over and checked off. "Do you have references from your previous employer?"

"I trained with the EVSA," he admits, "but if you're pressed for time, Professor Alina at the Voivode 2 southern hospital will tell you everything you need to know."

"Perfect. In that case you'll probably ship out to our training center tomorrow."

Which side of his personality is driving this, he doesn't know; whether he's proving something or pleasing someone he's not sure, but Carys asked and he promised he would. He promised and he damn well—

"Max?" The voice interrupts his train of thought where he sits on a hard bench in a nondescript hall, looking at a photograph he hastily thumbs away on his chip. "You can head on down to the kit room, where you'll be allocated your equipment."

"Thank you."

"No, thank *you*. We really need people like you to volunteer for the aid teams right now, particularly in the conflict regions."

"No problem." Time to do something. Time to live.

twenty-six

WHAT'S ON THE menu today—anything exciting?"

Max looks up from where he's preparing eight large vats, moving to stir each one in turn. He doesn't have a ladle so he's improvised with anything he could find. He thinks that might be part of the test.

They've been training in Voivode 9 for six weeks, during which time they've been subjected to more fitness and exercise routines than Max could ever have anticipated. Signing up to be a chef for the aid teams, he now sees, is not that different from signing up to be an astronaut. They still need you in peak physical condition, wherever you're headed. If anything, by comparison, the Space Agency training pales into nothing: here he's done push-ups, burpees, and planks, plus two-, five- and ten-mile runs daily, all while being shouted at. The EVSA made him fit on paper with cardio, using machines, but he likes the mindlessness of old-fashioned outdoor exercise. He likes being able to tune out and focus on getting through the moment. "Zen," they used to call it. He feels Zen. Endorphins are great.

Max prepares to be teased. "Stew."

"Again?"

"Lovely nutritious stew. If you're lucky, I might even throw in some croutons."

"Don't try passing off those chunks of stale old bread as croutons. You and your fancy talk," the trainee aid-team leader says, and Max smiles.

"It's good preparation for when we've got limited supplies."

"Won't be long," the new team leader says. "Then we'll be shipped out to the coast, where it's war-zone central."

Max hands him a bowl. "Oh?"

"The US coastal regions are a mess," he says, "everyone fighting for the higher ground and the water."

Max briefly wonders where Carys's brother might be but he pushes the thought away. "What did you do before this?"

"Carpenter. You?"

"Chef."

"Oh," says the team leader. "I thought . . ." Max looks at him, but the team leader decides not to finish his sentence. "Don't forget my extra croutons."

They sleep in the oldest university in Europia, the beautiful red-and-yellow-brick college buildings filled with glass and steel rooms. The upstairs dormitories have large glass walls and no blinds, so Max doesn't get much sleep, but at least this means fewer night terrors. The relentless routine of preparing meals and aid-team training sessions has distracted him from his default thoughts. At night he dares himself to see her, calling up the well-thumbed photograph: Carys folded into the crook of his arm, the fluttering digital flags of the Voivode Games behind them. A different climate, in what felt like a different life.

After serving breakfast Max joins a session covering essential first aid and nutrition taking place on the university grounds. On autopilot he mixes one spoon of salt with eight of sugar, adding five cups of drinking water to make a rehydration solution. The trainer—Kelly—nods in approval. "You know your stuff."

"I trained with the EVSA. Hydration is a big deal in space."

Having looked up Max's history, the trainer says mildly, "Yes, though I imagine water is trickier without gravity."

"They pipe most of it into your body via tubes. You can drown in your own tears if they fill up your helmet during a spacewalk."

The trainer looks shocked for a moment, then recovers, patting Max's shoulder and moving on to the next trainee. "Too much salt," she says. "Your patient will be retching on all that salt water."

Max makes the meals for his team, rotating with the other cooks across breakfast, lunch, and dinner. The volunteers are a nice bunch, though understandably preoccupied with their imminent move to the former United States. Every sentence starts with "when" and not "if"; there's a lot of big talk about what they'll do when confronted by rebels. The camp swoops on the little firsthand news, while secondhand rumors are rife, winding the new recruits into a frenzy. Many of them call home or use their downtime to call loved ones, the Wall Rivers lighting up the common-room walls.

Max longs to speak to somebody who knew Carys. Not someone who knew *of* her, not Aunt Priya or even Kent, who knew what she'd meant to him; he wants to speak to somebody who'd known her laugh or her ambition, who'd touched her. He's frightened she'll become an apparition, and part of the reason he looks at the photo from the Games so often is to hold her face at the front of his memory. He thinks about messaging Liu, but Liu hasn't called for a while. "Tell me your favorite Carys memory," he'd said at her memorial, and Max had punched him. Liu had tried again and again, but it was clear Max was going through too much to process. Liu finally gave him some space.

During downtime, Max messages Liljana on the MindShare. Surprised, she quickly replies. *The king of dessert*, she says, and it appears in red on a small section of the wall in the common room, where Max is sitting with a few others talking to their friends and family on separate Wall Rivers. *No longer an astronaut?*

Apparently not, Max writes back. *Now I'm the king of stew.*

At least you're the king of something.

How are you?

A pause. *I miss her.*

He closes his eyes. *Me, too.*

Nobody calls me Lili now that she's gone.

I know what you mean, he flexes. *Nobody calls me at all.*

There's a pause and he watches her type, waiting for it to appear. *You can call me, if you ever need to.*

Thanks. You can, too, he adds as an afterthought. *If I'm not in what's left of America already.*

Godspeed, she flexes, *and stay safe.*

Any sense of danger for Max feels confined to rumor or a vague, nebulous future—while his comrades talk in whens, not ifs, Max thinks only in minutes. The next ten minutes are dedicated to a two-mile run. The following twenty minutes are for cooking dinner.

ONE DAY MAX IS washing up sixteen saucepans, swirling water over the steel—nine minutes—when the senior trainer, who'd praised his rehydration technique, finds him in the kitchen. Max moves on to the knives, sharpening each blade one after the other, as she presents him with a request.

"You want me to tell them about the asteroid field," he repeats.

"Please," Kelly says, handing him the next knife in line. "You've got firsthand experience. A lot of people are scared."

Max rubs his temple with one hand, the sharpening steel still in the other. "You know I signed up to be a chef? That's not connected to what I did at the Space Agency."

She weighs her words. "The thing is, Max, with your EVSA training and your experience, you're the most prepared of us all."

"I'm not."

Kelly smiles gently. "Have you ever heard what happened to the first astronauts who saw Earth from the moon?"

He shuffles his thoughts. " 'One small step.' Nothing else springs to mind."

"They looked down at our tiny planet and saw that national borders don't really exist, and conflicts between people are unimportant because we're all here, together. They coined a term for it—the Overview Effect." She hands him the next knife. "People who've been to space and looked down on Earth have an overview that others don't."

Max sighs. "And you think I have it."

"Don't you?"

He doesn't want to say it's the type of cognitive shift that he probably wouldn't experience. He doesn't want to say that the only cognitive shifts he has experienced from space are grief, loss, and a lasting mental chaos he's trying to suppress with routine.

"I've seen you outrun the best here. You can improvise. You adapt.

Out of everyone"—Kelly gestures around, though they're alone in his room—"*you* should be leading the team. You should be team leader."

Max takes a minute to slice a culinary blade against the steel rod, thinking how to phrase it. "The thing is, Kelly—can I call you Kelly?—I'm not a soldier. And I'm certainly not a hero." Most heroics don't involve roast potatoes, he concedes.

"You won't have to fight."

He takes a deep breath. "I don't believe the aid teams should be armed."

"It's only to protect ourselves."

"Protecting ourselves shouldn't require force. Using force in Europia's name is no better than fighting a war in the first place."

"And who do you think won the war?" she asks.

"Who won?" repeats Max. "Nobody. You can't walk out victorious when you've maimed a continent."

"Exactly, Max. Exactly. And you think you don't have the Overview Effect." She shakes her head, laughing to herself. "Why don't you join the session tonight with the team leaders and see how you feel?"

"I'll think about it."

Kelly steps back. "And you'll talk about the asteroids?"

"I'll think about it."

"Good. Come to the quadrant at eight."

"IN WHOSE NAME DO you act?" Kelly calls, and the team leaders quiet down and turn to her.

"Not God, not king, or country," they call in response.

"In whose name?"

"My own."

Curious, Max walks out from the kitchen, untying his chef's apron and leaning against the brick wall at the back. Kelly turns over her wrist and activates the external Wall Rivers on the four sides of the courtyard, the university walls flickering to life.

"Team, it's time you saw a little more of the world you're going to visit. I'd rather you saw the real situation from me, instead of continuing to freak out over rumors."

The four walls are taken over with a livestream and the trainee team leaders are surrounded by the projection, straining in each direction to get a glimpse. "It's nothing you can't handle," Kelly says, "but I want you to be prepared."

A large Georgia Southern University sign, peeling and bloated, lies discarded by the road, the white wooden buildings long rotted away, but the gardens and a crumbling clock tower still stand. The camera stays stationary on this shot, allowing their eyes to adjust before the image rotates to reveal the rest of the landscape.

There's a gasp.

"What on Earth could've happened?" somebody wonders, appalled.

"Humans," says Max quietly, his heart rate picking up.

Potholes and craters line the earth, with black holes in place of buildings and cities—the verdant, lush green of Georgia is long gone. They see broken faces where there are none, because there is no evidence of life here, anywhere. Ash covers everything in a gray dust that drifts at ankle height in the wind, swirled by the movement of the camera. It takes them a moment to realize the ash is swirling over human remains.

"Six devices," says the trainer, her voice also soft. "Six nuclear devices, placed close enough to one another to create a chain reaction." She looks around at each of them as they crane to look at the devastation on four walls. "That's how humans did this. This is what they did to each other."

The frame lingers on the remnants of a skull and Max feels physically sick, his heart tap-dancing erratically against his rib cage. The camera track dislodges the skull so it rolls toward them and a tumble of brown hair unfurls down. Max jumps back. "Christ."

"Why did they do this—oil?" someone asks.

"Oil," says the trainee who'd teased Max about the croutons, "money, power, dominance."

"Shit," says one recruit. "Europia is the light."

Max feels the prickle on his skin rising, shifting from his spine to his temples, the sharpness of anxiety setting in. A murmur of agreement and approval goes up, but the tone is muted as the trainees continue to look out at the broken land. "Remember," says Kelly, "our only remit is to help people."

Max falls away from the wall, sliding apart from the group as the air in his lungs catches and begins to burn with panic. He leaves them behind, moving somewhere more private.

It wasn't supposed to be like this, he thinks. This experience was supposed to be hollow with the repetition of routine and regime. Max had gone to the aid teams as if drawn to a vacuum— somewhere with simple tasks and clean skills. Not like space. "I couldn't save you," he whispers, seeing the skull again behind his eyelids, as the swath of brown hair falls toward him and, in slow motion, merges with Carys, her tawny hair tumbling toward him the night they went to bed after the Games—"I've never wanted something this much in my life"—and a single tear streaks down his face. It wasn't supposed to be like this, he thinks. War wasn't supposed to be so *similar.*

Liljana? He flexes in desperation, activating his chip.

What's up? The response comes quickly, and he breathes out with relief.

I couldn't save her.

You did. You saved her when you met. She used to get really lonely.

I let her down. Max types out the most honest fear he has: *And I'm still letting her down now.*

Liljana switches to voice call, the *ping* jarring him, and he answers, surprised. "Hello?"

"You don't have to live up to anything," she says. "You just have to *live.* Look at you—helping people, cooking for those in need. You make people like me have faith."

"You already had faith." He leans against the red and yellow bricks, sweat beading along his back and across his forehead. "It's not what I thought it was, coming here. I thought I was being trained to feed and help survivors. But it's like . . . an army."

She waits.

"They want me to be a soldier." His voice grows thick. "They think I'm a hero."

"Max, you're a survivor. Carys thought you were a hero."

In the evening warmth of Voivode 9 he walks through ancient arches of the university into a paved garden. "Carys thought a lot of things about me."

"Don't you think you need to cut yourself a little slack? I don't think you're quite getting it. She held you in esteem, and you lifted yourself up to meet her expectations. She, likewise, did the same for you. Don't you see? You were the best versions of yourselves when you were together. She made you softer and more ambitious. And, in turn, Carys was stronger and happier with you."

"Maybe," he says, the pulse still tripping in his neck as the after-effects of a panic attack pump through his blood.

"So you might be lost without her, but she would have been just as lost without you."

"I'm not a soldier, Liljana." His voice cracks. "I don't ever want to hold two lives in the balance and decide who deserves to live."

"I understand," she says. "You don't want life to make that choice in your favor again."

"I wish I could undo it," he says, and his single tear is joined quickly by another as his heart breaks.

"People used to believe," Liljana says, "that we get the chance to repeat our lives. We live them, over and over, and the only way to move on is to make a different decision, to bring about a different outcome. It is only then that we reach a higher plane. So that awful moment you experienced is just one moment you can live again with a different outcome, every time, until you achieve the *right* one.

"You will make a choice when that moment comes again. You will make the only choice that can be made."

"I'd take it back if I could," he says desperately, and as Max thinks about two lives held in the balance, his mind spirals back, the frames unspool, and the reels come loose—

twenty-seven

THE LIGHT COMES toward them slowly, a phantasm of hope. "We're not going mental," says Max. "It's not a mirage."

"No, Max," Carys says softly. "It's not a mirage." Beneath them, the dust of the asteroid field swirls around the largest meteoroid some twenty yards below their feet. Beneath that, the world pours past, a weather system brewing over Africa. But Max looks at none of the natural phenomena, nor at the light of the satellite streaking slowly toward them. Instead, he looks at Carys, her tawny hair halo-braided and coiled inside her fishbowl glass helmet, the small white-and-yellow daisy tucked into the plait, tendrils loose around her face. Her hand is pale and bare against the dark of the universe. The white thread, knotted badly, floats in microgravity around her finger, and he stares at it, then returns his gaze to her face.

"Why are you looking at me like that?"

"Like what?"

She smiles, her face a little wonky. "Like you haven't seen me for months."

"Feels like years."

Carys touches his shoulder. "You look like you've been through the wars." His eyes drop to the thread around her finger and back to her face as he says nothing, and she nods. "We're going to stop at a Lagrange point soon."

Instinctively they bend their legs, like ballet dancers landing on a stage, and as they level with the stony asteroid they slow to a stop.

"Physics, eh?" says Max dutifully. "Always right."

"Apart from when they thought the Earth was flat." Carys grips his bare hand in hers, and he squeezes back. They take a second to feel the other's hand in their own before Carys looks up. "That asteroid is huge, up close."

"Huge," he agrees. "Can't believe we flew so near it."

"I'm sorry."

"Don't be."

Not quite ready to get into that, Carys asks a question to which she already knows the answer. "How much time do we have?"

"Now?" he says. "The sat is coming straight to us in six minutes, I believe."

"Six minutes. That's not long."

Max takes back his hand, more for convenience than as any kind of statement. "It's a lifetime," he says. "Do you regret it?"

"What, this? No," she says, too quickly. "Maybe. I don't know. Sometimes I wonder if it would have been better not to ask for a repeal."

Max makes a face. "The thing is, Cari, you didn't ask them. I did. Which makes everything that's happened my fault." She doesn't answer, and he bites his lip. "It's my turn to be sorry," he says.

"Don't be. I don't think we're so great apart."

The asteroid dust swirls up next to them, momentarily masking the streak of the satellite drone. "You're right," says Max, "I don't think we are."

Carys raises her wrist, splaying her fingers. "I'm going to try to contact Osric now."

"Good idea." He smiles at her.

She checks that the mesh is in place, looped over her knuckles, and begins to flex. *This is Carys Fox from the* Laertes *requesting immediate assistance. Do you read me?*

She waits.

I repeat: this is Carys Fox from the Laertes *requesting immediate assistance. Do you read me, over?*

"I'm not getting anything," she tells Max.

"Keep trying."

Please, Ric.

Her audio crackles to life with a *ping.* Hello, Carys. This is Osric.

"Osric," she breathes aloud, as the blue text fills the side of her glass.

I am communicating directly with the satellite's computer to patch this to you, Carys.

Thank you.

Is there anything you want to ask me to do with the drone, Carys?

No, thank you.

Are you sure, Carys?

Now, what was it we said, she flexes, *about adding my name at the end of every sentence?*

My apologies.

Thank you. Osric, am I right in thinking that in the instance of a catastrophe in space the EVSA comms records are a matter of public record?

A pause. Yes, Carys.

Everything we flex with you in our final moments is open to Voivodeship citizens?

Another pause. Yes, Carys?

Okay. Stand by.

"Cari?" Max asks.

"The satellite is one of our drones. It will be here in six minutes. You have six minutes of air, and shortly I will have two."

"Right, yes. I'm sorry—"

"It's fine. We had to try different things earlier. There was always a danger something could go wrong. If it hadn't been your propellant, I would've killed us with ozone."

"But you might've succeeded in making black oxygen, which is impressive."

She laughs. "Wouldn't that have been something? Take that, physics."

"I think it's technically chemistry."

"Very funny. Now listen, because I'm trying to be matter-of-fact."

Max is solemn. "I've noticed."

"You're going to survive, and fix the things we've begun to break." She takes his hand. "Because we started a chain reaction, whether we knew it or not. We drew so much attention to the one rule *we* didn't like . . . we eroded the sense of a greater good." She looks at him, urging him to understand. "I don't think Europia was a utopia for me. I never fit with the ideal of Individualism, but that doesn't mean I'm happy that it's breaking. So, please, Max. You need to go back and make it right."

"I can't do that, Cari."

She sighs. "I was afraid you'd say that."

"What you need to know is I've seen my life without you and, frankly, it's bleak."

"It might be okay."

"No, I know. I've seen it," he says. "My family won't forgive me, and I'll no longer have a place down there. The skills I have, the things I want to do . . . Nobody needs me if you're not there. I'm no hero without you."

Carys is contemplative. "But we broke it, Max."

"No."

"We did. We started turning them introspective on the rules." She reaches for him.

"That might be true," says Max, "and it pains me to say it, but any system that can be broken by me loving you must have been pretty fragile to begin with."

She exhales, placing her bare hand back in his. "Wow."

"I know."

"I don't believe it. Max Fox dismissing the utopia?"

"It's true."

"Also—sorry—did you just say you loved me?"

"Of course I do. I'm only sorry I didn't tell you more often. I should have told you every day."

"No," she says, her voice quiet. "Somehow it means more this way."

"I tried. Especially on the ship. I always liked the part in *Hamlet* where he writes a letter to Ophelia. I wanted to read it to you—I was trying to this morning."

"Oh?"

"Yes." He clears his throat.

"Doubt thou the stars are fire,
Doubt that the sun doth move,
Doubt truth to be a liar,
But never doubt I love."

Carys is visibly moved. "Are you quoting Shakespeare at me, Max?"

"Yes."

"Maybe we *are* hallucinating," she says. "They likely did program our oxygen to release more slowly at the very end."

"Shut up."

"I'm sorry." Carys laughs.

"Stop teasing." He grabs her and holds her to him, as best he can. "You're ruining the moment."

"I was just happy you said you loved me."

Max is still for a moment, then adjusts his suit in a moment of self-consciousness. "We need to get you ready."

Carys sighs. "Max . . ."

He scoots around behind her and makes a show of tapping her pack and adjusting the shoulder straps and cables. "There." He keeps himself behind her, and she raises her bare hand to her shoulder and he clasps it, perhaps for the last time. "Listen to me, Carys. You're going to have to change tubes briefly when your air supply runs out. I loosened it earlier—you just have to switch and screw the thread into the other air pack, all right? Turn it until it locks." He pats her hand. "Do you understand?"

"No, Max. I know what you're trying to do, and I won't let you.

You're not going to leave me under some white-knight bullshit. You're not giving me your pack," she says, turning so sharply he swerves to her side in reaction. "I won't let you do this. You don't have to save me."

"Cari, no," he says.

"I won't be the same person if I leave you here—so I won't."

He's shocked.

"Yeah," she says, her voice returning to normal. "But there's still time for you. You could get to the drone, get back to Earth. You'd see your brother again." She hardens her heart. "It's selfish of you to leave him so easily."

"Easily?" Max shouts. "You think any of this has been *easy*? Because living without you won't be easy either," he says. "I'm not letting you cut the rope between us to save *me*. You talk about me attempting to be a white knight, Cari, but you're no better."

"I'm sorry I destroyed the ship," she says in a swift change of direction, and he starts in surprise.

"Did you?"

"Yes. I went in too deep. I thought I could see—no, I *did* see—a route through the asteroids. A way out."

He raises his eyebrows. "An exit path? Whoa."

"I know," she says. "But I crashed the ship going for it. The hull was breached by a meteoroid, and then—you know the rest. I'm so sorry."

"Ah, well."

"That's it?"

"Not much we can do about it now," he says, looking around them. "But a way out? Cari, you did it."

"I risked our lives in doing so. And now we're stuck with each other."

"For two minutes, maybe less. Are you sure, Carys?"

"I'm sure. Are you?" They take a breath, neither wanting to count how many they might have until their last.

"We're set on this, then," he says sadly. "Neither of us wants to leave in that satellite."

"I definitely don't. Do you?"

"No," he says, resigned. "Without you I'm lost."

She sighs. "That's it, then."

"Yes."

"What do we do?"

"I think we take a moment," he says. "We watch the northern lights trip over the atmosphere, think about our families, thank our lucky stars, and say good night."

"That final?"

"We're running out of time, Cari. It's like we said an hour ago: we either let it happen *to* us, or we take the reins and end this ourselves."

"We end this ourselves," she echoes. "Right." Her bare hand reaches for his, and she takes a deep breath. "On three?"

"On three."

Their audio crackles.

"One."

"Two—"

"Wait!" Carys throws up her hands. "I always wanted you to think I was above needing to hear it or express it. I never pushed you to say it. But I want to tell you that I've loved you, probably from the moment you saved my potatoes, until right now. I'm sorry, but I do, and I want you to know."

Max takes a deep breath. "Love at first sight? Cari, *that's* romance. Thank you. I don't deserve it." Then he changes tack, unable to resist. "But I always knew you were pretending."

"And I always knew you were a peacock," she retorts, "but somehow we're still together."

"Yes, we are. Alone in space. No *pings* from Osric—"

"Osric. I nearly forgot." She quickly flexes the coordinates of the asteroid field exit path to Osric, to the best of her memory. She transcribes the briefest of maneuvers and the route that got Carys and Max out of the field, but which shattered their ship as they emerged on the other side. The blue text pulses and fades on the glass of her fishbowl.

"Alone in space," he repeats.

"We're nowhere, Max."

He smiles. "I suppose we are. And that's funny, because the true meaning of 'utopia'—it isn't down there, in 'a perfect place.'" He points toward Earth, slowly moving beneath them. "In Greek 'utopia' means 'no place.'"

"You're telling me that, for all their posturing, Europia sent us to an actual utopia?" She starts laughing.

"You know," he says, "I've wanted to go home since we got here. I kept believing our best days would be down on Earth. But despite everything, I've been so happy up here, with you. A perfect place isn't a political state or a philosophical movement. It's this, it's us." And very gently she begins to cry. *You've got me*, Max had said to her a long time ago. *Cari? I said you've got me*, though she'd never really believed it. But here he was, with enough air to live and get home; instead he'd chosen—

She stops.

Osric, she messages quickly, *I've sent you the coordinates for the way out of the asteroid belt. It's navigable, just about. I think you'll be able to leave Earth again, should you want. But before you do, tell them—*

Carys thinks about what she wants to say. She reflects on what her mother had said, or would say, or might have said, appreciating, at last, that Gwen would only have been half-right.

Tell them first love can break you. But it can also save you.

They watch the aurora borealis dance in the atmosphere across the Arctic and the northern territories, a spectrum of greens tripping and falling in the skies above their alternate-future homes—a future they will never know.

Carys's warning alarm beeps as they continue to watch the northern lights. "It's time."

"All right." He watches the top of the aurora, its red beams probing up into space, invisible to the casual spectators watching the blues and greens down in the northern hemisphere.

"Max, I . . ." She gestures at her space suit, the alerts lit up in red, her face apologetic. "I don't think I can." The idea of removing her own supply, even as it runs out, is terrifying.

"How about we do each other's?" He pulls her slowly into an embrace, his bare hand resting on the screw thread at her back. "Now put yours on mine."

She brings her arm up to the back of his head, laying her hands lightly on the glass of his fishbowl. Gently, she lifts her bare fingers, resting them on the tube at the nape of his neck. The white thread, tied loosely around her finger, hangs freely.

"No apologies," he says. "This is what we want."

She nods as her second warning alarm sounds.

"On three."

"No more countdowns, Max," she says, and he understands. "This is the end."

Very gently, without closing their eyes or looking away, with their arms raised and locked around each other, Max and Carys unhook each other's helmets, breathing in the chill of the dark.

Behind them, the light of the Milky Way burns like fire as a heaviness falls on their lungs; and, in the grip of each other's loving embrace, under the weight of a thousand stars, Max and Carys begin to dance.

acknowledgments

THANK YOU TO Juliet Mushens, the best agent and mother hen around, who sold this novel around the world and held my hand while she did so. Thanks also to Sasha Raskin, Nathalie Hallam, Sarah Manning, Howie Sanders, and Jason Burns at United Talent Agency.

Karen Kosztolnyik believed in the romance of *Hold Back the Stars* early—thank you to everyone at Gallery Books in New York, including Jen Bergstrom, Louise Burke, Jen Long, Kristin Dwyer, Molly Gregory, and also Nita Pronovost at Simon & Schuster Canada. Thanks also to the amazing Gallery marketing team: Wendy Sheanin, Liz Psaltis, Abby Zidle, Melanie Mitzman, and Diana Velasquez.

The team at Transworld in London: Darcy Nicholson worked tirelessly on this story with brilliant insight, patience, and good humor—thank you, Darcy, for making me a better writer. Simon Taylor has been a fantastic steering hand, along with the whip-smart team, including Sophie Christopher, Nicola Wright, Sarah Whittaker, Deirdre O'Connell, and Lizzy Goudsmit—thank you all.

In 2013, Richard Skinner, Director of the Fiction Programme at Faber Academy, told me unequivocally to finish the first draft of this novel. Thank you.

My friends and first readers: Katy Pegg and Kate McQuaile gave me their early thoughts and told me to carry on. Thank you for giving me the belief to do this. And to Dan Dalton, for rearranging the first page.

Ian George, John Fletcher, and the team at Paramount Pictures: having two careers is challenging but with your support, you made it easy.

My parents, Jane and Don Wood, provided the real-life inspiration for Carys's close relationship with Gwen. Conversely, Max's horrible parents were created by imagining every possible thing you would never, ever say. You're wonderful. Thank you, I love you.

My brilliant family: Sam and Liz, Amber and Ella, Finley and Sol, Poppy and Marley. Those last two are dogs, but dogs are part of our family . . .

And finally to Jonathan Hopkins, for the morning tea, deadline cheering, and human sloth jokes. This human sloth only went and wrote a book! Thanks for everything.

hold back the stars

KATIE KHAN

Introduction

In Europia, the individual comes first—relationships come later. Every three years, citizens are "rotated" to a new location to fully experience their youth and discover themselves as individuals, and romantic coupling is forbidden until the age of thirty-five. But when Max and Carys realize they can't stay away from each other, a series of life-altering decisions plays out to leave them stranded in space with only ninety minutes of oxygen remaining, struggling to deconstruct the choices that brought them face-to-face with their mortality. In *Hold Back the Stars*, Katie Khan explores the influences of family, the concept of freedom, and how our decisions can touch everyone around us.

Topics and Questions for Discussion

1. In *Hold Back the Stars*, the author uses dual time lines to tell the story of Max and Carys's journey to space. In what ways does this enhance the story? Which time line did you feel more connected to?

2. Carys and Max had radically different upbringings from each other. How do their philosophies differ on utopian ideals?

3. In Europia, the individual is prized above all else, yet there is a particular irony in a utopian society valuing individualism. In what ways does Carys see that, and how is Max blinded to it?

4. According to the Couples Rule, romantic couples are not allowed to form until an individual reaches thirty-five. How could this rule benefit our own society? How might it hurt it? How would the rule affect your own life?

5. Max says, "We show our true colors facing the end" (p. 75). Do you agree? Why or why not?

6. As part of a Founding Family, what kind of pressures was Max feeling during his relationship with Carys? Do you think he was justified in feeling the way he did in the beginning?

7. How does the author use details to highlight themes or plot points in each time line? For example, the origin of the crumpled daisy in Carys's ear does not become evident until after the two time lines converge.

8. Max's parents essentially excommunicate him after he reveals his relationship with Carys. Can you think of parallel examples in our own society of this kind of familial rejection?

9. Which "ending" seems the most realistic to you? What kind of choice would you have made in the same scenario?

10. How did Carys and Max each cope without the other? What did their coping mechanisms communicate about their personalities?

11. *Hold Back the Stars* confronts the idea of choice—or lack thereof—and the question of whether true freedom can exist in a utopian society. In what ways were Carys and Max free? How did their concept of freedom change throughout the story?

12. Neither Carys nor Max can live without the other in their respective "endings." Do you think it's possible that, for some people, time cannot heal certain wounds?

13. How do you interpret the last chapter of *Hold Back the Stars* in light of the alternating perspectives of Carys and Max?

14. What were the best examples of strong relationships in *Hold Back the Stars*? What made them strong? How did Europia foster—or hinder—forming relationships?

15. What do you think it means to do something for the "greater good"? Can a utopian society exist without its citizens striving for a common "greater" cause?

Enhance Your Book Club

1. If you could participate in a Rotation, where would you go? With your reading group, share your top five choices—cities, countries, islands, wherever!

2. Visit a local observatory with your reading group for a fun, engaging weekend activity. Ask every member to write down a star, planet, or galaxy he or she would like to observe. Don't forget to view Saturn!

3. Max says to Carys, "There's no better way to spend the last minutes of your life than talking to the best person you've ever met" (p. 165). How would you want to spend your last ninety minutes on earth? Share your ideal scenario with your reading group.

4. Would you send your children on Rotation, even a six-year-old son or daughter? Why or why not? Do you wish you had had an opportunity like that when you were growing up? Discuss with your reading group.

5. If you're thirty-five or older, how would your life have changed if you had waited until you were thirty-five to choose your partner? Discuss with your reading group what your alternative time line would have looked like in *Hold Back the Stars*'s Europia.

2. Wilhelmine Hartman
1895 Poland-1895 Poland

3. Gustav (Gus) Hartman
1877 Germany 1925 Detroit, MI
M1 Elsie Anna Walter 1883-1967
M2 Pauline W

4. Roelf (Ralph, a.k.a. One Punch) Hartman
1880 Germany 1974 Standish, MI
M Barbara Nigl 1886-1975

   1. Florence Hartman 1913
   M

   2. Helen Hartman 1915
   M Harold Neiman

   3 Clara Hartman 1916
   M

   4. Victor R. Hartman 1919-2006
   M Elwanda Ross 1929-2010

   5. Raymond A Hartman 1921
   M1 Esther Peeper
   M2

   6. Leslie C Hartman 1923
   M Verna Corp

   7. Robert E Hartman 1925
   M Carol Hagerg 1925

   8. Russell R Hartman 1928-2007
   M MaryLou

5. Rosa (Rose) O. Hartman
1882 Port Hope, MI – 1967 Cortland, NY
M Joseph Frank Fisher

   1.Cecelia M Fisher 1902-1982
   M Paul Kroberger 1896-1981

   2. Hazel L Fisher 1904-1988
   M George Wilcox 1900-1978

   3. William J Fisher 1906-1968
   M Jeanette Carrington 1905-1986.

   4. Dorothy M Fisher 1911
   M Franklin E Corl 1906-1982

   5. Frank G Fisher 1917
   M Wilhelmia

   6. Francis Fisher 1918

6. Emma Amelia (Amelia) Hartman 1883-1883

7. Bernard (Barney) Hartman
1884 Port Hope, MI – 1954 Standish, MI

8. Amelia Molly Anna (Molly) Hartman
1887 Au Sable - 1942 Standish, MI
M Ludwig (Louis) Christian Wegener
1883-1954

   1. Leonard W.Wegener 1917-2005

9. Edith Ida Amelia (Edith) Hartman
1889 Au Sable, MI – 1961 Standish, MI
M Louis Adrian Ireland 1893-1948

10. Otto Hartman
1892 Au Sable, MI – 1922 Monroe, MI
M Mamie Wognowski

11. Amil (Emil) Hartman
1894 Standish, MI – 1968 Standish, MI

12. Fred A. Hartman, Jr.
1896 Standish, MI – 1936 Standish, MI

MINNIE'S POTATOES

Laurice LaZebnik has a BS in Education from Central Michigan University. LaZebnik taught secondary school Art and English, worked in international marketing and sales and in the local community as a volunteer. A licensed pilot and real estate salesperson, the author balances a social life with her husband with caring for her two dogs.

Made in the USA
Middletown, DE
07 March 2016